Strange Business

by

Carol Leister

This is a work of fiction. Names, characters, places, and incidents are either the product of the author's imagination or are used fictitiously, and any resemblance to actual persons living or dead, business establishments, events, or locales, is entirely coincidental.

Strange Business

COPYRIGHT © 2015 by Carol Leister

Cover Art by *Debbie Taylor*

The Wild Rose Press, Inc.
PO Box 708
Adams Basin, NY 14410-0708
Visit us at www.thewildrosepress.com

Publishing History
First Black Rose Edition, 2015
Print ISBN 978-1-5092-0178-5
Digital ISBN 978-1-5092-0179-2

Published in the United States of America

I was being ridiculous.
I'd already taken the job without feeling dramatic about it. How life-altering could a personal assistant position be? Even *with* a boss as good looking and stomach tightening as Michael Àrsaidh. "I am absolutely ready to be a part of the Foundation."

"Well done, Gillian Burke, well done," he said, holding out his hand.

I had enough time to notice his firm warm grip before a sharp shock travelled up my arm and through my entire body, somewhat like static shock, but a hundred times stronger. Truth be told, rather more erotic, my body tightening and shivering at the sensation. The lights in the office seemed to brighten to an almost painful level, and I shut my eyes until it passed. When the room came back into focus, I sat in my chair with Michael back on his side of the desk.

"Right then. On to the business at hand," Michael said calmly, like the strange interlude never happened. "I suppose you'd like to know what we do."

I nodded, feeling completely at sea. Something about Michael made me feel dangerously off-balance. Not only because he was breathtakingly gorgeous, either. He had a quality, an oddness I couldn't quite put my finger on. Disconcerting and more than a little bit sexy, I decided the safest thing to do was play along and hope I understood everything at a later date.

Michael smiled. He had, I noticed once again, an extremely nice smile. "I've found through the years the best way to explain what we do is to be as open and direct as possible. Are you ready?"

"As I'll ever be."

"We are an agency for the supernatural."

Dedication

To my parents,
who always encouraged my imagination;
my fantastic network of friends,
(Anna, Kathryn, Kim, Dina, Wendie, and Trish)
for being both my beta-readers and my support system;
my son Charlie,
the light of my life;
and finally to my husband, Dave, my real-life angel—
thanks for being by my side, now and always

Chapter 1

An innocuous little box tucked away in the middle of my new-hire paperwork made me almost want to cry.

By checking the little box labeled "divorced" on the W-4 form, I realized more keenly than ever how much my life hadn't quite turned out as I thought it would, an epiphany I didn't expect to have on the first morning of my new job.

I admit to feeling less than excited about my career path, or lack thereof. Personal assistant to executive partner may sound good on paper, but it's only a fancy word for secretary, not exactly a glamorous position at the best of times. Still, I needed a job, and The Aeternam Foundation offered a surprisingly decent salary so, as someone with only one year of college and five years as a society wife on her resume, I had no cause to be anything other than extremely grateful.

Nevertheless, the box seemed to cement the fact that I, at twenty-six years old, was divorced and alone and marking a box on a form for a job nowhere near the glittering career I'd dreamed of in my youth or part of the life I'd thought I'd found when I got married at twenty. That box symbolized a whole new chapter in my life, one I didn't expect and never truly wanted.

In short, the box had a lot to say for itself.

I couldn't be completely sorry, though, despite the box. I chose to make the change. I might have done my best to ignore my husband's selfish and self-destructive behavior and continued living life as a rich man's wife. Thrown myself into charity work, perhaps, had some children, or at least a purse-dog, and made a life for myself despite my unhappiness, but I didn't want to live that way for the rest of my life. So I left, determined to make it on my own. If that meant fetching coffee for some VIP, then that's what I would do. I'd been on my own before and survived, and this time I would not look to anyone else but me to make my life a happy one.

Finally finished with both the paperwork and the introspection, I handed my forms to the unsmiling HR assistant and sat back down to wait. Before I could get too deeply involved in the two-year-old magazine lying on the table next to me, Angela, the woman who'd interviewed me three weeks ago, strode into the room, her hand out to clasp mine in a classic firm handshake.

"Good morning, Gillian, good to see you again, welcome aboard." Angela spoke as if she was in a hurry to get it over with. All her words came out in a quick burst without pause for breath or punctuation. "You'll get your ID badge later today, right now let me take you to your desk so you can settle in. Michael will be in the office in about an hour so you'll have time to get settled before he gets here."

Stifling the need to take a deep breath on her behalf, I attempted a smile. "Great," I said. "I'm looking forward to meeting him."

A tiny pit of anxiety opened in my stomach as I followed Angela toward my new workspace, worrying thoughts playing in my mind. *What if I fail at my job? Would my new boss like me? Would I like him? What if I never learn to pronounce his surname properly?*

I didn't get the chance to meet Michael Àrsaidh, the executive partner I would assist, during my interview process because he'd been away. Tentative questioning during my interview told me only he was one of the three partners in the company, and the second in command, with no indication as to his personality, or what I might actually expect from my new boss. I knew I'd handle things like sorting mail and answering the phone, but would he also expect me to wash his car and pick up his dry-cleaning?

I spent the intervening days between my hiring and my actual start date imagining all sorts of possible personalities for my new boss. I could only guess at his age and appearance, and in my imagination he varied in looks and personality, depending on my mood. Sometimes he appeared as a dashing, silver-haired modern gentleman who treated me with respect, other times an elderly man of outdated morals who treated me like a peon. Occasionally, I pictured him with a monocle, just for fun.

Angela continued to yap at me in her strange manner during the elevator ride to the thirtieth floor, and I desperately tried to keep up with all the information she lobbed at me at breakneck speed. I had to take lunch between twelve and two, Fridays were casual dress, no personal usage of the postage machine unless I paid back petty cash and so on. I nodded where I thought appropriate, hoping these rules were written down somewhere, because I had little hope I would remember them all.

The elevator reached the executive level as Angela finished telling me about the company's Internet policy, and as the door slid open I gasped in surprise, earning a curious look.

"It's a lot more elegant than I expected," I said by way of explanation.

Actually, elegant, as an adjective, barely sufficed as a description of the suite. The word awe-inspiring leapt to mind, though intimidating might be closer to the mark.

I looked around with admiration as I followed Angela, my sensible heels making a hollow clicking sound on the dark marble floor. The walls were covered in deep, opulent damask wallpaper, and adorned with oil paintings of men and women, I assumed former partners of the firm. The far wall was made entirely of glass, affording a breathtaking view of Center City Philadelphia, the Delaware River and even a bit of New Jersey.

Tasteful wooden file cabinets stood on either side of the large windows, each topped with verdant plants. To my right was a waiting area with comfortable chairs arranged along the wall, and to my left were three impressive-looking oak doors with discreet brass plaques on the wall next to them. The executive offices, I surmised, each office guarded by a desk where the other two assistants were already seated. They both looked up as I walked past, and I gave a nervous wave.

"This is where you'll work. We encourage our employees to personalize their workspace so feel free to bring in pictures or plants or anything else you might like to have."

"Okay, thanks." I sat down at the desk, feeling kind of foolish, wondering exactly what I ought to do first. Large and old-fashioned, made of actual wood, the desk was a far cry from one of those pre-fab models so popular in modern offices. I vowed to myself right then to never eat or drink anything while seated there because, being me, I'd spill it within five minutes and ruin the finish.

"So, sort things out the way you like them. Michael will be in soon, and he'll give you further instructions, welcome aboard again. We're happy to have you here." With those words, Angela gave me a brief smile and strode away. The anxious pit in my stomach grew as the elevator door slide shut behind her; I felt almost like a child being left on the first day of kindergarten, scared and alone and unsure what to expect of this new world.

Well, not completely alone. I glanced over at the other two assistants, busily at work, both dressed in expensive clothes and looking far more like the society women I used to socialize with than how I imagined a glorified secretary would look. They must have sensed me staring at them because they turned to look in my direction, almost in unison. I gave a nervous smile and waved, suffering another wave of "new girl on the playground" fear, wondering vaguely if there was some sort of secret handshake or something I would have to learn in order to fit in.

One woman simply nodded curtly and turned away, but the other woman offered a warm, friendly smile and came over to my desk, offering her hand in a non-secret, welcoming handshake.

"Hi," she said in a chipper voice. "My name's Valerie. You must be Gillian. Welcome aboard!"

Not terribly tall, and leaning toward the plump side, although the word "curvaceous" fit the bill better, Valerie looked like she could have been one of those pin up girls from the 1940s. She had vivid green eyes and auburn hair done up in a simple, braided ponytail, a style I never could manage. I couldn't help the slight pang of irrational jealousy as I looked at her. As a little girl, I used to fantasize about having green eyes and auburn hair, a combination I believed would make me look glamorous and exotic. In reality, although my eyes might occasionally look green in the right light, they mostly stayed decidedly an un-exotic hazel, and my light brown hair, the follicle equivalent of hazel, grew too thick and too curly to ever stay braided for long. For special occasions, my former mother-in-law coerced me into visiting a fancy salon where they forced my hair into an elegant style with a decent level of success. Sometimes when the mood struck me, I'd attack it with a straightener, but I didn't have the patience to do that on a daily basis. Generally, I kept it shoulder length and loose and let the curls fall where they may.

Eye and hair color aside, Valerie seemed the kind of woman I aspired to be, someone who knew exactly who she was, secure in her own looks and personality. I mean, I'm not unintelligent, and while I may not be a beauty queen, I've always been perfectly content with my level of attractiveness, but even on my best day I never quite managed to capture the same easy confidence and style of women like Valerie.

Okay, I have to admit to more than a little pang of irrational jealousy, more like a stab, but it passed quickly, as these things do. I returned her smile with my own, eager to get to know her better. "Thank you," I said, using my best confident and optimistic voice. "I'm happy to be here."

I must not have completely succeeded in the confident and optimistic thing, because Valerie gave me a sympathetic look. "I know this place seems intimidating," she said, "but that's its job. After all, the clients we have need to feel impressed, or they might not think the service they receive is worth the money they pay." She laughed, and I knew I would like her. She had a fantastic laugh, warm and rich, the kind of laugh that makes you feel a little better about life from hearing it.

I laughed along with her, even though I still didn't actually know what the Foundation did, and why it needed to make clients feel like they were getting their money's worth. The online advertisement I responded to described it only as a consulting firm, and Angela remained vague on the details during my initial interview. I wasn't terribly comfortable pushing the topic at the time, and when I accepted the position, it seemed idiotic to ask what the company I agreed to work for actually did, so the details of the business remained a mystery.

I couldn't even find anything on the internet about the Foundation, other than the fact, while it existed in some form or other for something like two hundred years, the Foundation opened here in Philadelphia about ten years ago. The lack of information annoyed me. I prided myself on my research skills, and not knowing things ahead of time grated on my nerves like a toothache, but I tried not to let it frustrate me too much. I knew I'd learn what the Foundation did as soon as I actually began working with them.

"Anyway," Valerie said, "I think you'll find the work here unique, to say the least, and I'm pretty confident you'll fit right in!"

Before I could answer, what sounded suspiciously

like a scornful laugh caught my ear, and I glanced over to see the other assistant glaring in our direction before turning back to her work, looking pointedly busy.

Like Valerie, she exuded an air of easy confidence and looked exactly like…well, how you'd expect a beautiful, confident, expensively-dressed blonde woman to look. The stab came back, a bit stronger this time. "Hey, Rachel," Valerie called cheerfully. "Come meet Gillian."

Rachel looked up, giving me the most calculating look I'd ever seen before flashing me a brief, insincere smile. "Hello, Gillian," she said curtly, then turned back to her work.

"That's Rachel Matthews. She's the assistant to the Foundation's president, so she tends to be the busiest of all of us. She's a nice person, once you get to know her," Valerie added, probably in an attempt to justify Rachel's lack of warmth.

"I'm sure she and I will get along fine," I said, not believing a word of it. I spent five years in high society, interacting with women like Rachel, and we never quite managed to gel, despite efforts on everyone's behalf. I wasn't going to hold out too much hope Rachel and I would become BFFs.

"Her position can be a bit more stressful than ours," Valerie continued, clearly trying to sell me on Rachel. "Samuel is the big boss, not only in Philadelphia, but all over the world."

Ah ha, I thought. I learned something. Apparently, we were an international company. Good to know.

"Now my boss, Ralph, he's as mellow as they come," Valerie continued, "but Samuel can be a bit intimidating. It takes a certain kind of person to take him in stride; someone who can hold her own with someone like him and not get nervous when he gets…scary. He's a good man," she added obviously trying to reassure me. "But intense. Now your boss, Michael, he's the kindest being I've ever met. You must have noticed that when you met him."

"I haven't met him yet," I said. "He was away when I interviewed. Angela said he'd be in soon though."

"Really? So you don't actually know…" Valerie looked slightly worried, but then she grinned. "Don't worry, you'll like him. Like I said, he's kind, very laid-back and friendly. He positively spoiled his old assistant. They went out to lunch together once a week and he…" A funny look crossed her face, and she faltered a moment. "It nearly broke his heart when she left."

"Why did she leave?"

"It…she retired. Anyway…I'd better get to work. Give me a shout if you have any questions or need anything." I got the distinct impression Valerie didn't want to talk about my predecessor. I realized much later it should have seemed odd to me, but at the time it didn't register as strange. Besides, by the end of the day, so many other things occupied my mind, vague allusions to a former secretary barely even made the list of my concerns.

Valerie trotted back to her corner of the room, and I busied myself by arranging pens and turning on the computer, hoping I looked like I knew what I was doing.

The desk was so organized already I didn't have much else to do. I kept opening and closing drawers and rearranging the Post-it notes until I forced myself to stop fidgeting. Instead, I stared at the vast expanse of my desk wondering what I could bring to, as Angela suggested, personalize my workspace. I glanced over at Valerie and Rachel's desks—Valerie's overflowed with various plants and an enormous candy dish full of bite-sized chocolates. Tasteful crystal vases and an obviously antique mahogany desk set graced Rachel's workspace. I didn't have any family I knew of—keeping a photo of my mother would only depress me—and I killed any plant I had in my possession for over a day. I didn't even have any knick-knacks, not being a collecting sort of a person. I briefly wondered if books counted as personal items, or if they'd clutter up the place, when the elevator door slid open again with a tasteful dinging sound.

Automatically, I looked up, curious if a client or another co-worker was coming in, and nearly swallowed my tongue.

Stepping off the elevator was easily the most handsome man I'd ever seen. Any words to do him justice hadn't been invented yet. I could describe him as tall and obviously well-muscled underneath his bespoke three-piece suit, and how nicely his dark brown hair curled gently and fell just below his ears, and his eyes were the most vivid blue I'd ever seen. I could even attempt to explain the way everything else seem to fade into the background as he entered the room, or the easy grace he exhibited as he crossed the floor, but none of that conveyed the sheer beauty of the man. It didn't translate. He was, in short, amazing.

When he stopped at my desk, I realized two things. One, I was staring at him, and possibly drooling and two, he was my boss.

"Good morning, Gillian," he said in a rich, almost musical voice tinged with a touch of a British accent. "I'm happy to meet you at last. Angela has high hopes for you."

"Thank you, Mr. Àrsaidh," I responded, praying I got his name right. Searching the internet led me to discover his surname was Scottish-Gaelic; not the easiest of languages to pronounce, but I did my best. "I'm happy to finally meet you, too."

He smiled a predictably dazzling smile "Please, call me Michael. It's much less of a mouthful."

I nodded, managing to suppress my sigh of relief.

"Why don't you grab us both a cup of coffee, then we can go over what you can expect from me?"

"I'd be happy to." I smiled, doing my best imitation of a seasoned PA, although I suspected I sounded more like a nervous schoolgirl talking to a cute boy. "How do you take your coffee?"

"Unsullied," he said, grinning. I probably looked confused because he added, "Black, please." I cringed inwardly, already feeling like I would never get the hang of anything around this place.

Valerie pointed me in the direction of our break room, a fully-stocked kitchen with a large round table upon which sat a basket full of fresh fruit. A granite countertop stretched the length of the far wall along with the mandatory microwave and fridge. It even had a stove, worrying me slightly. *Do people work such long hours here it's necessary to cook actual meals?*

I found the fancy coffee machine, and managed to make two cups of coffee without creating a horrible mess. I walked toward Michael's office with the coffee in hand, terrified at any moment I would slip on the smooth marble floor, spill the coffee, and make a fool of myself in front of Rachel and Valerie, but, fortunately, I made it back without incident and a deep sigh of relief.

Michael was working at his desk, but leapt up to help me with the coffee as I gingerly made my way into the room. "Thank you," he said, "and please, sit down, make yourself comfortable. I need to finish this up."

I perched on the chair opposite him, took a nervous sip of coffee, burned my tongue in the process, and did my best to look at ease. I don't think I succeeded.

Eventually, he put his pen down and stared at me for an uncomfortably long time, like he was sizing me up. I took another sip of coffee, trying not to squirm under his gaze, and pretended not to be uncomfortable with the scrutiny. "I apologize for not being here to greet you," he said at last. "It's been a busy few weeks. Are you settling in okay?"

"I suppose so. I just got here." Afraid I sounded a bit pathetic, I hastened to add, "I think I'll be happy working here, though. It's a beautiful office."

"Yes, it is. Samuel likes things to look expensive."

"Valerie said it makes clients feel like they're getting their money's worth."

"Yes," he said, flashing me another dazzling smile. "She's not wrong. She's been with us for…a long time now, so she knows how it works."

"What is it you, I mean, we do here, anyway?" I ventured. "I know it has to do with consulting, but I didn't have much luck finding out any details."

"We'll get to that soon. I want to talk about you right now."

I stifled a sigh. I always hated this part of any conversation, the "tell me about yourself" thing. I never knew exactly what to say, what image of myself was the best one to portray. I'm me. Any attempt to explain came out sounding kind of awkward. "What do you want to know? Where I grew up, that sort of thing?"

"No. I already know the basic facts about your life," he said, pulling out a file from his desk drawer and flipping it open. "Your mother had you at eighteen years old, and you never knew your father. In fact, your mother claimed she didn't even know his name. You and your mother lived with your maternal grandmother until her death when you were six. You have no siblings and no extended family, at least not any you have a desire to speak to. Your mother committed suicide when you were sixteen." He paused to flip a page as I sat there, stunned, a prickle of apprehension running up my spine.

How did he know all this about me, especially my mother's death? I never told anyone how she died, at her own request. We weren't religious, but my mother was raised Catholic, and in her note she begged me not to let anyone know the truth about how she died. She didn't want people to think she went to hell. The coroner's report held the truth, of course, but it seemed extreme for my employer to dig so deeply into my past that they actually found the report.

"Let's see, after her death, you emancipated yourself rather than enter into the foster care system, well done, by the way." He paused to smile at me. I didn't smile back.

"After your emancipation, you completed high school with decent grades, despite holding down an almost full-time job." He put the file down and turned his full attention to me, his disconcertingly blue eyes locked onto my own. I clenched my teeth in an effort to control my emotions, and fought the urge to look away.

"It couldn't have been an easy life, Gillian. It shows real spirit of determination. You rather remind me of..." A sad expression crossed his face, gone so quickly I thought maybe I'd imagined it, then he turned back to the damn folder.

"Where was I? Oh, yes. You studied at a community college for a year, but quit when you got married, and lived on the Main Line with your husband and his family until about a year ago, when you filed for divorce." He smiled. "You could have asked for a large divorce settlement, but you didn't, preferring to make it on your own. Again, well done. It takes courage to travel the hard path and even more courage to walk away from something familiar, even if that something brings you nothing but pain." He closed the file and slid it back in his drawer. "Now, why don't you tell me something about yourself I don't know?"

"What else is there to tell? I'm surprised your ridiculous file doesn't tell you what I ate for breakfast, or what underwear I chose for today." Maybe sarcasm wasn't the best way to go, but the depth of knowledge my new boss threw at me scared me half to death, and when I'm frightened I tend to get angry. It's easier that way. "You have no right...how could you possibly..." I took a deep breath. "Where did you find all of that information, and what business is it of yours?"

Michael didn't look surprised, or even particularly concerned at my outburst. He smiled. "It's my business to know about people, Gillian."

I took another deep breath, forcing myself to calm down. I didn't want to risk losing my job on the very first day, at least I didn't think I did, but the information in that file went far above and beyond anything an employer could, or should, possibly know. "Okay, I can understand knowing about my emancipation, or my divorce, but how could you possibly know about my mother? Or the fact I don't know my father? That's..." I fumbled to find the right word. "Personal. And I know for a fact it isn't in public records."

"It's my business to know people," he said again. "You must understand the Foundation deals with extremely sensitive issues, and it is imperative I know as much about the people to whom I entrust my clients, and myself. Once you've been here a few days, you'll see what I mean. Trust me."

My turn to do the scrutiny thing to him. Michael waited patiently as I weighed my options. I studied his face, reminding myself handsome didn't always equal trustworthy, although my gut told me I could trust him. Still, could I truly accept the idea that digging into the intimate details of my life was a necessary part of vetting me for the position? Did I actually have a choice in the matter?

"I guess I understand where you're coming from," I said carefully. "It's...creepy, though, you having a whole dossier on me."

"I'm sorry, Gillian. It might be invasive, but not unnecessary, believe me. Yours is the kind of background we look for in an employee; someone with few ties to the outside world."

I thought of the stove in the break room. "Someone whose only life is the job, you mean?"

"Not exactly. At least not the way you probably think. We don't expect people to spend every waking hour here, but due to the nature of our business, we find it better that our employees don't have too many attachments. Does that worry you?"

I leaned back in my chair, trying to wrap my head everything. I still didn't even know what the Foundation actually did, so understanding why they felt it important I had no life was difficult, to say the least. "It doesn't worry me," I said. "It's not exactly like I have a much of an outside life, anyway, to be honest with you." I rolled my eyes. "That sounds pathetic, I know, but it's true. I don't have any friends around here. Don't have friends anywhere." I waved my hand vaguely at the drawer containing my file. "Well, as I'm sure you already know, after my grandmother died we moved practically every other year. Mom was always looking for a better job, or a better town, anything. Running all the time, I guess. When I married William, I thought finally I'd be settled. Safe."

"But then he got restless," Michael said, his voice full of sympathy. "He began drinking excessively, experimented with drugs, had…" Out came the file again. "Several run-ins with the police, among other things."

I didn't even bother to wonder how he knew. "I thought I could handle that, too. He could do his thing, and I'd stay at home, have children, and hold the right sort of parties and attend the charity events his mother held. But…" I stopped, aware I headed into dangerous over-sharing territory. My boss didn't need to know the sordid details of the last days of my marriage. "It didn't happen. So I left, and I moved into the city."

"Looking for a fresh start."

"Yes." I smiled wryly. "I'm more like my mother than I care to admit, I guess."

"And now you're here, with us. And I think you'll find we're exactly what you're looking for, Gillian." He left his side of the desk to stand next to me, and I stood as well, feeling awkward.

I giggled nervously. "Is this where I learn the secret handshake?"

For an answer, Michael took my chin in his hand, gently forcing me to look into his eyes. In normal circumstances, at such an intimate touch from a boss, I'd bolt out of the room and straight to HR to file a sexual harassment complaint. Instead, his gesture left me feeling breathless and more than a little intrigued.

He spoke again, his voice low, almost hypnotic. "Gillian Burke. You wanted a fresh start, and you found one with me, should you have the courage to take it, and I rather think you do. If you stay with us, we will be all the friends and family you'll ever want or need, Gillian. We ask much from you; I won't lie to you, but we give so much more in return, and I can promise you a life beyond anything you've ever experienced."

As abruptly as the moment began, it ended. Michael released me from his grip and stepped backwards. "Do you think you're ready to be a part of the Foundation, Gillian Burke?"

When I was around ten, my mother and I were almost in a car accident. We were crossing an intersection and a truck ran the red light. I remember seeing the headlights rushing toward our car, and having this fleeting thought when the truck hit us, my life would change forever. Time slowed down, and I sensed two of me, the "me" before the accident, and the "me after." Fortunately, the truck stopped in time, and we were fine, but I'd never forgotten that moment, the feeling of my life splitting in two.

Only two other times in my life had I experienced that sensation. The first time, standing by my mother's open grave, deciding then and there I was not going into foster care. The other time was the day I packed my bags and left my husband's house for good. Now, standing in the well-appointed office of my new boss, I had the feeling once again, my life was poised to change forever.

I gave myself a mental shake and flashed him my most confident smile. I was being ridiculous. I'd already taken the job without feeling dramatic about it. How life-altering could a personal assistant position be? Even *with* a boss as good looking and stomach tightening as Michael Àrsaidh. "I am absolutely ready to be a part of the Foundation."

"Well done, Gillian Burke, well done," he said, holding out his hand.

I had enough time to notice his firm warm grip before a sharp shock travelled up my arm and through my entire body, somewhat like static shock, but a hundred times stronger. Truth be told, rather more erotic, my body tightening and shivering at the sensation. The lights in the office seemed to brighten to an almost painful level, and I shut my eyes until it passed. When the room came back into focus, I sat in my chair with Michael back on his side of the desk.

"Right then. On to the business at hand," Michael said calmly, like the strange interlude never happened. "I suppose you'd like to know what we do."

I nodded, feeling completely at sea. Something about Michael made me feel dangerously off-balance. Not only because he was breathtakingly gorgeous, either. He had a quality, an oddness I couldn't quite put my finger on. Disconcerting, and more than a little bit sexy, I decided the safest thing to do, was play along, and hope I understood everything at a later date.

Michael smiled. He had, I noticed once again, an extremely nice smile. "I've found through the years the best way to explain what we do is to be as open and direct as possible. Are you ready?"

"As I'll ever be."

"We are an agency for the supernatural." He stopped, waiting.

I carried on looking at him.

"With me so far?"

I nodded, waiting for the punch line.

"Many different creatures exist in this world far beyond the realm of what you call normal, Gillian, and we are their guardians." He paused, again, staring at me for a long moment. "I am, for want of a better word, an angel."

Chapter 2

The only thing I asked for during my divorce was enough money to find a place to live and not completely starve to death before I found a job. William was petty enough not to acquiesce, and I don't know what would have happened if it weren't for his mother. I'd always been led to expect all rich, society women were self-centered and snobbish, but instead my mother-in-law was a down-to-earth, genuinely kind woman, who liked me in spite of my background. She thought me a good influence on her son which, I realized far too late, was probably a warning sign.

Through her intervention, I received enough money to support myself while I got on my feet, and, again thanks to her, I had the means to buy what was locally known as a "trinity," a small row house consisting of three one-room floors. From the ground floor, tiny, twisting stairs led up to a small bedroom and a bathroom, and other stairs led down into the minuscule kitchen. The ground floor itself made up the living area. The entire place could have fit into my master bedroom in the house I'd lived in before the divorce, but for me it was exactly the right size. Like my own little nest, my house protected me, gave me a safe place, quiet and peaceful. Even better, I owned it completely, and it couldn't be taken away from me on a whim, like so many of my rented childhood homes.

After changing out of my work clothes and pouring a generous amount of wine, I returned to my living room, looking lovingly at all of the things that meant home to me, the oversized purple armchair I bought secondhand during my one year of college, the end table, once part of my childhood bedroom set, a tiny television and a bookshelf stuffed with books. They were mostly biographies, my books. I liked reading about other people's lives, real people who lived and laughed and cried and sometimes survived a much worse life than mine. It made me feel better.

These were the few possessions I could ever truly call my own, and they gave me the sense of peace I needed after a thoroughly confusing day. Comfortably real objects in a world made unreal.

I took a big sip of wine, and closed my eyes, still reeling from the events of the day. I'd thought the life I'd chosen would be simple and mundane. Instead, I found myself in Wonderland.

After telling me he was an angel, Michael sat there calmly, a small smile on his face, waiting for me to catch up on events. I continued to stare at him.

What else could I do? Saying "you don't look like an angel" seemed kind of flip and "shut the front door," my go-to expression of disbelief, probably too disrespectful. So I waited, sure any moment he would tell me what he actually meant by "angel."

"Okay, not an angel, exactly," he said, finally. "Not like what I'm sure you're imagining. No wings, no halos, no golden harps."

"Oh, wait," I said, light dawning. "Do you mean like the Make a Wish Foundation? Is that what we do here? Help people?"

"We do help people, yes, but it isn't what you'd call philanthropy. We're…guardians is a better word than angel. We help those you call supernatural, the ones who live on the fringes of the world, deal with the daily minutiae of life among mortals, and we protect mortals against the beings that would do them harm."

Okay, so not philanthropy then. I made an effort to wrap my head around his words. "What exactly is the definition of supernatural? Are you talking about things like witches? Vampires? Werewolves? Faeries? Zombies?" I faltered, running low on supernatural entities. "Ghosts?"

"Not ghosts," Michael said with a laugh. "Ghosts don't need our services."

I went back over my list. "So, yes to zombies? Really zombies?"

"Sometimes. Okay, they're not exactly zombies like you see in the movies. We call them 'revenants.' Revenants don't lurch around dripping blood and skin, eating brains like the movie version. They are spirits who return to their mortal body because they have unfinished business they need our help with. We don't get too many of those."

I didn't know what to say. Michael continued to smile, so I seized onto that like a life preserver. "You're kidding me, right? This is some sort of new person hazing thing?"

"I assure you I am being perfectly truthful."

"So there are zombies, sorry, revenants and vampires and, and stuff, and they come here. And I get them coffee?"

"Vampires don't actually drink coffee, but broadly, yes."

I didn't want to think about what types of refreshments I would offer a vampire, so I focused on something else. "And you said you're an angel? Or guardian, rather. What exactly does that mean?"

"It means I exist to protect the world from the supernatural, and vice-versa. I am here to make sure the balance stays balanced. We all are, Samuel, Ralph and I, and others of our kind who make up the Foundation. We, the partners, are all immortal, here to help those whose lives are also long or unusual to survive the modern world—we obtain, or in some cases, even create passports, birth certificates, that sort of thing. And when it is time for them to move on to a new location, we help them do that as well.

"In turn, we keep them in line. Vampires don't kill, faeries don't steal babies…and so on. If they do, they answer to us."

"Faeries don't steal babies?" My knowledge of faeries began and ended with Peter Pan, so this surprised me. "They actually steal babies?"

"Faeries are not nice. Something for you to keep in mind when you encounter one." He glanced down at his calendar. "Which is actually around eleven o'clock today, so be prepared. He'll try to charm you. Don't let him."

"Oh. Okay." I drifted on a sea of confusion at this point, and the only thing I could do was hang on, metaphorically speaking, and hope eventually something would make sense.

"Vampires come in at night, naturally, so on those days you are expected to work what we jokingly call the 'graveyard shift.' We try to schedule the local vampires all on the same day—it can sometimes be a long night, so generally you don't have to come into the office until around four, and aren't expected to come in until the afternoon the day after so you can sleep in. I understand sleeping in is a luxury most mortals enjoy."

"Angels don't sleep then?" I asked.

"No. No, we don't. Though"—he leaned forward as if imparting a great secret—"I'll admit to sometimes giving it a try. "

I attempted to laugh along with him, but I was still a bit too stunned to find angel humor terribly engrossing. He must have noticed I looked less than amused, because he cleared his throat and continued, "As for the rest of it, you'll learn as you go. Jump right in, it's the best way."

I didn't know what else to say. I kept waiting for him to say something, anything, to explain to me what he was talking about. I detected no hint of glee in his demeanor to indicate he was putting one over on his new assistant, no suppressed laughter. He sat there, looking calm and serene.

"Generally at this stage in the conversation, I'm asked to give some sort of proof," Michael said, grinning in amusement.

"Okay, then," I said. "Give me proof you're truly an angel."

Michael looked thoughtful a moment. "I want you to think of an object, something beloved from your past. Perhaps a toy you loved as a child, but have since lost."

"The music box," I said, astounded at how quickly the memory jumped into my mind. I hadn't thought about it in years. Gran's music box, the one thing in her house she would let me play with. It fascinated me as a child, and I loved it above all my toys. "Shaped like a Swiss Chalet," I said. "You know? Like a little cabin, with these beautifully painted flowers in flower boxes on each window, all red and green and white, and it had little piles of snow on the roof. I used to wish I could live in a house like that; some place cheerful and bright and beautiful." I swallowed the tears threatening to spill, feeling a bit foolish something so silly could stir such emotion. "When you lifted the roof of the house, it would play a song."

"What song?"

I frowned, trying to remember. "I'm not sure," I said. "I don't know if I ever knew the name of it."

"And what happened to the music box?"

"When my grandmother died, my mother sold absolutely everything in the house to give us enough money to make our first move, including the music box." Just six years old, I was old enough to feel a touch of resentment toward my mother and the unfairness of it all. It was the only thing I wanted to keep, but it got boxed up and shipped away with everything else from my childhood.

Michael nodded, his expression solemn, and held out his empty hand. No fanfare, no bells and whistles, just his empty hand and a moment later, my music box, not a copy; the actual music box once belonging to my grandmother. I saw the chip on the side where I'd dropped it when I was four.

Michael handed me the music box, and I took it gingerly, certain it would pop like a bubble when I touched it, but it sat solid in my hand. I recognized the weight of it, the rough texture of the tiny ceramic flowers as I ran my fingers over them. From somewhere deep in my memory came the same joy I felt whenever I got permission to play with it, and my lips curved in to a dopy smile.

Carefully, I lifted the lid and a tinny tune began to play. "Greensleeves," I whispered. "That's it. That was the song." Once again, tears filled my eyes, and I tried in vain to blink them away, embarrassed at the emotional display. "I'm sorry," I said, trying to laugh. "I feel like an idiot."

Michael stepped out from behind his desk to kneel in front of me. "It's understandable," he said softly, "and it does you credit. There's nothing wrong with a little sentimentality now and then." He brushed his fingers across my cheeks, wiping away some still falling tears, another startlingly intimate move I think took both of us by surprise. His vivid blue eyes darkened as his hand caressed my cheek, and I thought for a heart-stopping moment he might kiss me. I sternly reminded myself I'd sworn off relationships and sex, and as an angel, Michael was probably even more out of my reach than the usual boss/secretary out of reach-ness. Still, I wanted to put my own hand on his face and kiss him like my life depended on it.

Fortunately, or unfortunately, I honestly wasn't sure which, Michael seemed to pull himself together, and stood, his face returning to its original, professional expression. "It will get easier, Gillian, trust me," he said, returning to his side of the desk once more. It was safer there, I guess.

I wiped my face with my fingers, and sat up straighter. Trying to pretend like my entire world view hadn't been turned upside down. "I'm fine," I said. "And I guess I believe you. You're an angel, and we work with magical people."

"Don't be afraid to ask questions. Valerie and Rachel are old hats at this. They'll help you through the difficult bits, and by the time your probation period ends, none of this will seem strange at all."

Oh, right. My probation period. Angela told me the first thirty days were a trial period, to make sure I was right for the position. After Michael's startling revelations, it made sense. I needed the time to make certain the position was right for me. "What happens if I fail?" I asked, struck by a thought. "Do I simply walk away knowing all this weird sh…stuff exists, and you hope I don't give it away?"

"If it comes to it, Gillian, which I very much doubt, you will not be burdened with this knowledge in your future."

"How exactly will I not be burdened? I mean, do you do some sort of psychic mind trick on me or do you have me killed?" I laughed a bit, hoping I had actually made a joke.

"Mind trick," he said with a grin. "You'll be free to go back to your normal life, and you won't spend the rest of it looking over your shoulder making sure vampires aren't coming to get you, should you decide you can't handle life among the supernatural."

"Okay. That's good then, I guess." Knowing I could walk out the door and back into a normal life without any consequence gave me a sense of relief, though mostly it made me determined to survive this strange new world I found myself involved in. I may be many things, but I don't like to quit. Or lose.

"I have some letters I need you to type up," Michael said calmly, like we'd been talking about office work this whole time. "When Gerald comes at eleven, please let me know at once."

"Gerald being…"

"The faerie, yes."

Right. A faerie called Gerald. It just kept getting weirder. I took the papers he handed to me. A thought struck me when I reached the door, and I turned around. "If I do leave, and forget all about this, would vampires follow me?"

He laughed. He had a nice laugh. "No, they won't. As I said, we have a covenant with them. They don't hunt humans; we let them live."

There were dark harmonics to what he said, making my pulse race with a sudden rush of fear. Okay, I admit it was kind of sexy, actually, but in a scary way. Michael may be an angel, and probably on the side of goodness and righteousness, but I knew being good didn't automatically mean he was nice. "Right. Good. I'll just…I'll go type."

I found Valerie waiting for me when I returned to my work space. I smiled at her, placing the music box on my desk, still half-expecting it to disappear. It sat there, looking solid and ordinary, a piece of bric-a-brac to "personalize my desk," but it freaked me out. Glad as I was to have the box back in my life, it also proved to me I was well outside normal, and I still didn't quite know how to process all this new information.

"How did it go?" Valerie asked eagerly. Her expression told me she knew the content of my conversation with my new boss. "How are you feeling?"

I calmly opened the folder Michael had given me and shrugged, trying to convey the idea working for supernatural entities didn't faze me at all. "It's all a bit odd, but I'm fine, honestly."

She nodded toward the music box. "I see Michael did the memory thing. They like to give you something personal, kind of a welcome to the weirdness present. Mine was a china doll I'd coveted from afar when I was a girl." She smiled at the memory. "A schoolmate of mine owned it, and she quite liked lording over me her family had what mine didn't. I thought if I had that doll, I'd be as good as she was." She shook her head, smiling ruefully. "Silly, I know, but when Ralph gave me that doll, I knew no one would ever make me feel inferior ever again. I'd found the place I belonged."

A china doll struck me as a rather old-fashioned toy to be jealous of, but it wasn't my memory. "Did you find it hard to deal with when you first got here?" I asked instead. "If you don't mind telling me."

She laughed. "Oh, goodness! I didn't think I would survive my first week, but figured I should at least try. I decided I'd keep to myself, do the best job I could, and hope no one would hurt me. Then the first client came in. He was a kelpie." Her eyes softened at the memory. "He helped me through my first month, and I knew I would survive. And I haven't regretted it for a moment."

"What the heck's a kelpie?"

"A Celtic shape-shifter. They usually lurk in the rivers and lakes, or rather lochs, of Ireland and Scotland. Quite dangerous, actually, they used to lure people into the water and drown them. Most of the time, they look like horses, but when one has business with the Foundation, they come in human form. I nearly choked when he walked in, unbelievably handsome, I can tell you, and dripping wet. Charming Irish brogue." She sighed, looking wistful for a moment. "Those were interesting times, heck, they are still interesting times."

"And you like it?"

"Wouldn't trade it for anything in the world."

She looked sincere. It gave me hope. "How long have you been working here, anyway?"

"Oh, quite a while now," she said evasively. "So I'm here if you have any trouble coping. You'll do fine, though; I have a good feeling about you." She laughed again and rolled her eyes. "You should have seen the first two girls brought in to replace Michael's old assistant. Pathetic, they were. The first girl, after Michael told her the truth, ran out of his office and right onto the elevator. Didn't even stop for her purse. I tried to return it to her, and she refused to let me in. I wound up leaving the bag on her doorstep."

"She did?" I preened a bit, feeling a bit smug. At least I didn't run screaming from the room. Well, okay, the thought might have occurred to me, but I didn't follow through, so I counted that as a win.

"I know, right? What a silly girl. The second one made it until her first vampire, and never came back the next day. Oh, don't worry," Valerie said quickly, "she didn't get eaten or anything. We checked. She couldn't deal with the weirdness."

"I'm sure I won't bail," I said, hoping I sounded confident.

"Yeah, I don't think you will. I certainly hope not, anyway, you're pretty much the last chance for Michael."

"Last chance? Last chance for what?"

"Valerie!" Rachel's crisp voice interrupted. She'd

come over so quietly I hadn't even noticed her standing behind me. "We need to let Gillian get to work. We have a busy day ahead of us."

"Right. Sorry. Just shout if you have any questions," Valerie said, looking relieved at the interruption. The two of them went back to their desks, and I turned to my own work.

Shout if I have any questions? I had a million, starting with whatever Valerie started to say before Rachel interrupted her. I decided, however, to focus on the work Michael gave me, and pretend I knew what I was doing.

I found it difficult to concentrate on typing, however. The letters themselves were so bizarre to me I had to force myself not to sit there reading them with my mouth hanging open.

I learned a lot from those letters, that first morning. My first piece of correspondence was to Athena, as in the actual Greek goddess, informing her we had her paperwork ready so she could complete the purchase of a condo in Ardmore. Athena, currently employed as a physics professor at Villanova, went by the name Anna Owlsley; an amusing, if a bit obvious name I thought, but who was I to argue with the goddess of wisdom?

Upon questioning, Valerie told me many so-called mythological gods and goddesses, or creatures who called themselves so at any rate, existed and lived in various parts of the world, generally passing as humans and minding their own business. I spent a good half hour looking some of them up, in case a more obscure god should cross my path sometime in the future. It never hurt to be prepared.

The morning passed quickly, and I began to feel,

well, maybe comfortable was too strong a word, more like I could actually get through the day relatively unscathed, when the elevator dinged again, signaling a visitor.

For the second time in one day, I gasped in surprise, but this time one of dismay. Stepping off the elevator was my ex-husband, William.

Despite everything, a little thrill tingled through my veins at the sight of him, reminding me how much I once loved him. He looked exactly how he always did, ash-blond hair slicked back in its usual manner, his handsome face inscrutable. I stood up, willing myself to remain calm and professional, a woman standing on her own, independent and strong. I didn't want him to have an excuse to tell me, once again, what a mistake I'd made in leaving him.

And yet sometimes, I still struggled with the loss of our marriage. I loved him so much, once upon a time, and he'd been so kind and loving in return. I saw him as my knight in shining armor, rescuing me from the sadness and uncertainty of my early life. I truly believed with William I'd found happily ever after. Unfortunately, "ever after" lasted a little more than two years. William worked in his father's company, and came home to me every day at five, a fifties-sitcom husband. We honestly enjoyed each other's company; we needed no one else.

The change happened slowly. He'd call maybe twice a month to tell me some friends wanted him to go for drinks and did I mind? Before long, he spent the majority of his time with this bunch of disenfranchised rich people, bad seeds, his mother called them, whose idea of a good time was seeing how much trouble they could get into. Before I knew it, he'd beg me to go with him to some ridiculous night club in New York in the middle of the night, or scream at me because I'd questioned his drinking at nine in the morning. When he tried to use me as a bet in a poker game, I'd had enough.

My jaw tightened in frustration as he sauntered to my desk. How did he find me? I didn't credit him with having the brains to actually track me down, detective style. His mother must have told him. I mentally slapped myself on the head. Of course, she did. She still liked me, and made it a point to check up on me to see how I was holding up. When I told her I got the job offer, she was positively thrilled for me. William liked to check up on me too, in his way. He called me once in a while, usually when he'd been drinking, either begging me to return, or berating me for leaving, depending on his mood. I hadn't set eyes on him since the divorce finalized, though. He had to have a pretty good reason to come and face me in person. I swallowed tightly, silently preparing myself for whatever drama lay ahead.

"Hello, Gillian," he said in his familiar drawl. "Aren't you happy to see me again?"

"William, what are you doing here? Is everything okay?"

"Everything's fine. I miss you, that's all. Nothing has been right since you left me," he said, leaning so far over my desk I backed away.

"William…"

"No, I'm serious. I'm want you to know I'm so sorry for everything, and I'm hoping maybe you'll give me another chance. I promise I will do everything I can to change, I mean it. I thought we could have lunch, and try to talk things through."

I stared at him, familiar emotions sweeping through me. I wasn't sure if I wanted to tell him to go the hell away, or take him up on his offer, but as I opened my mouth to frame some sort of response something stopped me. I can't say exactly what, but something wasn't quite right. He looked like William, definitely his face, his voice, and his winsome little smile (the one that caused me to forgive him far more often than I should have), but something was off about him. His eyes looked wrong. They were the same pale blue I used to love, but he looked, not exactly cold, I'd seen William look coldly at me before (and not drunk or stoned because, believe me I'd seen that too), but empty, devoid of any kind of human emotion.

Now, I'd accused him of being devoid of any human emotion on more than one occasion during the crash of our marriage, but this was different. Nothing had changed in his looks, his face was still as familiar to me as my own, but I didn't see any trace of the William I'd once known, good or bad.

My computer dinged at me, and I glanced over to see the notification I'd set up to remind me of the eleven o'clock appointment. I almost laughed.

"Gerald," I said in a cool and professional, only slightly quavering, tone. "Michael is expecting you. Please have a seat, and I'll tell him you're here."

I'd spent part of the morning on Google, researching some of the legends about faeries, and one of the things I learned was they could look like anyone they chose. Why he chose William I could only begin to guess, but I knew, or at the very least was fairly sure, the person in front of me was not my ex-husband.

Luckily, I was right. The William in front of me looked startled for a moment, then dissolved, revealing a tall, thin man with pale green skin and bright red hair, rather handsome, in an otherworldly way. Handsome if you like green skin, at any rate. I thought of Valerie's kelpie, wondering if he looked anything like the creature in front of me. For all I knew, it *was* the creature in front of me.

"Well done," he said in a voice sounding almost like music. "First time in ages it didn't work."

"How did you do that?" I blurted before I lost my nerve. "How did you know who to look like?"

"I can read your thoughts, girl," said the faerie. He leaned over my desk until we were almost nose to nose. It took all of my willpower not to back away, I wasn't going to give him the satisfaction of showing him I felt frightened or uncomfortable. I mean I was frightened and uncomfortable, but I didn't want him to know, if I could possibly help it.

"He's prominent in your lovely little mind, my girl. I can see the pain he caused you, the pain he still causes. I can see the dreams he gave you, and the dreams he took away. It's all there, for those who know how to look. He's taking up quite a bit of your soul." He backed away, grinning like a cat. "I'd do something about that, if I were you."

"Please have a seat, and I'll see if Mr. Àrsaidh is ready for you." I spoke firmly, to keep my voice from cracking with emotion. So that's a faerie. Not nice, indeed. I only allowed myself to relax once Gerald entered Michael's office, and the door shut behind him.

"Wow!" Valerie called from across the room. "I'm

impressed. How did you see through his glamour?"

"His what?"

"Glamour. It's how they keep humans from seeing their true form. They think it's funny to trick us. God only knows what he would have said to you if you'd believed him. Who was it he imitating, anyway?"

"My ex-husband."

"Oh. Oh dear. Well, good for you. You saved yourself some pain, I think."

It didn't feel like it, I thought, but didn't say so out loud. I couldn't believe how much seeing William, or at least a William lookalike, hurt me. And what did he mean about him being prominent? I kept telling myself I was over my failed marriage, over William and his broken promises, but clearly I wasn't.

"You have good sight." This came from Rachel, which surprised me. "You notice things. That's important, in this job."

"Thank you. I'm glad you think so." Maybe she and I would be friends after all.

Rachel sniffed haughtily, and turned back to her work.

Okay, maybe not.

I turned back to my own work, still shaken from my encounter with Gerald. I suppose I should have known William wouldn't have bothered to track me down anyway. I tried not to dwell on the fact I harbored the tiniest bit of disappointment he hadn't actually come begging me to return, concentrating instead on the fact whatever Gerald tried to do to me, he didn't succeed. Score one for me.

I hoped I'd be on my lunch break before Gerald came out of the office again.

Unfortunately, a few minutes later my phone beeped at me, and Michael's voice came over the speaker asking me to please join them in his office. Steeling my nerves and stifling a curse, I went to see what else was in store for me.

Gerald sat in one of the two chairs opposite Michael's desk. He looked, insofar as I could tell, chagrined. Michael, for his part, looked stern. I took the other chair, scooting as far away from the faerie as possible without it being too obvious.

"Gillian," Michael said. "I understand Gerald unsuccessfully tried to deceive you. Is that correct?"

I glanced over at Gerald, who grinned at me. "Um…"

"Oh, go ahead, girl, tell the truth. It's fine by me."

"He came in imitating my ex-husband. I'm not quite sure why."

"Because a part of you wanted him to find you and beg you to forgive him," Gerald said with a wicked grin. "Oh, it's a small part," he added, apparently reading my mind again. I hoped he heard the curse words I threw at him. "I simply wanted to see how easily you would be swayed by his promises again."

"But why?" I almost wailed. "Why would you do something like that?"

"Because it's fun," said Gerald, "because human emotions are like wine to the Fey. Because you are in mourning and don't even know it—"

"Enough." Michael broke in, his voice stern and commanding. Immediately, Gerald sat back, looking cowed. "There are rules the Fey abide by, besides the one set down by us, and because you called him out, as it were, Gerald owes you a gift."

"I don't think…what kind of gift?"

"Anything you want," said Gerald in his musical voice. "Anything."

"Within reason," Michael added.

"Well, I…" Just when I thought this day couldn't get any weirder. "I can't think of anything I need or want."

"That cannot be true. All humans want something."

"Honestly, I can't think of anything I want right now."

Gerald looked thoughtful. "Are you quite sure? Let's find out, shall we? Look at me, Gillian Burke."

"Gillian, don't!" Michael's warning came a moment too late, and before I could stop myself, I looked into the faerie's eyes. As I stared, his eyes shifted colors going from gold to brown to amber to green and back again. My vision blurred, and I felt like I was drifting off to sleep, like a part of me floated away from my body.

When Gerald spoke again, he sounded far away. "Interesting. I see an old longing to know who fathered you, but, no, you have no wish to bring him into your life now. I see regrets, but no desire to change what is past. I see wrongs done to you, but no real wish for vengeance. How unusual for a human. I see wishes in your heart, but you reject all of them. You gave up on wishing a long time ago, didn't you, Gillian Burke? Isn't there anything you desire?" He gave a cold little chuckle. "Or anyone, perhaps? The field is wide open."

I admit I wavered a bit. William was the only man I'd ever been with, and in the year since my divorce I've experienced my share of lustful dreams, especially in the first, lonely days after I left, but pursuing a relationship, sexual or otherwise, wasn't something I wanted to deal with at this strange stage in my life. The memory of my first glimpse of Michael flashed through my mind, and I wavered for a moment before breaking away from Gerald's hypnotic gaze, hoping he didn't read my sudden and lustful thought about my new boss. I shook my head emphatically. "Just…promise you won't try to hurt me again, and we'll call it even," I said.

"I am already bound to that promise through Michael, here," said Gerald. "Okay, fine. You win. We'll put it on hold, for now. If you ever need me to grant you a wish, simply call my name, make your wish, and I shall grant it."

I nodded in agreement. It seemed safe enough. I certainly had no plans of ever calling on Gerald.

"Good. I'm glad that's settled," said Michael. "Gillian, why don't you take your lunch break while I finish up here?"

I nodded again, glad to get out of there and away from wishes and faeries. I needed something solid and real, preferably something with mustard on it.

The remainder of the day was comparatively uneventful. After lunch, I sat with Valerie to learn the computer system which, by the way, was somehow able to tap into every single database in the world with only a few keystrokes. I ended the day by basically forging a new pilot's license for a normal-looking woman who hailed from a completely different planet.

Weird day.

After I'd finished dinner, I put on my most comfortable pajamas, and curled up on my purple armchair, planning on seeking some semblance of normality from something inane on television. But the stress of the day, and two glasses of wine, caught up with me, and before I knew it I'd fallen asleep.

And I dreamed.

I dreamed of my wedding day. I stood in the vestibule of old historic St. Mary's Catholic Church, waiting to walk past the close to four hundred guests in attendance, none of whom I knew. The marriage of William Bradley III was a big event, and the most of the people who made up Main Line society wanted to see and be seen at the wedding, even though the majority didn't have a clue who I was.

I didn't care, though. I was too happy to care what the guests might think of me. I had finally found what I'd been looking for my whole life, stability, peace, a family who loved me. I saw William standing at the altar, waiting for me, and a tiny flutter of nervousness kicked up in my stomach.

Someone took my arm to lead me down the aisle, and I turned to see who it was. I had no family, no one to give me away, so I'd planned to walk the aisle alone. Next to me, smiling proudly, stood a tall, handsome man with long, platinum blond hair cascading past his shoulders and startling blue eyes eerily identical to Michael's. I didn't know him but, in the nature of dreams, he seemed familiar, like someone I should recognize.

"So, Gillian, are you ready for this?" His voice was gentle, with fatherly harmonics, but the sound of it sent a chill through my body, filling me with a sense of dread.

I wanted to turn and run, but my feet were no longer under my control.

The music swelled, and we began the long walk down the aisle. I struggled to stop, to pull myself from the stranger's grip, but it was like an iron band around my arm. My feet, following orders other than my own, continued toward the altar, and I was powerless to halt my progress.

The detail in the dream was incredible. The church looked exactly how it did during my actual wedding, right down to the ridiculous amount of flowers decorating the aisle, but with subtle and disturbing differences. As I passed them, the flowers withered and died, and the traditional wedding march being played on the organ sounded sinister and full of foreboding. Above, the white stars painted on the blue ceiling blurred and grew into angry-looking eyes, glaring down at me.

I tried to look at the people in the pews, desperately hoping to find someone who might help me escape, but as I passed, everyone turned away from me, hiding their faces in their hands.

As we continued the inexorable walk down the aisle, the lights above me flickered one by one. Again, I attempted to pull away, but the man next to me kept a firm grip on my arm. My heart pounded in fear, my breath coming in sharp gasps. The lights continued to go out as I passed under them, and I knew when I reached the altar I would be in complete blackness. The idea terrified me. I couldn't let that happen.

It took all my strength, but I forced myself to stop walking. The one lone light still lit shone down on me like a beacon of hope.

"No!" I shouted. "I'm not going. I'm dreaming, and I am going to wake up." I turned to face the man next to me. "Let me go."

In answer, he grabbed my chin, a mirror of what Michael did earlier in the day, but this time it was cruel, almost painful. His blue eyes blazed as he stared intently into my eyes, and his thumb traced a teasing pattern across my cheek for a moment. His touch filled me with revulsion, and I swallowed the bile rising in my throat. "Who are you?"

With a final caress, he released his grip. "I'm a friend. I simply want to help you, Gillian my dear. Believe me, the Foundation is no place for you. Forget Michael, he'll only break your heart. You belong here, safe with the humans living your normal, human life. Now let's get you back where you belong, with your loving husband."

The William at the altar turned to face me. I tried to scream, but nothing came out.

The face was William's, but barely, so ravaged as to be almost unrecognizable, the skin lacerated, one pale-blue eye hanging from its socket. When he smiled, a thin trickle of blood poured from his mouth. Once again, I fought against the bile rising in my throat. A few moments ago, I had to force myself to stop moving and now when I needed to flee, my feet stayed traitorously rooted to the spot.

The mockery of William reached toward me, holding a ring in fingers that were almost all bone. The ring itself was made of silver, and etched with intricate symbols. The ring, beautiful though it might be, terrified me almost more than the fleshless hand holding it.

"Don't be shy, Gillian. It's time to wed." The man beside me grabbed my hand and forced it toward

William's, and I knew if he put that ring on me I would be lost forever. I struggled, but I was still trapped in the grip of the blond man at my side.

The ring was almost at my fingertip when a white-robed figure leapt in the way, knocking the bloodless hands away from my own.

I turned to see Michael, wearing the minister's garb. "Gillian," he said, his voice urgent. "You must run. Now!"

My body back under my control, I turned and raced up the aisle, stumbling slightly as my legs tangled in my long, petticoat laden skirt. As I ran, the blond man said, "Yes. Run. Run now. But before you do, tell Michael I'm coming back." His cruel laugh echoed through the church, mocking me as I stumbled toward the exit. "Tell him we are all coming back!"

I woke up, my heart pounding, feeling confused and disorientated. Usually when one wakes from a nightmare, the terror of the dream fades in the face of the gaping plot-holes and nonsensical events. Awake, what was so terrifying in the dream is not even a bit frightening, but this time the terror stayed with me.

Everything was still, no sound in my house except the ticking of the old clock sitting on top of the bookshelf, telling me it was half past three in the morning. I sat in my chair until my heart rate returned to normal, and I'd almost reached the stage where I could laugh at my silly dream and go to bed properly when I heard it, a whispering voice seemingly coming from everywhere at once. The susurration got louder and clearer and, finally, I made out the same four words repeating, terrifying me to the core of my soul:

We. Are. Coming. Back.

Chapter 3

Alice may have believed six impossible things before breakfast, but six was way over my limit. I could just about handle the fact my boss was some sort of angel and a faerie owed me a favor, but believing some disembodied voices shouting at me in the middle of the night was too much. Which was why, when I woke up the next morning, I put the strange noises I thought I heard down to nothing but aftereffects of the bad dream. I rationalized the dream as stemming from too much wine on top of a confusing day.

The rest of the week went by quickly. There was quite a bit for me to learn, naturally, but as the days went on, I managed to get a good handle on things. Interesting how quickly the strange and unusual becomes commonplace.

Well, not exactly commonplace. Dealing with the supernatural continued to astound me. Every day brought some new revelation, but by Friday, I felt pretty confident in my ability to deal with the extraordinary whenever it cropped up.

Then I met my first zombie.

Sorry, *revenant*.

She didn't have an appointment. Apparently, they're not good about that sort of thing, what with being dead and all. She came to see Ralph Darthair, not Michael, so I relaxed and watched as Valerie, a seasoned professional, made the zombie comfortable before she went to inform Ralph of his client's arrival.

I'd never been a big horror movie fan, but based on the general pop culture knowledge I'd collected over the years I always assumed zombies lurched and drooled and slurred their words. Or word. As far as I knew "Braaaainnnns" was the only thing zombies ever said.

This zombie looked, let's face it, she looked embalmed, but didn't otherwise look like a corpse. Clothed in an elegant and weirdly immaculate dress, she certainly didn't look like she'd clawed her way out of a grave recently.

I tried to concentrate on the social security form I was currently forging, but my gaze kept drifting back to the zombie as she sat quietly in our waiting area, flipping through a magazine. Was there a big hole next to her tombstone where she crawled out, or did she teleport here? Did anyone notice? Were people running around in a panic at her absence? What did she think about being a zombie?

She must have sensed me staring at her, because she turned to look at me, giving me a slightly disturbing smile. I smiled back, ashamed at my gawking then, gathering my courage, I went over to speak with her.

"Hello," I said. "Can I…er…get you anything?"

She shook her head. "Thank you, no." Her voice sounded rather labored, like it took extraordinary effort to speak, but I heard the humor in her tone when she added, "I don't think I could actually digest anything anyway."

"I hope you don't mind," I said after a moment, "but I'm new here, and I'm still learning about…things.

May I ask how you came here? I mean, how did you know to come to this office?"

She shrugged, and her arm made a sort of cracking sound. I tried not to show I noticed. "I woke up knowing." She turned to look directly at me, and for the first time I saw a glimmer of a horror movie zombie. Her eyes burned with an expression of anger so intense I found myself taking a step backwards. "I was killed. Robbed and left for dead on the street. I died for no good reason, and my murderer walks free. I want justice, and I will get it before I rest."

"Oh." I fought the urge to run, and tried to smile. "I hope Ralph can help you, then." I wanted to ask what kind of justice she expected, if she meant arresting the guy or settling for ripping his arms off, but I wasn't quite sure how to phrase the question.

She must have read the question in my eyes, because she actually laughed. It sounded painful. "I expect your firm to use their resources to find the person who did this to me. When I know he will answer for his crime, I believe I will be able to rest."

"Did you…" I took a deep breath, not sure how to ask the question. "Did you, do you remember going to heaven or anything?"

"I remember being killed, and seeing myself lying on the ground, and the blood, and watching as my murderer ran away, my purse in his hands. I remember seeing my funeral, and my family walking away from my grave." She stopped, and it looked as though the memory was painful for her. I instantly regretted asking the question.

"It's okay," I started. "You don't have to…"

"I felt a great pull and found myself back in my

body again, knowing I must come here, to the Foundation to find Ralph Darthair. He will listen to my plea. Once I know your people will find my killer and avenge my death, I will go. Where, I don't know yet." She gave another painful-looking smile. "I hope it is somewhere good."

"Well, good luck," I said lamely, then nearly fled back to the relative safety of my part of the office and pretended to be busy looking for a file. She seemed nice, for a dead person, but I still felt uneasy for reasons I couldn't quite define. I hated being judgmental so early in my career, but I didn't think dead people should be walking around. It didn't seem right.

A few minutes later, Valerie ushered the revenant into Ralph's office, and I breathed a sigh of relief, rather like I'd narrowly escaped something dangerous.

The simple data entry I'd been tasked with left a large part of my brain free to ponder things, and kept replaying my conversation with the zombie in my mind. What exactly was the Foundation's policy on helping zombies achieve justice? Did we go to court? I imagined telling a judge the information presented came from the dead woman, and giggled. That probably wouldn't go over very well. Personally, I'd be happy if we sent someone, maybe a vampire or one of the minor gods, to exact revenge on whoever killed her, although the Foundation probably had a more ethical solution in mind. Eventually, overcome with curiosity, I knocked on Michael's door. "Do you have a minute?"

"What can I do for you, Gillian?" he said, smiling and waving at the chair opposite him.

"I have a question."

"About the revenant, I presume?"

"Yes. I'm trying to understand…everything, I guess." I laughed. "I'm not quite sure where to start."

Michael put his pen down and leaned back in his chair, giving me his full attention. "Begin at the beginning," he said with a grin. I couldn't help but grin back. I recognized an *Alice Through the Looking Glass* quote when I heard one.

I took a deep breath, trying to figure out which question I needed answered first. Tough choice. "That woman, the zombie…sorry, the revenant, said she's here because she was murdered, and she wants us to help find her killer. She said she found herself back in her body, but I thought zom…revenants were created by other people, voodoo and dead chickens and whatever."

"Sometimes quote unquote zombies are created, that's true. Those we actually call zombies, not revenants. Fortunately, there aren't many people who have that kind of power, and the ones that do…we're talking dark magic in that case. The Foundation does not look kindly on those who use dark magic, and we will stamp it out whenever we can."

"So a created zombie is different than, er, our client?" I made a mental note to find out the revenant's name. It seemed disrespectful to continue to think of her as a thing. She's still a person, albeit a dead one.

"Correct," Michael said. "Created zombies are more like puppets, generally without sentience and controlled solely by the one who created it, whereas revenants, like our client, exist because they have a strong reason to stay in their body. Being murdered is a pretty strong reason to stay around."

"But lots of people are murdered," I said. "How

come the world isn't knee deep in zombies…revenants?" Who knew saying "zombie" was such a hard habit to break?

"Having that sort of will-power is extremely rare, which is why we don't get too many revenants seeking our services. Most people don't have the strength to continue on after death. I imagine it's because, for most people, dying is a relief, even if they are murdered." A strange look passed across his face at this point, but before I could analyze it, he continued. "However, on rare occasions, there are those whose, let's call it a life-force, is so strong it keeps them from fully dying until they are satisfied."

"What if we can't help her? What happens then?"

He looked thoughtful for a moment. "We'll help her, don't worry. It's basically a matter of…manipulating some people so they find the person who killed her. It's so much easier to solve a murder when the victim can point out her killer."

"Think how short the murder mystery books would be," I said, and Michael laughed, pleasing me much more than it probably should have. "But what if, hypothetically, we can't help a z…revenant. What happens? Will she stay un-dead forever?" I pictured our client lurching through the streets of Philadelphia, seeking revenge on the person who murdered her.

"The life-force can only sustain the body for so long. It will slowly drain away until, eventually, the body becomes lifeless once again. They become less and less aware as this happens, which is where the idea of the lurching zombie comes from."

"Do they eat brains?" I asked, only half-jokingly.

He didn't laugh, which worried me. "The ones like

our client don't. They still retain the same morality and humanity they had when they were alive. Made zombies usually work for someone for dubious reasons, and the best use of a made zombie is as a weapon. They are stronger than a human and even many supernatural creatures, and they don't stop fighting. They don't eat brains, but what they can do isn't usually pretty."

I shuddered and hoped I'd never meet a made zombie. I hesitated, then plunged ahead. "I have one more question, if that's okay?"

"Only one? Go ahead, ask away."

"How did she know to come here? She said she woke up knowing. How does that work?"

"Ah, that's even more complicated to explain. Let's call it 'magic' for now, okay?"

"I suppose so."

"Don't look so downcast. It's not that I think you can't handle the answer, but you need a bit more experience working with the Foundation before the answer makes any sense to you."

I smiled. "Fair enough."

"Is everything set up for this afternoon?"

I had already become accustomed to Michael's abrupt subject changes, and mentally shifted gears from zombies to staff meetings with only a modicum of effort.

"Yes." I went through the check list in my head. "I ordered the cookie platters and the fruit; the new pens and personalized notepads came in yesterday, so I'll put them at each seat. Should I put coffee in an urn, or will people get it themselves?"

"They can bring their own coffee," he said. "No point in spoiling everyone."

A couple of hours later, I was alone in the conference room, making sure each seat included a pen and a pad of paper, and arranging a couple of pitchers of water on the table. The cookies looked delicious, but my stomach was too full of nervous butterflies to think about sampling one of them. I would meet all the company leaders for the first time, and I wasn't entirely sure what to expect. I knew a few people, of course. Angela from human resources and Stacey the office manager, but for all I knew IT was run by a robot and vampires ran the marketing department. In short, I had no idea what to expect during this meeting.

Stacey arrived first. "I'm always relieved to have time away from my desk," she said to me cheerfully, grabbing a couple of cookies from the tray. "You have no idea some of the ridiculous phone calls I get. Honestly, if one more person asks me if I want to buy toner, I'm going to seriously consider turning them into a newt."

I liked Stacey. She was in her mid-forties, extremely cheerful, and a witch, a real, caldron-stirring, broomstick-riding witch. She'd already offered to turn my ex-husband into a newt, which I turned down after a few moments of internal struggle. When I asked her why a newt, she said because she was a Monty Python fan. She also collected cat figurines.

Angela arrived next, followed by her unsmiling HR assistant, Lisa, who Valerie told me was fairly new to the company, having joined a couple of years ago, and simply a non-magical human. My tentative questioning revealed Angela was also human, although, based on her speech patterns, I still wasn't completely convinced. If she were from another planet or something, I wouldn't be surprised.

Michael and Ralph arrived soon after, chatting in low tones, followed by Valerie. Ralph was as handsome as Michael—it must be an angel thing—but in a different way. His wore his ginger hair closely cropped and was shorter and stockier than Michael. He looked more like a football player than an angel. I hadn't spoken much to him, but he seemed kind enough. He gave me a friendly nod before sitting down and turning his attention to his phone.

My first real surprise came when the two men from the Accounting Department walked into the room. I thought at first they were identical twins, but a moment or two of observation indicated they were even more identical than twins. Twins generally exhibited slight differences, even if one needed to look hard to find them. However, the Accounting Guys were completely identical to the absolute minutest detail. They had exactly the same short, graying hair, dark skin and deep brown eyes. I estimated them at least six foot four, and underneath their expensive-looking, identical black suits lurked bodies of weightlifters. They looked more like CIA agents than accountants, but from what I understood their job went above and beyond normal accountancy. The Foundation occasionally had to create new identities for clients from scratch. It made sense to entrust serious, if scary-looking, people to make sure the money was legit, or at least looked legit.

Their clone-like bodies might have been odd enough, but after a few moments of observation it got even odder. As I smiled nervously at them, they nodded, flashed me identical smiles, grabbed a cookie, and poured water into their cups in complete and perfect synchronization.

If they had actual names, I never learned what they were. They were addressed only as the Accounting Guys.

Shortly after the arrival of the Accounting Guys, a small man, kind of wiry-looking, and so full of nervous energy he practically vibrated, came bounding into the room, introducing himself as Roger, the IT Manager. "Hey there!" Roger said, shaking my hand vigorously. He had a curious way of speaking; the words came out in little bursts, almost like yaps. "Good to meet you. How's your computer treating you? Any problems you let me know, okay? Good."

He didn't seem to be a robot although with his wire-rimmed nerd glasses and white button-down shirt, he looked more like he played the part of a computer geek than actually being one. He grabbed a handful of cookies, waved cheerfully at Valerie, then sat down next to her, giving her a positively cheeky grin. I had the strangest urge to pat him on the head.

Everyone sat down, chatting lightly and filling plates with the cookies and fruit. We were waiting, I assumed, for the president of the Foundation, Samuel Gwaladr. Perhaps the Foundation had a requisite for partners to have nearly unpronounceable surnames. I hadn't seen him come in the office at all which puzzled me slightly until Valerie told me he had a private entrance into his office and rarely came out into the main area. I didn't have the nerve to ask why. He was the boss, reason enough I supposed.

I didn't know what to expect with Samuel. I knew Ralph and he were the same type of being as Michael, angels or guardians or whatever, but as the leader,

Samuel was more, well, powerful I suppose is the right word. Michael said when it came down to it, Samuel's word was law, and everyone, partner and supernatural creatures alike, couldn't help but obey him.

My imagination drew Samuel as a tall, imposing figure, all flashing eyes and authoritarian airs, but when he walked in, followed closely by Rachel, he was nothing I expected.

Instead of the intimidating giant I envisioned, Samuel was slight, not much taller than Rachel, with pale, practically translucent skin and hair so blond it was almost white. Still as handsome as Michael and Ralph—definitely an angel thing—Samuel nonetheless struck me as an unassuming sort of person, someone you wouldn't look twice at if you passed him on the street. He looked more like an accountant than the accountants.

There was no question he was the boss, though. As soon as he entered the room, everyone got quiet, all eyes turning to him. He sat down at the head of the table, and nodded regally, signaling the start of the meeting.

Michael stood up. "Welcome everyone to the monthly meeting of Aeternam Foundation. I realize having a meeting on a Friday afternoon can be difficult. I'm sure most of us are already thinking about our plans for the weekend, so I promise this will be as painless as possible, and then you can pick which happy hour to go to."

Everyone giggled dutifully, and I imagined what my co-workers might do for fun at the weekend. I easily saw Rachel visiting the art museum, and Valerie having drinks with friends, but I completely failed at visualizing the partners doing anything as mundane as going to a movie or grocery shopping. I bit my lip to suppress a giggle. It would be like seeing your teacher outside of school, mind-blowingly out of context.

I couldn't even *begin* to guess what the Accounting Guys did for fun. Looking at them surreptitiously from beneath my lashes, I tried to envision them hanging out at a bar or going to a ball game. It didn't work. I couldn't picture them doing anything outside the office, with the possible exception of assassination. They had that kind of look.

I mentally shrugged, leaving that mystery for another day, and turned my attention back to Michael. "As you know," he said, "My assistant Barbara left us a few weeks ago. I know we were all quite fond of her, and she will be missed." Everyone murmured in agreement then bowed their heads, as if observing a moment of silence. What the heck happened to my predecessor? I'd tried to find out several times from Valerie, but she wasn't forthcoming. I thought perhaps she died, but why would that be a big secret? Unless, of course, something supernatural killed her, and they didn't want to freak me out. The thought was logical enough to disturb me.

Moment of silence over, Michael continued, "However, we were fortunate enough to find Gillian Burke, who has already proven herself as Aeternam material. Please, make her feel welcome."

Now everyone applauded, making me blush. I was grateful when Michael cleared his throat and moved on to the next order of business.

Considering what the Foundation did, one might think the meetings would be full of interesting tidbits, but once you got past the subject matter, the nature of the business was still business, in other words, rather dull. The Accountant Guys spoke after Michael, droning on about taxes and investments and the general state of the finances, and other boring things that didn't sound any less boring in unison. I jotted down notes on my notepad when appropriate, and tried not to yawn too loudly.

Their lecture over, I turned my attention to my notepad with the intention of flipping to a new page. Instead of the financial information I thought I been copying, I'd written, "We are coming," over and over again.

I bit my tongue to keep from crying out, and carefully looked around the table. No one else seemed to have any issues. Ralph was in the middle of explaining new policies being created by the Foundation to help overcome some of the more difficult Homeland Security measures that had cropped up in recent years.

In short, everything still looked like we sat in a perfectly normal business meeting; people contriving to look alert and interested, despite the meeting stretching into its second hour. People nibbled on the remaining cookies, laughing when Valerie made a Lucky Charms joke after Ralph mentioned a family of leprechauns who needed help immigrating into the States.

I noticed Michael looking at me, and I grinned sheepishly, feeling like I'd just got caught daydreaming in class. Show him what happened, I told myself sternly, but when I looked back down at my notepad I nearly shouted out loud, managing at the last minute to turn it into a cough. Gone. The strange words were gone.

All my notes were back on the page, including the badly drawn cat I made at a particularly dull moment in the meeting. I scribbled my name a couple of times on a new page, then stared at it, waiting to see if the words would morph into something else, but the writing on the page remained frustratingly non-mysterious.

Ralph finished his spiel then Samuel, who hadn't spoken a word during the entire meeting, rose from his chair. All noise in the room ceased, and everyone sat a little straighter. Now for the keynote, I thought.

A thunderous knocking interrupted Samuel's greeting, echoing throughout the room. Before anyone could react, the door opened with such force the hinges splintered off the wall, forcing the door into the room with a resounding crash.

There in the doorway stood the revenant from earlier, oblivious to the fact she'd knocked our door down.

"Mrs. Anderson, I already told you we would do everything in our power to bring your murderer to justice," Ralph said in a kind, firm voice, almost like talking to a child. "So please, go back to your grave; you are in good hands. Don't worry about the door; I am sure you were unaware of your own strength. We will take care of it."

The revenant didn't move, and a prickle of worry crept along my spine. She seemed different, somehow. Wrong. When I first saw her she looked, well, dead, but still human. Now, standing in the ruined doorway, she looked more like the horror movie zombie I'd imagined. Her eyes, intense but friendly when I first met her now seemed blank and empty, almost like the human part of her got switched off somehow.

"April Morgan Anderson." Samuel's voice touched me like a caress, making the hairs on my arms rise with goose bumps. I wrapped my arms around my torso protectively when he spoke again. "You do not belong here, April Anderson. Go back."

Samuel spoke gently, but the command was evident. No, not a command, more like a magical impetus, brooking no arguments and impossible to disobey. I actually found myself moving toward the door before I managed to gain control. I wasn't the only one, either. Even Michael stirred in his chair, and Angela had to hold Lisa back.

I clearly watched it work on Mrs. Anderson. Head bowed, she turned and headed back through the ruined doorway. I thought that would be the end of it, but then she stopped—pardon the expression—dead, almost like she'd run into a wall.

"Mrs. Anderson." Samuel's voice took on a harder edge, and I shivered as the magical command zapped through the room. "You must go now."

With jerky movements, Mrs. Anderson took a few more steps forward. It looked to me like she had to force herself to move, but at least she moved.

A general sense of relief filled the air as Mrs. Anderson lumbered out of the room, but my own sigh of relief caught in my throat when, with a loud, anguished wail, the revenant turned and lunged straight at Rachel.

Chapter 4

Someone screamed. It might have been me. Rachel initially managed to fling herself out of the way, but the dead woman moved deceptively fast and soon closed in on the terrified Rachel. Next to me, I heard Stacey muttering something and flipping through the book of spells she always kept with her, but everyone else seemed frozen with shock. The zombie, and I found myself not correcting the term, almost had her hands around Rachel's throat when I heard a growl come from my left. I turned to see Roger the IT guy in a crouch, his teeth bared and fingers curled into claws, his wiry hair standing on end.

Before I could process this new piece of weirdness, Roger sprang across the table and lunged at the zombie, knocking her away from Rachel. He and the zombie went flying across the room, hitting the wall with such force it left a dent.

I didn't see what happened next, partly because of where I stood, but mostly because my eyes were closed. Sounds of teeth tearing into flesh reached my ears, and my fevered imagination pictured the zombie ripping into Roger's throat. I swallowed hard to keep from vomiting, covering my ears for what little good it would do. The sound of tearing flesh mixed with a cacophony of moans and growls still filtered through, filling my mind with all sorts of gruesome images.

An anguished yelp forced me to open my eyes in time to see Roger fly straight up into the air. He landed on the heavy conference table so violently the table cracked in half, and lay there as still as death.

Valerie screamed as the zombie struggled to her feet, turning again toward Rachel, still cowering on the floor behind Samuel.

She, or it, was completely unrecognizable from the woman I'd spoken with in our office just a few hours ago. Bits of skin and some kind of liquid covered her once immaculate dress. Deep scratches shredded one side of her face, and much of her neck was gone, leaving her head to tilt at a strange angle. White bone showed through the strips of flesh on both her arms, and her left leg bent at an unnatural angle. One ear remained attached to her head only by a thin strip of flesh. Yet still she lumbered toward the cowering Rachel. I bit back the urge to scream. What good would it possibly do?

"Michael, Ralph!" Samuel shouted from behind me. "Now!"

The partners stood in a circle, fingertip to fingertip, whispering in a language that sounded vaguely like Latin, but older, more arcane. The whispering words echoed strangely throughout the room, and once more the hairs on my arm stood on end.

The zombie's labored progress halted abruptly as she hit some sort of invisible barrier. I swear I even heard a crack as her head smashed against something unseen. She turned around, only to meet the same resistance, looking like a macabre version of a mime pretending to be stuck in a box. I covered my mouth with my hands to keep myself from bursting into hysterical giggles.

Meanwhile, the chanting got louder and louder, and as the strange syllables reached a crescendo, the zombie let out a terrifying wail. An anguished cry, full of pain and fear and sadness and loss, mixing with the chanting like a chorus in a way that might be beautiful if it weren't so terribly sad.

"What's happening?" I asked Stacey. She'd stopped flipping through her book and watched the three partners with admiration.

"They're binding her; they're the only ones who can. That's not strictly true." She waved her book. "I could do it, but it wouldn't last as long. What they do is permanent."

I looked back at the zombie, trapped in the invisible box, her body rocking back and forth violently, like someone caught in an earthquake. "What do you mean permanent? What's going to happen to her?"

"I don't know. Some people might say she was sent to Hell, but as a Wiccan I don't believe in hells. It's possible her soul, or at least whatever is driving her body, will disappear. I honestly don't know."

I looked back at the zombie, feeling sad for some inexplicable reason, and that's when it happened. What "it" was I could never articulate, but I know I saw something shift in her expression. The emptiness left her eyes, replaced with one of pain and fear. Despite the ruined flesh, she looked less a horror movie zombie and more like something human. As human as someone could look with her head nearly severed from her body, anyway. I don't know exactly what possessed me, but before I knew it I cried out, "Wait! Stop! Don't hurt her!"

The three men turned to look at me, surprised. "Look. Look at her face. That's Mrs. Anderson! She was already murdered once, just don't…" I faltered, not sure exactly what I wanted to say. "Don't hurt her anymore."

The three men held a whispered conversation then Samuel walked over to the zombie and said something I didn't catch. She didn't respond, but a tear slid down her cheek. Samuel nodded, resting his hand on top of her head.

As I watched, entranced, a yellow glow surrounded the woman, and one by one all her wounds sort of retreated into themselves, like a film being rewound, until she was whole once more. She turned to me, still surrounded by a golden light, and said, "Thank you." The light grew in intensity, forcing me to turn away until the light faded away. When I looked back, she was gone.

The entire incident took less than five minutes.

"What an interesting way to end a week." This came from Roger who, to my amazement, sat up in the remains of the table, grinning. Valerie rushed over to him, and helped him disentangle himself from the wreckage of the table. I noticed she and Roger held onto each other a little bit longer than necessary, and mentally filed it under mildly interesting things to think about later.

"What on earth is going on here?" Angela demanded. She looked equal parts frightened and angry, standing in front of Lisa like a shield. Lisa, for her part, looked positively terrified, not that I blamed her. She kept staring at Samuel like he was the most frightening thing she'd ever seen, making me curious about her role in the Foundation, and how much of the supernatural part of the business she saw on a daily basis.

Michael gave a tired shrug. "I am not quite sure yet."

"She wasn't a made zombie, though," Valerie said. "I talked to her. She came here looking for help. How did she turn into that…that…thing?"

"It can happen," Ralph said. "Someone with strong magic could easily hijack a revenant and bend it to his will." The three partners shared such a meaningful glance I thought perhaps they already had a suspect in mind.

"Gillian Burke." Samuel stood in front of me, and I yelped in surprise. I didn't even see him move. I stared up at him, lost in awe. The power, or magic, or whatever you want to call it still emanated from him, almost like a physical force. "Why did you tell us to stop?" he asked me.

I swallowed nervously, wondering if perhaps I'd done something wrong, Samuel's quiet voice and inscrutable expression didn't give anything away.

"I just…" I faltered, not sure how to explain what I saw, or thought I saw. "I saw something in her eyes. When I met her the first time, she looked alive, or alive-ish at least, but when she came in here she looked empty. Then when you were…" I waved my hand, trying to indicate something I didn't have the vocabulary for. "She changed, like a light coming on in a darkened house." I shrugged. I could barely explain it to myself rationally, let alone to a room full of people more experienced in supernatural affairs. "She looked like a person again." I thought about that for a moment. "Well, a dead person, but still human."

To my relief Samuel smiled, and seemed to understand what I was ineffectively saying. "You have good sight," he said, placing what I'm sure he thought was a comforting hand on my shoulder, but Samuel was too awe-inspiring a figure to be comfortable, and I resisted the urge to flinch away.

Before I could say anything more, he turned and held his hand out to Rachel, helping her to her feet. She looked unharmed, if rather disheveled, but grabbed onto Samuel's hand like a drowning victim. I didn't blame her; I'd have a hard time staying cool if a zombie attacked me. "That thing came for me, Samuel. Does that mean…"

"We'll discuss it later, Rachel. Now is not the time."

"But Samuel…"

He gave her a brief hug, and whispered something into her ear that seemed to please and upset her at once. She pulled away from him, and it looked like she wanted to argue some more, but he gently shook his head. "Come. You need some tending to."

He turned to me again, giving me the briefest of smiles. "You've done well. I think Michael is in good hands." To the rest of the staff he said, "I think, considering the circumstances, we can close the office a bit early today. Have an enjoyable weekend, everyone." With a final, inscrutable glance at Michael and Ralph, he left the room, his arm around Rachel's shoulder.

"All right! Happy hour time!" Roger shouted, pumping his fist in the air. I wasn't sure I'd be in the mood for company after being smashed into a table, but

Roger was obviously made of sterner stuff. "Eulogy here we come!"

Stacey and Valerie cheered in agreement, while Angela and Lisa declined. To my surprise the Accounting Guys said, "I'll get my coat." I didn't think they would do anything as human as drinking in a bar, and the image of them getting drunk in unison made me grin, imagining the reaction of the other people in the bar, with two enormous and intimidating men moving and drinking in perfect synchronicity. Would it cause a commotion, or would everyone else be too busy with their own drinks to notice, or care?

The others bustled around, talking about the bar and making jokes about whose turn it was to pay, reminding me of my days growing up, ever the new girl in school, standing alone on the playground as the kids laughed and played around me. As a grownup, I knew I should put on my big-girl panties and invite myself along, but I couldn't quite work up the nerve to do it. So I hovered in the background, ostensibly picking up pens and coffee cups so as not to look too pathetic as everyone began to file through the broken doorway.

"Gillian, are you coming?" Valerie called to me, and I smiled gratefully at her.

"Oh, yes, of course. Absolutely," I said, hoping my voice didn't sound as relieved as I felt, and followed after her, trying not to grin too broadly. We had survived a zombie attack, after all. In the grand scheme of things being invited to hang out with my co-workers was a minor victory, but it filled me with a warm sense of contentment.

Eulogy turned out to be this tiny, two-story bar in the historic part of Philadelphia known as Old City, one of my favorite parts of Philadelphia. Home to Independence Hall and the Liberty Bell, Old City retained its Colonial feel, with small, brick-fronted buildings and cobblestone streets. I loved the feeling of stepping back in time while walking through that part of town. Roger was surprised when I mentioned never visiting Eulogy before. I'd never been a bar-hopping kind of girl, and when I moved to the city, I didn't have anyone to hop with so I wasn't overly familiar with the Philly hotspots.

We arrived a little after five, the tiny pub already crowded with people eager to start their weekend. I followed my group up the narrow stairs, and into a slightly more private room where we crowded around a long table, I realized with amusement, made from a coffin. Even in the private room, the noise level made it difficult to hear anyone around me. I resigned myself to simply nodding politely whenever it seemed someone spoke to me, when Stacey made a complicated gesture with her hands, and the sounds of the bar faded away. "I put us in a circle," she said to me by way of explanation. "Now we're protected in case of any more zombie attacks and, more importantly, we can hear each other over the sound of the drunks. It's kind of a bonus."

"Don't people notice? I mean, when the server comes to our table, won't she notice there's no noise?"

She snorted derisively. "You'd be amazed at the things people don't notice."

Valerie laughed. "That is so true. Trust me, Gillian, after a few weeks, seeing the things we see on a daily basis, you're going to wonder how people so blind actually make it through the day." She and Roger sat across from me, hands clasped, and I silently congratulated myself for guessing their relationship status correctly.

"You've had an eventful first week at any rate," Roger said to me after everyone settled in place. "So what do you think of it all? Do you think you can go the distance?"

A pregnant pause followed his question as everyone turned to look at me. "I don't see why not," I said finally. "After all, I survived a zombie attack; I think anything else will be anticlimactic." I must have given the right answer, because the atmosphere at the table lightened in a way that emphasized the importance of Roger's question. That puzzled me a bit. I couldn't quite grasp why it mattered so much. Maybe they were tired of Michael's assistants fleeing the scene every five minutes.

Conversation then turned to the zombie attack, but not in any kind of serious way. There were ridiculous zombie jokes, laughter and good-natured teasing of Roger for going after her. I joined in with my own jokes, enjoying myself thoroughly, basking in the companionship of my new colleagues. For the first time in a long time, I knew I belonged somewhere, and the notion filled me with a warm, contented feeling. What's a few zombie attacks compared to finding a group of real friends?

The server came then, and we ordered our drinks. Not being a big fan of the taste of beer, on Roger's advice, I ordered the cherry-like Kestel Rouge, and he got Abbaye De Saint Bon-Chien. "I like the name," he said to me with a wink.

I thought about it a moment. *Chien* was French for

dog, if I remembered my high school class accurately. This begged the question I didn't know exactly how to broach.

"Go ahead," he said, apparently reading my mind. "Ask me."

"Are you a werewolf?"

"Yep. Born and, if you'll pardon the expression, bred."

"Do you turn into a wolf at the full moon and all that Hollywood stuff?"

"Yep! When the moon is full I have no choice but to turn. The rest of the time I can shift whenever I want."

"And do you…" Again, I struggled to find a way to phrase the question in a way that didn't come across as insulting or idiotic. I saw Valerie listening in, an amused expression on her face, and I wanted to get it right. "Does anyone have to chain you up or anything?"

"No." He glanced at Valerie. "Not for the full moon, anyway." They both giggled, and I blushed. "No, my sort of werewolf is the kind who knows exactly what's going on. I'm perfectly capable of not ripping someone's throat out when the moon is full."

"And you heal easily, as evidenced by today's activities."

"Yep, it takes more than the walking dead to hurt a werewolf, no fear there. I live much longer, too. Yet another bonus."

Valerie chimed in. "Understand, it doesn't mean there isn't the other sort. Roger is a born lycanthrope; that's fancy talk for werewolf, but others are…cursed, I guess is a good enough word, and those are the ones you need to watch out for. Those are the ones our

Foundation keeps an eye on and, yes, chain up when necessary."

"So it's a bit like the zombie thing—there are horror movie monsters out there, but they're created by someone on purpose, to do harm?" When Valerie nodded I continued, "Does that mean most of the supernatural people the Foundation deals with are naturally, um, supernatural?"

"Not supernatural. That is a human term," the Accounting Guys said, startling me. They'd been so quiet I'd almost forgotten they were there. As imposing as they looked, I noticed they seemed to fade into the background when they wanted to. Yet another eerie thing about them. "What we are, and what we do is part of the natural world. But you are right. There are things out there who wish to upset the balance of the natural, and those are the ones to fear."

"Come on guys," said Stacey. "Cool it with the ominous talk, there's no reason to scare her."

"There are portents. Look at what happened today. It is a warning."

"Come on, nothing like that has happened in over three hundred years," Stacey argued. "Not since Salem."

"It does not mean it cannot happen again. Evil never dies."

I half expected the lights to flicker, or the room to thicken with eldritch cold. The Accounting Guys' in-unison speaking, coupled with talk of evil not dying practically begged for special effects lighting.

Fortunately, our beers arrived, and conversation drifted into more normal territory. Well, as normal as possible considering the company. No one else seemed unduly concerned with the Accounting Guys and their warnings, but I couldn't get it out of my head. I kept thinking of the notepad, and the strange message that appeared on it. In the drama of the zombie attack, I'd almost forgotten about it, but the Accountant Guys' warning about portents and evil made me wonder if something sinister truly was going on.

"Hey, Gillian, are you okay? You look worried." Valerie's voice cut into my thoughts, and I shook my head.

"Sorry." I almost told her about the notepad, but stopped. I'd mostly convinced myself I'd imagined the whole thing and, while it might be childish, I didn't want her to think I couldn't handle the strange goings-on at the Foundation. I didn't want her, or anyone at the table, to think less of me, and freaking out over a probably imaginary threat wouldn't do my reputation any favors.

"I'm wondering what portents I should look out for," I said instead. "Is it something that's going to happen, or something that happened already? Is there truly evil lurking around every corner, or is the Accountant Guys' nature generally ominous and freaky?"

Valerie laughed. "Definitely their nature."

For the rest of the evening, every time I tried to find out more information as to what evil the Accounting Guys were worried about, or what incident happened three hundred years ago, Valerie bought me another drink until all my questions were drowned in a sea of alcohol.

When we finally left Eulogy, at last call, I found myself standing on the sidewalk with the Accounting guys. I decided I'd try one last time to get some answers.

I hoped they'd be a bit more forthcoming than Valerie. At the least, they couldn't distract me with another drink, since the bar had closed.

"You said today was a warning." I blinked. The copious amounts of alcohol I'd consumed meant I occasionally saw four Accounting Guys, and it made it difficult to concentrate. "Who is warning us?"

"We do not know."

"But look. The zom…the reva…the dead woman, Mrs. Anderson. She was fine…" I stumbled a bit over the use of the word "fine" to describe a dead person. "…when she first came in, but then she changed and got all attacky." I paused. The word didn't sound right. "Attackable? Attacking. Evil. Do you think the…the…thingy that took control of her did it only to warn us?"

"Today was a warning and an attack." They must have anticipated my next question because they added, "We do not know exactly what forces are behind today's attack. We only know it will be the first of many."

"But why?"

They looked at me again, their twin gaze disconcerting. "Because, Gillian Burke, there are things who hate everything our Foundation stands for; creatures who wish for chaos and evil to walk this earth, for wickedness to reign. The innocent always pay the price."

With that, they walked across the cobbled street and disappeared into the night. Literally. When they got to the corner of the block, they faded away into nothing.

Six impossible things? Alice was an amateur.

I woke the next morning with a raging hangover, and the urge to find the grave of Mrs. Anderson. I knew I'd never forget the look on her face when she transformed back from the mindless zombie, and the look on her face right before she disappeared. Bad enough she was murdered, the idea of her body being used in someone else's crime after her death made me sad. I wanted to take something to honor her. Laying flowers on her grave seemed like the least I could do.

I dedicated much of my morning to research until I discovered she'd been buried at Laurel Hill. Impressive, considering Laurel Hill was an historic cemetery, full of all sorts of rich and vaguely famous dead people. More research told me I could take a bus to the cemetery, but my aching head made that idea particularly unappealing. Living in the city, I had no real need to drive anywhere, leaving car rental as my only option. Sorting all that out meant it I didn't reach the cemetery until late afternoon.

I wasted more time trying to find directions to her grave site, and then got completely distracted by the cute little gift shop and museum. The cemetery itself was fascinating, a sprawling marble forest with towering obelisks and imposing crypts. Hilly too, and I was more than a little out of breath by the time I got to the central part of the graveyard where Mrs. Anderson was buried.

As I crested the top of the hill, I saw one other person standing near a headstone, a tall man with long blond hair practically glimmering in the afternoon sunlight, contrasting with his dark clothing. His face I couldn't see clearly, but the bit I saw was rather handsome.

So intrigued by this mysterious figure, I didn't see the low stone wall surrounding a grave and tripped, sprawling ungracefully onto the manicured lawn. When I regained my feet and my dignity, the man was gone.

His sudden disappearance didn't strike me as odd, although if I hadn't been so embarrassed at tripping in a graveyard while ogling a handsome man, I might have been more worried. There were so many structures, he could have disappeared behind one of them when I wasn't looking, and at the time it didn't seem terribly important to me.

Much later, I realized how wrong I'd been.

At long last, I found Mrs. Anderson's grave at the foot of the hill I'd walked up, looking serene and undisturbed, no sign of her having climbed out of it recently. At least it proved her family didn't have to fear her body being stolen or something. That was a relief.

I'd brought a bouquet of wildflowers I bought at one of those little sidewalk carts in the city, and placed it at the foot of the grave marker, a pretty headstone that simply read, April Anderson, Aged 54, Beloved wife and mother. Tears filled my eyes, both for her, and for the children she'd left behind. Once again, my thoughts turned to my own mother, but as always, I pushed the thought aside.

I sat down in front of the stone, wondering exactly what I should say. I never understood why people talked to tombstones as a general rule, but in this case, I thought it possible she might just hear me.

"Hi, Mrs. Anderson…April. It's me, Gillian, from the Foundation." I looked around, feeling embarrassed.

I'd thought for a second someone was listening in.

"It's beautiful here," I continued, "quite peaceful and serene. I think your family will find some measure of comfort when they come visit your grave, and I hope you found peace and comfort in…well, wherever you went. Don't worry about the bast…" I stopped. Cursing in a graveyard seemed disrespectful. "Man that killed you. The Foundation will bring him to justice, providing closure for your family, and I also wanted to say I'm sorry you were hurt, both when you were killed, and yesterday, in the office. What happened to you…" I broke off, again, certain this time I'd seen someone standing near me for a moment, but the area was completely empty.

Another website I'd found told me the cemetery was haunted, and after the week I'd had, I didn't doubt it. I told myself ghosts wouldn't be any bother, but I couldn't shake the uneasy feeling settling over me. I shook my head to dislodge my disquieting thoughts, and turned back to the headstone to murmur a final goodbye.

As I stood to leave, I thought I saw out of the corner of my eye someone standing near me, but when I looked, there was nothing but gravestones and grass.

"Right," I said out loud. "You're being oversensitive due to the whole zombie thing. Jumpy. And you drank more last night than you have in ages. You're imagining things." I walked firmly and purposefully to where I hoped I'd parked my car. "Enjoy the beautiful autumn day. Focus on history and architecture, and not ghosts and zombies for a while. And stop talking to yourself. You look crazy."

My only slightly insane pep talk helped calm my

nerves. I relaxed and began to enjoy myself when, just for a second, I was certain someone walked right next to me.

I shuddered. *Beautiful day or no, I'm going home. And, quite possibly, jump in bed and pull the covers over my head.*

I walked faster, my heart thumping in my chest and goose pimples on my arms. I told myself I had no reason to feel frightened; even if a ghost was nearby, it couldn't hurt me. I had it on good authority. Then I remembered what the Accounting Guys said, about something evil using other creatures to do their dirty work, and I scared myself all over again.

Then I saw him, or it, standing a few feet away from me. Not the good-looking blond guy from before; this one was darker, more indistinct. All I saw was what looked like a tall man wearing a long trench coat with a wide-brimmed hat shadowing his face. His eyes were lost in the shade of the hat, but I knew he was looking right at me. Nothing about the man looked frightening, yet my blood ran cold with terror.

No, more than terror. Every nervous feeling, every scary dream, every frightening moment I'd ever experienced flooded my mind, nearly knocking me to my knees. I felt every negative emotion pouring over me like fog. I couldn't move; I could barely even think. I closed my eyes for a moment, willing it to go away. When I opened them, the man stood closer. There was no earthly way he could have walked or even run so quickly but there he was, inches closer than before.

Everything I'd ever been afraid of, every unexplained noise, imaginary monster under the bed, every nightmare I ever had washed over me like a tidal wave, streaming from the mysterious creature in front of me. It stood as still as the grave markers surrounding it, making no move to come toward me, but I knew if I shut my eyes again, even only for a moment, he would come for me, and I would be lost forever.

I couldn't help it.

I closed my eyes.

And a hand touched my shoulder.

Chapter 5

Too frightened to even scream, I stood there like a rabbit in the path of an oncoming car, completely paralyzed with fear, waiting. For what, I didn't know. An evil laugh, perhaps, or possibly my life flashing before my eyes, such as it was. I didn't expect to hear a familiar voice say gently, "Gillian, relax, you're safe now."

The shriek building up in my throat died, and I cautiously opened my eyes.

The cemetery was gone, replaced by the familiar and comforting walls of Michael's office. I turned around to see Michael himself, his blue eyes full of concern.

"What…how?" I stared at my boss, who looked perfectly normal, if out of uniform in khaki pants and an oxford shirt as opposed to his usual three-piece suit. I'd never seen him dressed casually before; it was almost like seeing him naked. That image struck me as funny, and I started to giggle. It bubbled out of me, unbidden and impossible to stop. Stress relief, I assumed.

"I'm sorry," Michael said, he sounded far away. "It's not an easy way for humans to travel, but I needed to get you out of there fast."

He stood close to me, extremely close, looking incredibly sexy despite his worried frown. I felt light and fuzzy, like I'd been drinking. Maybe I was still drunk from the night before, or simply having an elaborate dream.

"Wow," I said. "Did you know you are really, really good looking? I mean, angels, right? Michelangelo with thingies, the halos. He didn't do you justice." I reached out my hand, touching his cheek. Completely inappropriate, but I didn't care, nothing made much sense anymore. Everything was absurd, my whole life, and I laughed until my sides ached, and couldn't stop.

Michael looked alarmed, not amused or even insulted, and I knew something was wrong. My laughter turned into wracking sobs, and I clung to Michael in terror as I tried desperately to gain control over myself. Michael grabbed my arms so tightly it hurt and stared hard into my eyes. "Gillian Burke. Sleep."

And I did.

I woke up on Michael's sofa, a soft afghan covering me, feeling calmer, if still a bit disorientated. The window outside reflected the night sky and the twinkling lights of the city. Apparently, I'd been asleep for several hours. I struggled into a sitting position, checking my mouth for drool, and tried to make sense of what happened.

Michael came in, carrying tea. "Oh, good, you're awake. How are you feeling now?"

I accepted the tea he held out to me, and shrugged. "Okay, I guess. Kind of baffled." I remembered what I'd said to him right before I passed out. "Embarrassed, mostly." I took a deep breath. "Look, I didn't…"

"Don't fret. You were not yourself." He spoke in a reassuring tone, but I think we both knew I absolutely meant the things I'd babbled at him, and I wanted to bury my burning face in my hands for an hour or so, until the embarrassment passed. "I am such a dork," I muttered.

"Gillian, believe me, I'm not upset at your words," Michael said, sitting on the coffee table across from me, and flashing me cheeky grin. "Quite the opposite, I assure you."

Another time the possibilities hinted at in that comment would have thrilled me, but at the moment I was too mortified to do anything other than blush again and resolve to wipe that interlude from my memory.

"I'm sure you have a million questions."

"A million and one, actually." I took a sip of the tea, savoring the sweet taste as it hit my throat, wondering briefly if it was some kind of magical angel brew or normal human tea. Either way, it cleared the remaining dregs of fear I'd experienced, and I felt much better.

"I can't promise I can answer everything, but I'll do my best."

I thought for a moment, sipping my tea, wondering where to begin. "Okay, question one. How did I get here from the cemetery?"

"Magic," he said with a smile.

"Meaning it's too complicated to explain."

He nodded. "It is rather difficult to explain in a way that would make sense. I suppose you could say one of our powers is teleportation. That's an inaccurate description, but it will do. I don't do it often, especially not with a human passenger. As you learned, it doesn't sit well with the human psyche. Personally, I prefer to travel like a mortal, walking, driving, or taking a train.

It keeps me grounded. Samuel, on the other hand, hates commuting, so he does it rather regularly."

That explained why I never saw him come into the office. Private entrance, my foot.

"Okay, question two. How did you know I was in trouble?"

"Magic. Okay, sorry," he added quickly when I threatened to throw my tea at him. "We were keeping an eye on April Anderson's grave, and saw you there." His expression turned grave, and I tried not to notice how sexy he looked when he was being serious. I'd embarrassed myself enough for one day.

"What happened in the cemetery? What was that thing?"

"You were attacked by a…generally, we call them 'shadow men' for lack of a human term. Frankly, I'm rather surprised you saw it. They are always around, on the edges of the world. Humans sense them, but never see them. I think it was as surprised as you when you noticed it. You have good sight."

"People keep saying I have good sight. If it were true, why haven't I ever noticed anything like them before? It's not like I haven't been in a graveyard before."

"Working with us has unleashed your natural talents. It tends to. Stacey didn't exhibit any talent for witchcraft before starting with us, for example."

I knew I shouldn't get distracted from the matter at hand, but the subject was too fascinating an idea to let go of. "Seriously? Do all humans have hidden, er, talents?"

"No, not everyone. We try to hire the ones who do. Angela, for example. She was a nurse, and coming here has given her a more, let's say supernatural lift to her healing talents. I'm not saying she performs miracles, mind, but she's more skillful now than the most talented mortal doctor."

"What about Roger?"

"He was always a werewolf, but that's not why we hired him. He's one of the best IT managers in the city. His family…that's a story for another day."

"Oh." I wanted to follow that line of thought, but there were more pressing things to deal with, and I reluctantly put aside any further questions about my co-workers. For now. "So what's a shadow man, then?"

Michael took a deep breath, and ran a hand through his hair in a distracted manner, obviously trying to find the best way to explain. I fought the ridiculous urge to run my own fingers through his hair, telling myself firmly to grow up and control my raging hormones, and waited patiently for him to speak.

After a moment he said, "What were you afraid of when you were a little girl?"

A strange question, but probably relevant, so I thought carefully before I answered. "Being left behind, mostly. My mother liked to move around, as you know. She'd get, well, sad, I guess, and decide she would be happier somewhere else. I always thought one day she'd decide I made her sad, and leave without me." I shrugged. "And I guess she did, eventually, if you think about it."

"Ah." Michael cleared his throat, a strange mixture of sympathy and amusement crossing his face. "I mean something a bit less complex, more like something you'd consider an irrational fear."

I took a big sip of tea to try to cover my

embarrassment. Then I laughed. I had to either laugh at myself or melt into a puddle of shame. I never told anyone that particular fear, not even the psychologist I was forced to see as part of my emancipation process. "I guess that was more of a psychological fear, huh?"

Michael reached out like he wanted to offer a sympathetic pat on my shoulder, but instead his hand dropped to his lap. Maybe my inappropriate remarks earlier made him change his mind about touching me, in case it set me off again. I brushed the thought aside. That way madness lies. "I'm not crazy about spiders."

"That's not exactly what I meant, either," he said. "What I mean is, when you were young, were you afraid of the dark or anything, or monsters in the closet? Things grown-ups told you didn't exist. That's the kind of fear I'm talking about."

I thought about it a moment. "Mirrors. Well, not all mirrors. Bathroom mirrors. Someone told me the Bloody Mary story once, and ever since I turn the light on right away, the second I enter a bathroom. I have this irrational fear..." I paused, thinking of the adventure of the last few days. "At least I hope it's an irrational fear, I would somehow accidently summon her or something, if I went into a bathroom in the dark, even though logically I knew it wouldn't happen."

"That's what you saw. Shadow men are the face in the mirror, the fear of the dark, the monster under the bed. They are around, as I said, lurking at the edges of the world, all the time. Adult humans have developed defenses against them, logic, pragmatism, that sort of thing, but children can sense them. That's the reason they are so afraid of their closets, or sleep with nightlights. They know those creatures wait there, the darkness behind the light."

Only in my imagination did the room darken and get colder, but I pulled the afghan more tightly around me anyway. "Last night," I said, and was it only last night? It seemed like a million years ago. "Last night at the bar, the Accounting Guys said something about creatures who thrive on chaos, or something, and they fight against the Foundation. Was the thingy in the cemetery one of them?"

He actually looked a bit impressed. "Good guess. They are part of it. You'll find shadow men live off fear. The stronger the despair, the sadness, the anger, the fear, the more they feed.

"There are so many things in the world to keep them in check—science and logic and philosophy, especially now, so they mostly live off scraps, in a way, trying to siphon off fear whenever they can. What they want is to see the world shrouded in darkness and living in terror, so they can feast to their heart's content. And they aren't the only ones."

"And so you fight against them."

"When needed. There are others who wish to see the world in chaos, those who wish to let the shadow men run free to feed and destroy. These…creatures thrive on chaos and disorder and hatred and fear. Millennia ago, my kind fought them in our own world, and we stopped them, sent them into a different dimension as punishment. We thought they would be trapped there, but, unfortunately, there are too many other dimensions, too many ways to cross from one plane to another. They invaded this world time and time again, and each time we must stand and fight them, send them back to their own world once more." An expression of weary sadness crossed Michael's handsome features. "But they always find their way back."

We are coming back. The memory of those words hit me like a freight train. I'd convinced myself I imagined them, that night I dreamed about my wedding day. But those same words appeared so mysteriously on my notepad right before the zombie attack, and I knew I couldn't avoid the truth any more. I didn't imagine them. They were real, and they were telling me something.

As much as I wanted to believe that dream and the voice I heard was nothing but a product of an eventful first day on the job, I realized now I probably shouldn't do that anymore. My world had expanded, and I could no longer take refuge in the adult belief boogeymen were make believe. I looked at Michael's worried face, and my whole body seemed to flinch with remorse. "Um. There's something I didn't tell you."

I recounted my dream, and the words I heard as well as the ones that mysteriously appeared and disappeared on my notepad, and when I finished he looked even graver. "You should have told me about this straight away," he said, his voice stern. "If I'd known there were warnings, we would have prepared accordingly."

I felt my face go hot, like it always did when being reprimanded, and retreated, as I tend to, into anger. "I'm sorry," I said as coldly as possible. "But I'm still new at all this stuff. I didn't think it all actually happened. Why would I? I mean, it's not like I have the habit of waking up from a bad dream and saying, 'Oh, it must mean evil creatures from another dimension trying to communicate with me.' I didn't know it meant anything."

I took a deep, calming breath. "You said when we grow up we forget about the…the magic that's around us. I spent the last ten years or so thinking like a grown-up. I have to relearn thinking like a child."

For a moment, Michael looked like he might argue with me, but then the tight expression on his face softened, and he smiled. "You're right," he said. "You couldn't have known. I apologize. Still, in the future, should you have any other dreams, even if it seems silly or unimportant, please let me know."

I promised to do so. "So, do you think that's what the voice meant?" I asked. "Did it want me to know the shadow men things are trying to destroy the world?" It sounded ridiculous even as I said it, like comic book dialogue, but Michael nodded seriously.

"Not only the shadow men. There are others, as I said, and if they succeed, even those in the supernatural world will suffer." He gave a bitter little laugh. "Although, there are those who chose to fight by the side of the, let's call them Creatures of Darkness, because they believe if disorder reigned, they could unleash their true nature without fear of reprisal from the Foundation."

A look of weariness crossed his features as he spoke. He told me he had walked this world for centuries. Did he ever want to give up and rest?

I tried to imagine having infinite time stretching before me. My mother couldn't even last through her own natural lifespan. What was it like to live for hundreds of them? It must get so tiring, sometimes, and lonely.

"So how often do these things try to take over the world?" I asked, trying to distract myself from maudlin thoughts. "Is it a constant battle or, is it more like a special, one-night only event?"

He smiled a bit at my comment. "It is rare. Oh, there are always little struggles. Small creatures trying to do harm, we can keep those in check rather easily, but a real battle doesn't happen too frequently. The last big battle we fought was over three hundred years ago. I hoped, as always, that battle would be the last." He sighed. "It never is."

"What happened?" I asked quietly, almost afraid he wouldn't tell me.

"In this case, prejudice and ignorance and fear opened the door to let the shadow men in, and the shadow men are almost always precursors to a bigger attack. A small group of bored and repressed young women created panic in their village, and the shadow men fed on the fear and caused it to spread. We were lucky, we stopped them before it spread too far, but by the end, nineteen people were dead, and many lives ruined."

"Stacey mentioned something last night," I said, light dawning. "She said it hadn't happened since Salem. Those things created the witch trials?"

"They did. It's what brought the Foundation to this country, as a matter of fact. When we arrived, we saw the New World rife with openings for the shadow men and their…compatriots, as well as a home for regular supernatural people looking for guidance and help, so we…branched out, as it were."

I wanted to ask if he, personally, was there at Salem three hundred years ago, but it wasn't the time.

The list of things I wanted to know was getting ridiculously long, and I had to prioritize.

"So," I said after a few moments' contemplation. "Did shadow men make Mrs. Anderson attack Rachel?"

"No. They lack the intelligence to successfully execute such a plan. There's someone else behind this latest attack. He…" He broke off, frowning. "However, the fact you saw a shadow man by her grave in the cemetery…I don't trust coincidence." He looked at me thoughtfully for a moment. "Why were you at Mrs. Anderson's grave, anyway?"

I thought for a minute, trying to figure out the best way to articulate what I'd attempted to do. "What happened to her seemed so cruel to me. She was a normal person, a wife and a mother, and not only was the poor woman murdered, but then someone used her to try to murder someone else. I wanted…well, I wanted to apologize, I guess, to tell her I was sorry about what happened to her, both before she came and…afterwards." I shrugged and sighed in frustration. "I can't explain it. I don't know that I had any solid reason for doing what I did. I just needed to…oh, I don't know…tell her, we were going to do everything we could to grant her last wish." Michael didn't respond, but stared at me so intensely I felt a blush blaze across my cheeks. "Silly of me, I guess." My breath hitched in surprise as Michael moved off the coffee table where he'd been sitting to sit beside me on the sofa.

"Gillian," he said, and the way he spoke my name made me go wobbly in places I didn't think wobbled. "You have a good heart as well as good sight. I'm glad we found you." He placed his hands on my cheeks, and rested his forehead on my own. My breath caught in my throat, startled by the intimacy of his movement and the rush of heat through my body at his touch. "I wish your employment here wasn't fraught with so much drama and excitement so early in your career. In other circumstances, perhaps, we could…" He pulled away, and I found myself once again caught in his intense blue-eyed stare. I opened my mouth to ask him what he was about to say when, suddenly, his lips were on mine and all thoughts fled.

Soft, almost a whisper of a kiss, and bits of me seemed to float away on a cloud of ecstasy. The practical part of my brain tried to point out kissing my boss might be a colossally bad idea in the long run, but I ignored it. After the harrowing experience in the graveyard, I think I deserved a kiss or two. I closed my eyes, practically melting into Michael's arms, surrendering myself completely to the moment.

The phone rang shrilly, breaking the spell. Michael pulled away to answer it, and I collapsed against the sofa, wondering, for probably the four billionth time that week, what just happened.

"That was Samuel," Michael said. "He and Rachel are going to meet us here." Instead of coming back to the sofa, he sat in his chair behind the desk, indicating the personal part of the evening was over. I hoped my disappointment didn't show on my face.

"They are? Why?" I asked, leaving the sofa to sit in the chair opposite the desk. If he wanted to get all professional, I would, too.

"Because, if our theory is correct, you and Rachel are in even more danger until we find this…new threat and stop it."

"Why exactly would they try to hurt me?" I asked. "It's not like I'm a big player in the Foundation. Is it because I'm new?" I chewed on my lip a moment, thinking over the last, rather crowded twenty-four hours. Mrs. Anderson, the zombie, attacked Rachel, not me. I hadn't given that too much thought. Too many other things vied for my attention at the time. Based on my one week of working with them, I'd assumed she and Valerie were normal humans like me, but now I suspected that might not exactly be the case. "Does Rachel have some sort of power to stop this…whatever it is?"

"Not exactly. It's…complicated," Michael said. "Rachel was, is human, as you are, but she's at a…certain point in her career with us that makes her more vulnerable to attack." He ran a tired hand across his face. "I thought we'd moved quickly enough to prevent something like this from happening, but apparently I was wrong. It didn't help the first two hires were…unsuitable."

I stared at him blankly. Seeing my expression, Michael laughed. "I'm sorry. I'm babbling, I know. It will make sense soon, I promise. I wish…I don't know if this is will be easy for you, Gillian."

"Let me see." Ticking the list off with my fingers, I said, "Since I started here, I gained a wish from a faerie, witnessed a zombie attack, met a werewolf, got chased by the boogeyman in a cemetery and teleported." And kissed by my boss, I didn't add. "I'm pretty sure I'm running out of things to surprise me."

He laughed. "True. I'm not worried so much about you being surprised, but I fear you will be angry."

"Why would I be angry?"

He took a deep breath. "What we are, what I am…we look human, but we're not."

"Yeah, I know. You're an angel."

"I mean what I look like, what I truly am, is nothing like what you see before you. We chose these forms long ago, but in order to retain them we need…" He stopped, sighing. "This part is never easy to explain. Do you remember your first day? When I took your hand?"

I nodded, remembering the shock, and the lights. "I thought at the time I imagined it," I said, then laughed. "I need to stop thinking that, don't I? I'm guessing there's a bit more to it. Was it something magical?"

"Yes. In order to remain corporeal and invulnerable, we need to bond with a human, to absorb a part of their soul."

It took a moment for the words to sink in. "You took my soul?"

"Not exactly. I exchanged a bit of my soul for yours."

"But you didn't ask me. What if I didn't want you to?"

"Thus the reason for a thirty-day probation period. It gives you time to get used to everything, and gives me a chance to see if you're suitable. Those two women before you, the ones who couldn't deal with what we did here, they both left within the thirty days, their souls intact, completely unharmed, and able to continue their normal, if mundane existence."

"So, what happens at the end of the thirty days?"

"Normally, that's when we'd have this conversation, and you decided if you wanted to leave, or if you wanted to make the relationship permanent."

"Oh." We sat quietly a few moments as I pondered this new information. "And what happens after it becomes permanent?"

"Once the decision is made, it's binding. There's no going back. But, Gillian, it has its reward, I promise you."

"What's the reward?"

"Like I said, you get a piece of my soul in return." He ran his hand through his hair again, obviously a nervous habit, one I found interesting and once again, totally endearing. I didn't think angels got nervous. "How old do you think Valerie and Rachel are?"

Taken aback at the abrupt subject change, I answered the best I could. "Around my age, I guess, maybe a bit older, twenty-eight, twenty-nine?"

He smiled. "Rachel was born in 1799. Valerie in 1882."

"What? You mean they're over…" I stopped. Math was never my best subject. "Old?"

"Yes. When you bond with me, you will stop aging. Rachel was around twenty-seven when she joined us in 1826, and Valerie twenty-eight in 1910 when Ralph chose her as his conduit."

"Oh." I couldn't think of anything else to say. "So if I accept this job permanently, I'd never look older than I am now?"

Michael nodded. "In addition, you will not get sick. Any injury you sustain will heal almost immediately, and you won't die."

"Forever?"

He looked sad for a moment. "No, not forever, but for a couple of hundred years or so at least. My first…" An unreadable expression briefly crossed his face, and then he continued. "My first assistant stayed for just over two hundred and fifty years."

"Then what happens?"

"A discussion best left for later, I think. Right now, we must focus on the problem at hand. Samuel and Rachel should be here any moment now, so we can talk about what to do next."

I wasn't thrilled with the answer, but I agreed anyway. What else could I do?

We didn't wait long. Rachel and Samuel appeared a few minutes later, I mean literally. One minute empty space, the next Samuel and Rachel stood by the door. Rachel looked completely composed, despite the fact a zombie tried to kill her a day ago. I also noticed, ruefully, Rachel seemed perfectly comfortable with being instantly transported from place to place. *She* didn't burst into hysterical laughter, but simply dusted some imaginary lint off her expensive, navy-blue sweater, giving me a smile that didn't quite meet her eyes. Michael indicated we should all sit around the small table in the corner of his office, and we did. I didn't know if I was on the clock, administrative assistant-wise, and if so, should I offer to get coffee? I decided against it, and sat down, feeling a bit nervous about what life-changing thing I might learn next.

Samuel spoke first. "I hope you are recovered from your rather exciting afternoon," he said to me formally. I nodded. "Good."

"Did Michael explain to you about the bonding?" Rachel asked me.

"Yes, he did. He also told me you've been around for a while."

She rolled her eyes. "Whatever. Did he tell you the

rest of it? Why that zombie attacked me, and why you, apparently, are being stalked by demons? Did you even ask?"

"Rachel, don't take your frustrations out on Gillian. She is not to blame," Samuel spoke calmly, but I heard the warning in his voice.

"I know it's not her fault. It's Barbara's fault," Rachel said spitefully. "If she wasn't so weak-willed, none of this would have happened, and you wouldn't refuse to let me choose…"

"I'm not refusing, Rachel. I don't agree that it's time…"

Obviously an old argument, the two of them spoke over each other, seemingly forgetting Michael and I were in the room.

"You act like I'm going to choose—"

"You don't know what you are going to—"

"I do know, Samuel, I've always known. Why won't you trust me?"

"I do trust you, but you don't understand. You may think you know, but when you're faced—"

"Excuse me, but can we get back to the matter at hand?" Michael said firmly, and Rachel and Samuel settled down, looking slightly embarrassed. "For the first time in our history, we have two human conduits open to attack, and I'm afraid there are others aware of that fact, and will use it against us. We need a plan."

"Wait, why are we open to attack?" I asked. "And what does that mean, exactly?"

"You and I are not permanently bonded yet, and until we are you are still…mortal, for want of a better word. And Rachel, it seems, is reaching the end of her tenure with us."

"Huh. Tenure," Rachel said bitterly. "Did he tell you, Gillian, ultimately the link will break? Did he mention there will come a time when you've reached the end of your lifespan? Because that's what's happening to me!" She turned toward Michael. "Barbara made this happen, and you let her, and now I could die without…" She faltered under Samuel's withering gaze, and looked down at her hands. "Sorry," she muttered.

"The point is," Michael said, ignoring her outburst. "Since the two of you are open to attack, you can both be killed, and if you die…" He hesitated, and glanced over at Samuel, who nodded slightly. "If you die, then we, Samuel and I, are vulnerable, and the barriers between this dimension and the others will weaken."

"And if the creatures break through," Samuel continued in his soft voice, "The world as you know it may very well end."

Chapter 6

I tossed and turned that night, trying to get comfortable in an unfamiliar bed, but sleep wouldn't come. Eventually, I gave up and decided to find the kitchen. Maybe warm milk or something would help me sleep.

The luxury condo, in which I now found myself, sat on its own pier on the waterfront at Penn's Landing off South Columbus Avenue, offering a lovely view of the Delaware River and the refurbished Camden, New Jersey waterfront. Although the condo offered all kinds of fancy amenities, already I missed my own place, with my own things.

To be fair, I couldn't fault the logic behind the idea of Rachel and me taking residence in the Foundation-owned building, as Michael and Samuel both assured us it would be safer if we stayed together. "We put protection around both of you individually, of course," Michael explained, "but it will be far stronger if you stay together as much as possible."

After a few minutes of reflection, I agreed, if reluctantly, but Rachel argued, complained and made me feel as wanted as ants at a picnic until Samuel finally managed calm her down enough to get her to acquiesce.

Thus, my Saturday night involved getting used to a luxurious condo and a two-hundred-year-old roommate who seemed to hold me somewhat in contempt. Not exactly the way I thought I'd spend my weekend.

I made it to the kitchen, only stubbing my toe twice in the process. I turned on the light, wincing at the brightness, hoping I hadn't woken Rachel. Something told me she was not the type to take kindly to being awakened in the wee hours of the morning.

After some trial and error, I found hot chocolate, and made myself a cup, contemplating once again the strangeness of my new life. I had to admit, though, it beat being married to William. If I were married, I'd probably still be awake in the middle of the night, afraid my husband was dead or in jail. Or I'd be up in the middle of the night arguing with him once again about him coming home late, and me never being any fun. Or I'd be up in the middle of the night crying because he threw something at me and walked out. This time, at least, my only worries were a grumpy housemate and supernatural bad guys trying to kill me.

I drank the chocolate, contemplating trying for sleep again when I heard a noise, and saw Rachel standing in the doorway.

She looked beautiful, obviously one of those people who even sleep with class. Maybe the whole magic bonding thing had something to do with her good looks and poise, and when my probation ended I, too, would exude effortless beauty. That would be nice. "Couldn't sleep either?"

She shook her head and went to one of the cabinets, pulling out a bottle of scotch. "Hot chocolate will not help you sleep," she said a tinge of humor in her voice. "Whiskey, definitely."

"I don't like to drink." I thought back to Friday

night and added, "Much."

"Maybe you should start. It might make everything easier." She poured two generous glasses and sat down across from me.

I accepted the drink and took a tentative sip, trying not to choke on the burning sensation of the whiskey as it settled on my tongue.

We sat in silence awhile until she said, "Go ahead and ask me. I know you're dying to."

"Ask what?"

"About me, my life, my impending death. You know, girl talk."

I laughed, and she cracked a smile. She was much nicer at three in the morning. "Well, I don't want to know anything you don't want to tell me."

"I don't think, at this point, I have too many things to hide."

"Okay." I thought a moment. "Tell me about your life before this. How did you wind up working at the Foundation? I didn't think women were secretaries in those days. I thought you were stuck being housewives and governesses and stuff."

She took another long sip of scotch. For a moment, I didn't think she'd answer, but then she put her drink down, yawned, and began.

"Apparently, you read too much Jane Austen and not enough Charles Dickens. Many women worked. Granted they weren't glamorous jobs, but we worked when required. My parents died when I was…" She stopped and gave a rueful chuckle. "It's been so long I can barely remember. I think I was ten or so. Anyway, I got farmed out to a nearby family, where I worked for my keep." A pained look crossed her face for a moment, and I frowned in sympathy. I could easily guess she didn't have an easy childhood. "When I was old enough I went into service, as they say. I worked in the house of a local prominent family, right here in Philadelphia."

"You've been in Philadelphia for two hundred years?" I interrupted.

"No, no. I began here. The company moves around, you know. At some point, people notice the lack of aging amongst the staff, so we try not to stay anywhere more than twenty years. When we moved back here ten years ago, it was the first time I'd been here since…I started. I was actually kind of glad to be home again, more or less. So much has changed, but there are still parts of this city exactly as I remember them, although now it feels…" She stopped, pouring more scotch into her cup. "Anyway, I worked for this family, and Samuel came to dinner one day. He…I couldn't take my eyes off of him. I knew right away something was different about him, and I wanted to know more, but my place was to serve the dinner and the tea and go back to the kitchen. So imagine my surprise when he followed me there.

"I thought, at first, he wanted to take advantage of me." She gave an exaggerated leer, and I giggled. "It had never happened to me before, but I heard stories. But no, he wanted to offer me a job. He saw something in me, he said. I was already in my late twenties, unmarried and likely to remain so, and my life held nothing more than domestic drudgery. Perhaps, if I were lucky I might become the head housekeeper someday, but I couldn't aspire to anything more than that." She sighed, and then smiled. "The pay was much higher than I'd ever get as a housemaid and the work much more interesting, so of course I said yes."

"How did you feel when you found out about what really went on?"

She laughed. "Terrified. I was raised to believe certain things, and to me the things the Foundation did were ungodly. I thought perhaps working there would put my immortal soul in danger." She rolled her eyes expressively. "The first supernatural I ever saw was a vampire. He was young and handsome, and he hadn't quite made his 'no humans' pledge to the Foundation yet so, and if Samuel hadn't shown up at the right moment, he'd… Let's just say I would have completely fallen for his charms." She grinned. "Does that surprise you?"

"It does, actually," I said honestly. "You don't strike me as the type to fall for that sort of thing. I mean, you seem so strong."

"Maybe I am now, but then, not so much. Anyway, it made me determined to show Samuel I could handle myself, so I plunged ahead. I made mistakes, but I learned from them, and I never regretted my decision to join, not for one minute."

"What's it like living for so long, and seeing so many things change?"

"It's not as shocking as you might think." She gave a one-armed shrug. "I mean, things have changed since you were born, right, but you don't go around being shocked at them. Things change so gradually, one doesn't notice them. I mean, if I'd left Philadelphia in the 1830s and found myself here, in the present, a second later I'd be freaked out, but living through it? You accept the changes and move on. Besides, for the most part, change is good. I can tell you things like indoor plumbing were quite welcome."

"What about family or friends? Wasn't it hard when they died and you didn't?"

She shook her head. "My parents were the only family I knew. I had a great aunt floating around somewhere, but she didn't bother to find me after my parents died, so I didn't have any reason to keep in touch. As for friends, my life wasn't conducive to making friends. I had no one in my life to worry about, even in the beginning. That's one of the things they look for in a conduit, you know. It's easier for someone with no ties to the world to live outside of it, as we do."

I nodded, remembering Michael saying something similar on my first day. "So how do you…why do you think you're at the end of your…um, lifespan?" She looked sharply at me, and I worried for a moment I'd gone too far.

"I didn't know… Not at first. I knew conduits didn't last much longer past two hundred years or so, and I've made it well past two hundred already, but I didn't feel any different. Then the zombie attacked me, and it wouldn't have done so if I wasn't vulnerable. We conduits can't be killed, you know, once the bonding is complete. I confronted Samuel, and he finally confirmed it, just today. My time is coming up."

"How did he know?"

"As far as I know, the partners sense the bond weakening. And then they…" She hesitated, staring hard at me for a moment. "I'm not supposed to tell you this, but I will anyway. When your time comes, you are given a test. You get to choose if you want to continue to live or cross over. If you choose to live, that's it, you are immortal. Forever and ever. So far no one has ever chosen to live." She drained the last of her drink. "So far," she repeated, almost to herself.

"So is that what happened to Barbara? Her time came up and she chose to die?"

I got another sharp look. "Not exactly." She gave an exaggerated yawn. "I think I'm tired enough now. I'm going back to bed. See you in the morning."

I wanted to ask her more questions, but obviously Rachel was finished being friendly for the time being, so I said goodnight and headed back to my own room. I felt a bit better about our situation. Rachel was pretty easy to talk to once she let her guard down, despite her rather prickly personality. I enjoyed having the opportunity to know her better, to understand her more. We weren't as different as I'd thought at first.

With the scotch still swimming around in my stomach, I knew sleep would be pretty much impossible so I went out onto the terrace overlooking the Delaware River, for some air. I leaned over the balcony, staring blankly at the darkness of the river, ignoring the cold and thinking about everything Rachel told me. If I stayed with the Foundation, I too would live for at least two hundred years.

Admittedly, the idea of never aging had a definite appeal. I liked the thought of not having to worry about gray hair, wrinkles or bad knees, but what would my life be like a hundred years from now when everyone I ever knew was dead and gone? On the other hand, maybe they would finally invent flying cars. Or hover boards.

My thoughts turned, as they often did in the dead of night when I couldn't sleep, to my mother. Would she have been happier if she knew she had more time to keep looking for the happiness that always seemed to elude her, or would the time only drag her down? She spent her whole life moving from place to place, looking for something or someone to fill a void in her life. She never talked about it, at least not to me, but I sensed it.

Growing up, there were many times when I did something in hopes of bringing a smile to my mother's face, either by dating a boy I knew she'd like or joining the cheer squad. I tried to change my personality into the kind of person I thought she wanted me to be, but it never worked. I was miserable, and she was still unhappy, and we'd wind up packing up and moving at the end of the school year anyway, looking for happiness somewhere else. And, eventually, she gave up and went to find happiness in death.

A sudden noise below me jolted me out of my reverie, and I looked down where I saw the shadowed figure of someone standing on the balcony below, a fellow insomniac I assumed. I caught a glint of blond hair as he or she, I couldn't tell for certain, leaned against the balcony's railing, very possibly staring up at me. I gave a little wave and opened my mouth to say hello when something splashed loudly in the dark water below, and I peered down, trying in vain to see what it was. When I looked back at the balcony below me, the person was gone. Another splash echoed in the river, louder this time, and I turned my attention back to the dark water, trying to determine what could have made that noise. A fish would be the logical assumption, but I was hard pressed to think what kind of fish lived in the Delaware that could make a noise heard from five stories above it. It occurred to me, belatedly, maybe I wasn't safe, standing in the dark, with who knows what kind of supernatural creatures out to get me. With that disquieting thought, I went back inside, trying hard not to run.

Sunday passed uneventfully, Rachel stayed in her room most of the day, and I spent my time searching the internet for information about the aquatic life in the Delaware. Happily, I learned the river could sustain life, but it didn't hold anything much bigger than striped bass which I found worrisome. It might be my paranoia talking, but the loud splash I'd heard worried me. What if it was something trying to find a way to get us? We were safe here; I was assured of it, but after my encounter with the shadow man in the graveyard, I had a hard time finding the assurance terribly reassuring. I trusted Michael, though, and focusing on that trust got me through the rest of the day.

Back in the office on Monday, my first task of the day was to set up identities for three women who wanted to settle in Colorado. Rachel even offered to help me; our late-night bonding session went a long way to thaw our relationship, apparently, but I waved her away. It might only be my second week, but I felt pretty confident I could handle the work on my own. It wasn't hard. As I said, our computer system easily hacked into anything and then it was basically a matter of filling out forms.

I admit the clients themselves were rather disconcerting, even though they sat across from my desk, waiting patiently for me to finish my work. I did my best to act like I'd been dealing with Norse immortals for ages. They were tall, extremely tall, and quite beautiful. The fact they were, technically, personifications of fate I decided to ignore. I was afraid if I asked about it, they'd tell me something horrible about my life. You never know, with gods.

I finished my work, and checked it over, trying not to sigh in relief that I did everything right. I wanted to come across cool and in control, not nervous and worried. Something told me they weren't exactly fooled.

Nonetheless, I pressed on, using my most professional voice as I handed out their new identities. To the eldest I said, "You are now Ursula Norn." I handed her a passport, a driver's license and a debit card. She nodded and smiled, and rippled, like a reflection in a puddle being stirred up. When it stopped, she hadn't changed in any drastic way, but she looked more human than she did a moment ago, like she'd hidden her supernatural side somewhere safe.

I clamped my mouth shut, hoping she didn't notice my look of utter surprise, then turned as quickly as I dared to the other sisters in an effort to hide my astonishment. "You are Vera Norn, and you are Scarlett Norn."

"Scarlett?"

"I'm sorry, it's the best 'S' name I could think of that sounded at least a bit like your real name. I can change it, if you'd like."

She smiled. "No, thank you, dear, it is a perfect name. I'm pleased."

Ursula leaned forward. "You're facing a big challenge soon, my dear, a test and a challenge, but rest assured you have the skill to face it."

"Um…thank you?"

"Follow your heart. It will lead you to the right places." Then she added, in a far less eldritch voice, "Should you ever want to take a holiday, do come visit us in Colorado. It's quite lovely there; I think you will enjoy it. We're looking forward to the quiet ourselves."

I thanked them, and they left, and I sighed heavily, feeling vaguely like I'd narrowly escaped with my life. I wasn't quite sure why, they certainly were nice enough. Must be a fate thing.

Valerie, watching from a discreet distance, came over to my desk, smiling. "Nice job, Gillian. You handled everything wonderfully. No one would know this was only your second week."

"Thanks. I think it went well."

"Have lunch with me," said Valerie. "Tell me your side of what went on this weekend, and why you and Rachel are housemates all of the sudden." She looked over at Rachel, chatting on the phone. "She isn't being terribly forthcoming."

I hesitated, unsure if I had the right to tell Valerie about the events over the weekend, but Michael never said I had to keep it a secret. Besides, it didn't seem fair to keep her in the dark, so I agreed to lunch.

"What did Rachel tell you?" I asked later, when we were settled at a nearby deli. I didn't want to upset Rachel by telling tales out of turn, and I certainly didn't want to damage our tenuous friendship sharing something Rachel told me in confidence.

Valerie took a large bite of her sandwich before answering. "She said you and she were in a bad place right now, due to the fact you are in the early days of your...employment, and she is probably reaching the end of hers." She sipped the last of her soda, the straw making a slurping sound as she dredged the last of the drink.

Watching her eat was an education. She ordered enough food for two people, and wolfed it down with every sign of enjoyment. "One of the other bonuses of this conduit thing," she told me, probably noticing my expression, "is I can eat all I want and never gain too much weight. Besides, before I found Ralph I was poor as a church mouse, so I remember what it means not to have enough to eat. I make it a point never to feel that way again." She shoved a handful of chips in her mouth and waved at me to continue. "So, go on, you and Rachel are vulnerable and therefore Michael and Samuel are as well, right?"

"That's about the size of it," I said, and told her about the threat of the shadow men, and the creatures who want to break through and destroy the world. To my surprise, she didn't seem too worried.

"I've seen our boys in action," she said. "During the war…the Second World War, I mean, there was this infestation of beings who fed on human misery…not the shadow men, not like you saw, more like supernatural carrion birds. They attacked wounded soldiers and fed on their suffering until there was nothing left. The Foundation, and our boys, took care of them in no time. And then there were the Nazis…"

To my disappointment, she waved her hand, saying, "It's a long and complicated story. My point is there is nothing they can't handle. After all, it's only three more weeks for you, and you're safe, and we can't be sure about Rachel. For all we know, those baddies are guessing about her, since she's been around so long. She might have ten years left at least."

I recognized denial when I heard it, but I decided to let it go. "I thought maybe Michael would be safe if I accepted the terms early," I said. "But he said that was impossible. He said I had to wait the thirty days."

"Yeah. Magic is weird. Once something is Written; and that's written with a capital W, mind, that's it. No changes are possible."

"I wonder…" I hesitated, remembering the argument between Rachel and Samuel. "I wonder if Rachel wants to choose early, but she can't, because it's not time."

Valerie shook her head. "No, that part is different. She can make the choice at any time."

"I thought Michael said after the thirty days, I couldn't change my mind."

"That's between working with us and going back to your old life. After the thirty days, it's a choice between living and…" She stopped, looking uncomfortable. "Oh heck, you need to know this sooner or later. When it comes time to leave the Foundation, you leave this world. When a conduit's end comes, they are given a test of some sort—I'm not entirely sure what it is, Ralph won't tell me."

"Rachel mentioned something," I interrupted. "She said something about making a choice and either coming back and living forever or…"

"Dying," finished Valerie. "The reason Samuel doesn't want Rachel to choose yet. I don't think he's ready to lose her."

"She told me she knows she'll choose the live forever option."

"Everyone says they'll choose to stay," said Valerie sadly. "But no one ever does."

A sobering thought. I took a bite of my sandwich, unsure of what else to say. After finally getting to know and even like Rachel, it made me sad to think she might die soon.

"Oh, did Michael tell you yet?" Valerie said as cheerfully as if she hadn't been talking about the imminent death of one of our colleagues. "Tomorrow night we're meeting with some of the local vampires."

"Oh," I said. "Good?"

"Of course, it's good. It means we get most of tomorrow off. I thought we ought to have a slumber party tonight. I can stay with you and Rachel. I'm dying to see what the condo looks like. The Foundation bought it a few years ago, but I haven't gotten a chance to see it yet. We can have pizza and beer and do each other's hair and make prank phone calls to boys. It will be fun!"

I smiled. I couldn't help it. Her enthusiasm was infectious. "Yeah. Yeah, it would be fun."

Back at the office, Valerie filled Rachel in on the idea of a slumber party, and she agreed, albeit with much less enthusiasm than Valerie.

As for me, I looked forward to it more than I'd cared to admit. I'd never had close girlfriends growing up, and all the women I'd known as an adult were acquaintances at best. I didn't quite know where I stood with Rachel yet, but I thought Valerie and I were well on our way to being actual friends.

Michael seemed to like the idea of our girls' night. I'm not sure exactly how he heard about it, since he and the other partners were out most of the day, but before we left, he handed me a company credit card and told me to use it to order pizza and beer and anything else we might want for our girls' night. "Maybe we men will stop by, serenade you from below, or whatever it is boys do these days."

I laughed. "I don't think they serenade. They probably just bring beer and play video games."

"I don't think video games are exactly my speed."

"You could…" I stopped, feeling awkward. How could I possibly tell him how much I'd love to spend time with him outside work without sounding pathetic? I didn't think it possible. For a moment, I thought perhaps Michael would make the suggestion himself, but instead he gave me a gentle pat on my shoulder and said, "Have a good time tonight. I'll see you tomorrow."

I waited until he was back in his office before I sighed in frustration, and went to find Valerie and Rachel.

That evening the three of us sat cozily ensconced in the large living room, dressed in our most ridiculous pajamas, Valerie's idea, eating pizza, and drinking a bottle of expensive wine Rachel found in the cabinet.

"We should have ordered extra garlic bread," Valerie said. "You know, in case one of the vampires forgets himself tomorrow."

"Does that stop them?" I asked, trying to sound only casually interested and failing. Truth be told, I was more than a little bit nervous about meeting an actual vampire.

"No, I'm kidding about the garlic, it doesn't actually stop vampires, although if we smelled garlicky enough it would probably keep regular people away, too." We all giggled. "Holy water doesn't work, either, although any religious symbol stops them, providing the person holding it truly believes."

"Okay, no to garlic and holy water, yes with conditions to holy symbols. What about the stake through the heart thing?"

"Darling, a stake through the heart would stop anyone," Rachel said, grinning.

We all laughed again, and I leaned back against the chair, feeling mildly drunk and fairly happy.

The good feeling faded a bit when my phone buzzed, and I saw my ex-husband's name on the screen. I excused myself, and went into the kitchen to answer. I wanted to ignore the call, but knowing William, he would keep calling until I finally answered. I couldn't keep my phone turned off for the rest of my life. Better to talk to him and get it over with.

"Gillian, what's going on?" he said, without even a hello. "I've been to your house three times, and you're never there. Where are you?"

"You've been to my house? Why?"

"I wanted to check up on you, make sure you're okay. I…I miss you, Gilly, I really do."

I took a deep breath, steeling myself. This was his consolatory phase, which meant he'd probably been on a drinking binge recently.

"What do you want, William?"

"Where are you?" he persisted. "Why aren't you at home now?"

"How do you know I'm not at home now? Oh, never mind. I'm…I'm with my co-workers. I'm fine. What did you want?"

"I want you to be happy, Gillian. I'm sorry everything didn't work out between us, and I know you think it's my fault." I stifled a sardonic laugh. *Even when he's trying William can't take the blame.*

"Anyway," William said. "Maybe…maybe we can meet for drinks sometime?" I flashed back to Gerald the faerie. He hadn't been too far off the mark with his impersonation of William.

In the months after I finally walked out on him, William sometimes showed up on my doorstep, full of regret, and swearing he would be a better husband if I gave him another chance. He brought me flowers and took me to nice restaurants, telling me how much he loved being married to me. I fell for it every single time, and as soon as I let my guard down and began to think we might be able to work it all out, he'd go right back to his old habits. Eventually, I wised up, but here he was, trying again.

"I have to go, William. Take care of yourself." I hung up before he could say anything else, before the ball of tension he always inspired in me got any bigger, wondering if there'd ever be a day where dealing with my ex-husband didn't leave me with the urge to throw something through the window.

I went back into the living room, and my bad mood immediately evaporated. I didn't need William, and I didn't need to worry what he thought about me, or if he approved with the way I lived my life. I had friends, a good job I enjoyed, and as a bonus, I now knew the world around me held more wonders than I ever expected or even hoped for. Life, I thought, was pretty good.

Then I saw the rain.

It had been raining most of the night, a steady pouring rain that makes a person glad they're staying indoors, and I hadn't paid much attention to it, but now…

"You guys," I shrieked. "Look! Look at the rain!"

As I stared in horrified fascination, the water droplets dripping down the large picture window coalesced into a vaguely humanoid shape, forming two giant fists of water that began banging on the glass so hard I couldn't believe the window didn't shatter immediately. "What is that thing?"

"Elementals!" Rachel screamed. "Someone sent elementals!"

Valerie and Rachel jumped up, and as one person we darted out into the hallway.

"Wait!" Rachel cried as we ran toward the elevator, stopping us in our tracks. "Where are we going? If we go outside, they'll drown us before we're two steps out the door."

"Stay here in the hallway?" I suggested.

Rachel shook her head. "No. There's no protection out here. They can come through the windows in every room. We need to get back inside. We have protection there. We should be safe. We're supposed to be safe!" I heard the annoyance in her voice, and whole-heartedly agreed with it.

Out of options, we went back into the condo. I looked toward the window. The elemental was still there, but no longer banging on the glass. Its hands and face were pressed up against the glass, like a macabre version of a child looking into a toy store window. "What's it doing now?" I asked.

"It's trying to find a way in. All it needs is one drop, and it can get inside, and will drown us," Valerie said, sounding surprisingly calm. "We need to go into the back bedroom. There's no outside door there. It might be more water tight. Come on!" She ran toward the back room, fumbling for her phone.

Unfortunately, two more of the creatures stood at the bedroom window, their watery fists banging almost rhythmically on the glass in eerie counterpoint to the torrential raging storm. Feelings of helplessness battled with terror as I watched the elementals trying to reach us. Valerie, obviously keeping a clearer head than I, was on the phone, yelling at Ralph we were in trouble and he needed to send help immediately.

If I understood how the whole conduit/partner thing worked, Valerie couldn't die, so the elementals held no threat to her. I pictured her floating in the water, unable to die, watching as I, and possibly Rachel, drowned. I wouldn't wish that on anyone. No wonder she looked frantic.

"The protection should hold," Rachel said, but I don't know if she was trying to convince me or herself. "It has to."

Almost in answer to her words, little spider web-like cracks raced across the window, and a moment later tiny drops of water slid through the spaces, dripping slowly down the wall. We stood, paralyzed with fear, unable to do anything more than watch. Faster and faster, the water crept through the widening cracks until the window shattered into a million pieces and water poured in unchecked.

The water reached our waists in a matter of moments. I tried to wade my way to the door, but the water surrounding us didn't follow any laws of nature, shifting and flowing in several different directions at once, making it extremely difficult for any of us to move.

We tried to stay above the swirling water, but at the rate it was rising it would soon reach the ceiling. Already tiny waves lapped at my face, making it difficult to catch my breath. We could do nothing, but wait for watery death.

I tried to decide if I should say a prayer, or just wait for my life to flash before my eyes when a green blur cannoned into the water next to me, racing around us at a dizzying speed. The water receded as quickly as it accumulated, leaving us back on solid floor, damp and terrified, but alive.

The elementals, gathering themselves back into their vaguely human shape, turned to face their attacker, a gigantic, sea-green horse.

I barely had a moment to register this new piece of weirdness when the horse, or more accurately, the horse-shaped thing, galloped around and around and around the elementals, forcing them into the middle of the room until they huddled together as Rachel, Valerie and I had only moments ago. The horse raced around them in ever tightening circles, herding them toward the window. Finally, the elementals merged together into something I could only describe as a cresting wave then, roaring like the sea, disappeared through the window and into the night.

A moment later, the horse disappeared and in its place stood a tall, handsome man with skin the color of sea-foam, wearing nothing but a devilish smile…

Before I could process this new development, the creature winked and said, in a strong Irish brogue, "Hello, Valerie, me darlin'. It's been a long time!"

Chapter 7

The next day, Valerie, Rachel and I arrived at the office around 4:30, bleary-eyed, but ready to face whatever the day held for us. I was still a bit anxious to meet an actual vampire, but after what had happened to us, something as mundane as a vampire on business seemed like child's play.

After all, it's not every day one is rescued by a kelpie. A kelpie called Declan, even, who, much to my surprise, was the same kelpie Valerie met when she first started with the Foundation. She was thrilled to see him. So much so, our near drowning on the fifth floor of a condominium didn't seem to worry her much anymore. She couldn't stop grinning.

After the elementals disappeared, Declan chanted some kind of spell he told us reinforced the protection already around our condo. Then he poured us all a glass of Irish whiskey and regaled us for hours with stories about his life in the "old country" until we were dry, and calm enough to sleep.

Due to either Declan's charm or the whiskey, I don't know which, I slept like a baby, and awoke invigorated, ready to write off the night's adventures as another side-effect of working with the Foundation, and eager to face whatever the day had in store for me.

Rachel, on the other hand, was still furious. As soon as we got off the elevator, she stormed into

Samuel's office.

"So much for protection!" she shouted. "You force me from my home, make me stay with Gillian"—I tried not to feel hurt at the comment—"and I may as well have stayed at home and taken my chances."

The door slammed on Samuel's reply, and Valerie and I exchanged slightly amused glances. "I'm glad I'm not him," she said, grinning like a Cheshire Cat.

"So, Declan," I said, trying to sound casual. "You were…friends?"

"Yes. Yes, we were"—she made air quotes with her fingers—" 'friends' for quite a while. But it ended, as these things do, and we both moved on. We're still, ahem, friends, occasionally, when he comes to the country."

I wondered, not for the first time, about the exact nature of her relationship with Roger. They were fond of each other that much I knew, but I suspected Valerie wasn't quite a one-man woman. I admired her for that. I could barely handle one man, supernatural or no. I might ask her for some pointers one day.

"Good thing Declan was around last night," I said, pulling out a file under "V" and flipping through it. "Otherwise…"

"Oh, he works for the Foundation sometimes. I called Ralph and, obviously, he called Declan."

"I guess I should thank you, then. If you hadn't thought to call Ralph, who knows what would have happened."

"I'm sure something else would have come up," she said confidently. "It usually does."

I sat down at my desk and turned on my computer, when a thought struck me. "Um, didn't you tell me kelpies tend to drown people?"

She giggled. "Not anymore they don't, not if they want to stay on the good side of the Foundation. Anyway…got to get going before my bloodsucker gets here." Valerie's client needed to plan his "retirement" from his law firm, since he'd been there for over fifty years. Vampires were pretty adept at using special effects to age themselves when needed, Valerie explained. "It's amazing what a little makeup and hair coloring can do."

"Oh…hey," Valerie added, mugging furiously. "I don't know what's worse, that he's a vampire, or a lawyer. Badumbum!"

I giggled. "Stick to your day job."

I turned my attention to my own vampire. According to the file, Michael's client planned to travel around the world, so he needed us to update his passport, create some vaccination paperwork, get his apartment sublet, and other details necessary to make sure he maintained his cover as a normal, un-fanged human. Michael also used these meetings to make sure the vampire wasn't breaking the covenant by, well, eating people, and would meet with him when I finished.

As I worked, I entertained myself with visions of what sort of vampire I would meet. Michael didn't say, and popular culture had so many different versions of vampires, I didn't quite know what to expect. Would he be a beak-nosed, hunched figure with long fingernails or the standard tall, dark and opera-cloak-clad vampire? Perhaps he was the angst-ridden, soulful type, working as a policeman as a form of redemption. Did his face get all bumpy before he attacked? Would he, lord help us, sparkle?

By the time our client arrived, I thought I had prepared myself for almost any vampire version possible, but I didn't expect to discover I already knew him.

Not personally, of course, but I immediately recognized the person who stepped off the elevator at 5:30 as one of the hottest new magicians in the country. I glanced at my notes. Sure enough, the name on my paperwork matched that of the magician. I hadn't made the connection before—why would I—but it was most definitely him. I'd seen him on several television specials where he wandered around doing street magic, all during the day, so that meant vampires didn't die when exposed to sunlight. It also proved he didn't sparkle. That was a relief.

He reached my desk in literally a blink of an eye, displaying his vampire speed; score one for popular culture. I mentally congratulated myself for keeping my professional cool instead of yelping in surprise, and introduced myself without sounding like a complete fan girl. "It's a pleasure to meet you."

"Gillian?" He leaned closer, peering intently at my face. "Wait. You're not the girl I met the last time."

"Um, no," I said. "That was Barbara, probably. She's no longer with the company."

"How odd, I remember her telling me she'd only been with the company a decade or so, let me think, about thirty years ago I believe. I thought you conduits hung around longer than that."

"Thirty years?" I said, surprised. "Are you sure?"

The vampire shrugged. "Fairly certain, yes." He smiled. "She liked my card tricks. I'm sorry she's gone so soon."

I murmured something vague in response and handed him documents to sign. I hadn't given much too much thought to my predecessor. I assumed Barbara simply reached the end of her natural tenure, or at least close to it, but the fact she'd only been around for forty-odd-years raised some interesting questions. It explained what Michael meant when he said for the first time the Foundation had two vulnerable conduits. I hadn't thought much about it at the time. There had been a lot on my mind lately after all, but now I wanted to know what happened to Barbara.

And whatever happened, I hoped it wouldn't happen to me.

The vampire signed the last form. "There," he said in a satisfied voice. "Done and dusted."

I took the forms, and put them in an envelope. "So, you're going on some sort of world tour, I take it?"

"I am. I'm quite looking forward to it. There are some cities I haven't been to in decades. It should be fun."

"So how does a vampire become a famous magician with his own cable show anyway?" I asked, handing back his documents.

"Oh, I've been a magician off and on for years. It's in my blood, if you'll pardon the expression." I rolled my eyes, and he laughed. "Every couple of centuries, I can't resist showing off a little. It's all legit, most of it, anyway. I learned most of my tricks from some of the most talented human magicians in history. The other stuff is me using my mystical vampire powers," he added, lending a thick Hollywood Transylvanian accent, which made me laugh.

"So when you're doing all those levitating tricks you're…"

"Actually flying, yes."

"Isn't that cheating?"

He pulled an exaggerated affronted face. "It's the opposite of cheating. I say I'm doing magic, and I am."

I giggled, imagining the reaction of the general public if they knew what they saw was more than a sleight-of-hand trick. "One more question, if you don't mind." He nodded acquiescence, and I continued, "Obviously daylight isn't an issue, since I've seen you in daylight on television, but I thought vampires couldn't be photographed or filmed, or see themselves in mirrors."

"Myths, all of them, based on varying religious beliefs throughout the ages. People believe we're soulless, and therefore can't be reflected, because at one point in time some religion believed a mirror reflected a person's soul. And sunlight generally represents all that is good and pure in the world, so it kills us evil soulless monsters." He did the Transylvania accent thing again. "We're weaker during daylight hours, we can be hurt or even killed, which is why we stick to the nightlife, but the sun doesn't turn us into ash. We can see ourselves in mirrors, and have no problem crossing running water, which is good, because otherwise my world tour would be seriously cut short." He gave me a smile so charming I actually flipped my hair at him and giggled before I could stop myself. I now understood why Rachel nearly got taken in by a vampire in her early days. He had a charm about him quite hard to resist.

Still, while he was extremely personable and nice, I saw something of the predator in his eyes and I knew,

Foundation or not, he could be dangerous if I wasn't careful.

After giving me his autograph at my request, I called Michael who came out to usher the vampire into his office, allowing me to prepare for our next client, a female vampire who wanted to buy a house in New Jersey.

As I worked, my mind kept drifting back to what the vampire told me about Barbara. I tried to convince myself it wasn't important and not my problem, but the fact Barbara left only half a century into her tenure seemed extremely odd to me. Or rather, why she chose to die, actually, since that's apparently want happens when a conduit leaves. Why did Michael let her? From what Rachel said, the partners did not encourage their conduits to choose before the time was up.

A minor mystery in a sea of much more important ones, but I knew Barbara's story was important in some way. It had to be connected to this whole "bad guys breaking through the barrier" thing. Besides, I really, really wanted to know exactly what happened, for my own peace of mind, if nothing else.

Around 2:30 in the morning, our last visitor left, and I finally caught Michael and asked if I could speak to him for a few minutes.

"Yes," he said. "We do have to talk. Please, come into my office." Warning bells went off in my head at the somber tone of his voice. Besides, nothing good ever comes from the words "we have to talk."

To add to the tension, he also closed his office door and sat behind his desk instead of on the sofa, which indicated he wanted to talk seriously.

I took the seat across from his desk, my body

shivering in nervous anticipation. I flashed back to my junior year of high school when I got fired from the fast food restaurant where I'd been working; the manager had a similar look to the one on Michael's face. I swallowed the worry clogging my throat, and tried to smile. "What do you need to talk about?" I kept my tone light and cheerful, hoping my attitude would change his, knowing it wouldn't.

"I want to apologize again for that incident with the elementals," Michael said, still strangely formal. "It shouldn't have happened, and I'm sorry it did. We try to anticipate everything, but it isn't always easy."

"How did those elementals get in, anyway?" I asked, relieved he didn't start the conversation with "I'm sorry, but…" Besides, I wanted to know. "Declan—the kelpie guy, who saved us, said nothing went wrong with the protection around the place, but they still got in."

Michael frowned. "We thought our protection was enough, but obviously the elementals found a crack. Water is an insidious element; all it takes is one drop to make it through, one tiny drop, and the rest can follow."

"Hey, it wasn't all bad," I said, still trying to lighten the mood. "I got to meet a kelpie. That was kind of cool."

"Gillian, I just…" He sighed. "I think it might be best if we terminated your employment."

And there it was. A whooshing sound filled my ears, and I felt the blood draining from my face. "Are you, is this, are you actually firing me?" I asked, wincing at the whininess in my voice. "It's not because I'm doing a bad job, is it? I know I typed up a document wrong for Ms. Windle, but I caught the mistake right away, and I fixed it, so she can still buy the house in Jersey. She didn't seem upset or anything." Which was a good thing. Ms. Windle might have looked like a middle-aged housewife, but she was still a vampire, and didn't strike me as someone who took disappointment well.

"No, that's not it at all. You're doing a wonderful job here." He smiled, softening his severe expression, but he still looked grim. "Truly. I'm not firing you, and I'm not saying you are lacking in any kind of way. But all this…what happened last night made me think it isn't fair to ask you to deal with all of this on top of everything else."

"But you said if I leave, you'll die."

"I won't die. I will lose my mortal form temporarily, but I can't die." He looked sad for a moment, and I thought again how hard it must be to live as long as he did.

"You can be hurt, though. Rachel said if something happened to either of us, you and Samuel would be vulnerable."

"I'll at risk, certainly, but I don't think it will be anything I can't recover from."

"If I left, and something happened to you, the whole world could be in danger." Great, I sounded like a comic book character again… Still, something *was* using my and Rachel's situation to try to break into our world, and I didn't think they planned to give everyone kittens.

Besides, as much as I tried to convince myself otherwise, I had feelings for Michael, and I didn't want to leave him. Not when I thought there might be a whisper of a chance we could have more than a professional relationship. The idea of not seeing him every day struck me with an almost physical pain.

"Saving the world should not be your burden," Michael said. "Not at this point in your life. Please, Gillian, think about it. It might be for the best."

"I have thought about it." I took a deep breath, trying to align my thoughts so they made sense. "Every day I think about how confusing and dangerous my life is now, and I get scared, I do, I won't lie. Still, when I think about my life before I came here, and the life I thought I'd have, I'm not frightened anymore. I know if I left here I wouldn't be chased by water elementals or shadow men; I wouldn't be teased by faeries or flirted with by kelpies. I'd be safe. On the other hand, I already met a world-famous magician vampire, and some Norse gods. Oh, and a Japanese Karura." That one was interesting. A god with a human body and the head of a bird, at least when he wasn't wearing glamour given to him by the Foundation. He came to us because he wanted to expand his koi farm in Delaware. I liked him. He told the most ridiculous jokes.

"If I left here, I might be safe, but I'd be bored," I continued, "and lonely. I'm not sorry I'm here. If I could make my permanent choice thing, I'd do it right now. I like this job, and I like the people, so no. I'm not going anywhere."

I stopped, embarrassed. That was a much longer speech than I'd planned.

Michael looked for a moment like he wanted to argue, but then he smiled, a proper smile this time, and I knew there'd be no more talk of me leaving. "Good. That's good. I want you to remember you still have a choice, at least for a few more weeks. If you change your mind, let me know, and I'll take care of it. But I must admit, I'm glad you said no. You're shaping up into a capable assistant, and I'm glad. I…I'm very pleased with your work so far."

"Thank you," I said, flushing with pleasure at his words. I stood up to go, then remembered I had an agenda of my own and sat down again. "There's something I need know, though, and I hope you can tell me."

"What is it?"

"What happened to Barbara?'

He looked nonplussed, as well he should. "Barbara? Why?"

"Because I found out she was only here for something like fifty years, apparently, and you said once the bonding was complete it couldn't be broken, I couldn't decide a year from now I didn't want to do this anymore." Michael nodded in agreement, and I continued. "Recently, Valerie told me the only choice a conduit could make would be to, well, die. So I presume that was the decision Barbara made. Is that why Rachel and I are in danger now?"

He sighed. "You are extremely perceptive, Gillian. You're correct. Barbara's leaving was unexpected, and it saddened me, so I suppose I didn't want to dwell on it."

"You don't have to tell me," I said quickly, feeling a bit guilty for bringing it up.

"It's okay. You deserve to know." He took a deep breath. "As I told you before, we like to find people who have few ties to the outside world. It's better not to have too many loved ones when one becomes effectively immortal, Gillian. It's a painful thing to watch the people you love grow old and die without you." He paused, as if he wanted me to say something, but I had nothing to say, so he continued. "When Barbara started with us a few decades ago she was, like you and the others, an orphan, with no extended family. She had, however, given birth out of wedlock a year before starting with us, and gave up her baby for adoption. There weren't open adoptions then, and she didn't seem interested in knowing what happened to the child. She told me she knew the child had a good and loving home, and didn't need to know anything more.

"I should have known." He stopped again, taking another deep breath, obviously struggling to keep his emotions in check. I fought the urge to reach over the desk to hug him, and simply waited for him to continue. "I should have known being a mother never goes away. Unbeknownst to me and the other partners, a year or so ago, the grown child found Barbara, and they maintained a correspondence. Then, a few months ago, Barbara got word her child died in a car accident."

"Oh, that's so sad," I murmured. "She must have been devastated."

Michael nodded. "She was heartbroken. When she confessed to me what happened, she asked me…begged me…to let her leave. She couldn't bear to remain in the world any longer. She'd lived for almost a century at that point, give or take, a normal enough lifetime, she said, and she didn't think she could stand living any longer. We argued about it for days. I told her she would get past her grief, and find happiness again, but she kept insisting she wanted to go. Finally, I gave in. I told her she could go."

Sympathetic tears welled in my eyes, not only for

Barbara's heartbreak and Michael's difficult decision to let her go, but because of the inevitable comparison to my own mother, who, at thirty-four years old, decided life was too difficult to bear and left via a bullet to the head. Barbara's situation may have been wildly different, but she still made the same decision as my mother.

"What did she do?" I asked, wiping the tears off my cheek and doing my best to compose myself. "Barbara I mean. What exactly happens when a conduit leaves?"

He sighed. "You're not supposed to know this, not until your time, but I think recently the rules changed enough I may as well tell you. When your time comes, a Door appears. The conduit must step through that Door and face a choice, either stay where the Door leads, or come back to this world, and stay forever."

I heard the capital D for door, and visualized a big, gothic structure creaking open to reveal something horrible beyond it. "Where does the Door lead?"

"The best way to describe it is that it's kind of like taking a shortcut to…heaven, I suppose you could call it. It's where…we're pretty certain it's where humans go when they die. It's wonderful there," he said, sounding wistful. "And no one has ever made the choice to stay here with us after seeing it."

"So Barbara picked the afterlife over eternal life, then?"

"Yes, she did. I imagine she simply chose to stay with her daughter, and her parents, and people who love her, and I honestly can't fault her for that. We don't have much to offer in comparison to that sort of happiness." He looked so sad, once again, I wanted to reach out and hug him.

"The problem is, as you know, the partners are vulnerable when not bonded. We've always managed to stagger it so only one of us is between assistants at a time, but Barbara upset the balance. I should have paid more attention to Rachel. She'd been with us long enough I should have realized she was nearing the time of her…" He hesitated, obviously as uncomfortable as the rest of us in acknowledging Rachel's possible death. "Her decision, and would open Samuel up to attack as well. But I didn't, and I let Barbara go."

"What else could you do?" I said. "Barbara was hurting, and you helped her. You can't blame yourself."

"Oh, I think I can," he said with a bitter smile, "but there's nothing I can do about it now, except hope we get through this intact."

"We will. I know it. I know all this…" I waved my hand vaguely. "It will all be taken care of. We've already survived three attacks, and the second week will be over in a few days, and before long I'll be permanent and you'll be safe, and I'll be safe and Rachel…" I stopped, not sure exactly what to say about Rachel. No matter what happened, she's still reaching the end of her lifespan. "Anyway, I know we're going to survive this. Valerie has faith. Rachel has faith, and I have faith."

He had such a bemused look on his face, I thought perhaps I'd made him uncomfortable with my admittedly vehement declaration, and I silently smacked myself for getting carried away.

"And I thank you for your faith in us," he said finally, his smile assuring me I hadn't gone overboard in my declaration. "And for your faith in me. I promise you, we won't let you down."

"I won't let you down, either."

"I know you won't." We smiled awkwardly at each other for a moment. Before I could say anything else, Rachel came in the office looking particularly smug.

"Are you done?" she said, smiling at me. "Because if you are, we can walk back to the condo together."

I looked at Michael, who nodded. "Yeah, I guess I am. I'll get my stuff."

We said goodbye to Michael, and Rachel and I headed outside. I admit feeling a little bit jumpy walking the darkened city streets either from fear of another attack from the forces trying to kill Rachel and me, or simply the result of spending several hours with vampires. As nice as they were, vampires still had the reputation for lurking in dark places, and hunting at night after all. Several minutes passed before I noticed Rachel smiling like she hadn't a care in the world, and acting much more cheerful than at the beginning of the night. In fact, she looked extremely happy, and I told her so.

"I am. I had a good talk with Samuel. Did you know there's a story, a legend almost, about us? About people in our position, anyway, the conduits." She didn't wait for me to answer. "I gather Michael told you the specifics of what happens when a conduit reaches their time limit?"

I nodded. "He said in history no one has ever chosen to come back after seeing what was there."

Rachel shrugged her shoulders. "That's true. But those other people aren't me. I've always known I'd choose to stay here. I mean, what's over there for me?"

I thought about it a moment. "Family, maybe?

Your parents? Maybe they're waiting for you there."

She made a derisive sound. "Look, I barely knew them when they were alive, and that was over two centuries ago."

"Well, I suppose there's eternal peace and happiness."

"Maybe, but it doesn't mean we'll never find eternal peace and happiness here. I've been pretty happy over the years after all. My life is here. My family is the Foundation. But that's not the point. The legend says if a conduit makes the choice to come back into the world, to live forever, then her partner will no longer need a conduit. He will become even more powerful, more invincible than ever, and you know the best part?" Rachel stopped walking and turned to face me, her expression intense. "The conduit, the former assistant, will become a partner."

I stared at her for a long moment. "Is that true?"

"I don't know for sure," Rachel said. She resumed walking, so quickly I had to scurry to keep up. "But I'm going to find out."

"What do you mean?"

"I mean Samuel finally admitted my time was coming, and agreed to let me choose."

"Rachel, you can't," I said horrified. "Not yet."

"I can and I will. In a few days, I'm going through that Door." Her smile looked eerie in the lamplight. "And I'm coming back out. I swear it."

Chapter 8

"But, Rachel, why do you want to do this now?" Valerie asked for the third time in five minutes. The three of us sat at a nearby café having a late lunch before starting work that afternoon. Rachel took the opportunity to tell Valerie her decision. Valerie did not take it well.

"Come on, Valerie, you knew this day would come eventually," Rachel said calmly, taking a bite of her chicken salad. "I'd have to do it sooner or later."

"Yes, but now? It isn't quite your time yet, Samuel said so."

"Samuel was wrong. He didn't want to admit it."

"Can't you at least wait two more weeks until Gillian is confirmed?" Valerie turned to me, apparently hoping I'd back her up.

"Give it up, Valerie," I said tiredly. "She's made her decision."

"Yes, I did, and I promise you it will be okay. Don't you understand? If I do this now, when I come back, we'll be safer than ever. Samuel will be even stronger, and I'll be there, able to fight alongside him…them."

"But you don't know you'll come back, you really don't. I know, I know…" Valerie waved her hand impatiently. "You say you will, but we don't know what's on the other side of the Door." I'd told Valerie what Michael said about the Door. I figured I knew the secret now, and Rachel knew the secret, probably knew it all along, honestly, so it didn't seem fair Valerie didn't. "It might be overwhelming. You could just as easily decide to stay there, and you know it."

I turned my attention back to my sandwich, letting the argument rage around me. Last night after we'd gotten back to the condo, I had a sort of epiphany and it ran basically like this: I wasn't going to worry about it anymore. I would take each day as it came, every day, for the next two weeks until my probation ended, and I became a permanent conduit. I didn't know if Rachel would return, but she believed she would, and that was good enough for me. I told Michael I had faith, and I did. I needed to let that faith carry me thorough the next couple of weeks.

A shadow crossed my plate, and I looked up to see our server hovering over us. "Can I get you anything?"

"No thanks," I said, "We're fine." I smiled briefly at him, and turned back to Valerie, now trying to bribe Rachel. "Seriously, Valerie," I said. "Do you honestly think offering a date with a leprechaun is helpful?"

"Are you sure I can't do something for you ladies?" I looked up at the server again, about to tell him to please go away, and noticed something sinister in his polite smile. Something was definitely wrong. We were regulars at the café and good tippers, so I didn't think it was something as mundane as him spitting in our soup.

Worried and suspicious, I leaned back to look directly into his eyes, and what I saw shook me to my soul.

His eyes were black, pure black, and where pupils

should have been there were flickering flames.

"Something hot, perhaps?" he said, his voice now tinged with menace. I cried out, stopping Valerie mid-harangue. She took one look at the server and shoved me aside, forcing me to the ground. The server's hand lashed out, quick as a snake, grabbing Valerie's neck. She stiffened, her face going white with pain.

"Let go of her!" I immediately grabbed at his wrist to release Valerie, only to experience a searing heat so intense I yanked my hand away, whimpering in pain.

It may have been an ineffective rescue attempt, but I managed to distract the server long enough for Valerie to twist out of his grip before collapsing, insensible, to the ground.

"Valerie!" I scrambled over to her, fear and worry thrumming in my heart. She couldn't die, I reminded myself, but she looked as still as death, her neck covered in blistering burns.

A noise behind me brought me back to my own inherent danger, and I threw myself backwards as the server, or whatever he was, leaned over me, his empty eyes searching my face. "We are coming. You cannot stop us. You will not stop us."

I was sure it would attack me like it did Valerie and frantically searched for something I might use as a weapon. To my surprise instead of attacking me, the thing turned away, reaching instead for Rachel

I screamed a warning, and she scuttled, crablike, away from the server-thing, missing its hands by inches. I looked around wildly, hoping someone would come to our rescue, but everyone else in the restaurant carried on with their lunch in complete oblivion to the drama playing out at our table, a fact almost more disturbing than the actual attack. Whatever was happening, we faced it alone.

The server's wild swing at Rachel caused his hand to hit the tablecloth, which burst into flame, giving me an idea. I sprang for the fire alarm, fortunately located near our table, muttering a prayer to whatever god might be listening that my impromptu plan worked.

Claxon bells rang, and water sprayed down on the diners from the sprinklers. Now people paid attention. Amidst the panicked customers rushing out of the restaurant, the server-thing fell to the ground writhing and screaming, his skin sputtering and hissing until steam rose from his body, like a campfire being doused with water.

I gaped at the sight in horrified fascination, gratified my plan worked so effectively, but my relief was cut short. The sprinklers shut off as quickly as they'd begun. The server-thing gave a great shudder and stood up, growling.

It didn't look remotely human any more. Horns sprouted from its head, and ears stretched upward, looking more wolf-like than anything else. Its fingers elongated and curved into talons, and flames, literal flames, spouted from its body in all directions, making it look like it wore the most dangerous fur coat in history.

All this I noticed in the few moments before my brain shifted into gear. I grabbed Valerie by one arm and tried to pull her up, but she was still unconscious and therefore dead weight. "Help me!" I hissed at Rachel, who looked almost catatonic with shock. Fortunately, she snapped out of it, and together we managed to pull Valerie upright and stagger out the door.

We took off down the street, the server-thing hissing and screaming behind us. We weren't far from the office, but I had no idea if we'd make it before it reached us again.

"Now would be a good time for a kelpie to show up," I panted. Valerie was heavy. "Or a vampire maybe? Anyone?" But the streets remained annoyingly empty of anything supernatural other than the thing following us.

Hope fluttered in my breast as we neared our building and Valerie, thank goodness, looked like she was recovering from the attack. As soon as she got her footing, she took the lead, dashing toward our office building like all the devils in hell were after her. Which they probably were.

The three of us burst through the door and right into the Accounting Guys, who, I swear, weren't there a second previously. "Get behind us," they ordered, and we happily complied.

Not a moment too soon, either. I didn't even have time to catch my breath before the glass door of the building bubbled and melted away, and the server-thing hurled itself into the lobby, hissing and snarling.

It stopped short when it saw the Accounting Guys, and, insofar as I could tell, a look of panic crossed its face. For a moment, it looked as though it considered running away. That hopeful thought fled when, howling and snarling like a rabid dog, the thing raised its arm and sent a scorching jet of flame flying toward us.

Before I could even take a breath to scream, the Accounting Guys waved their right hands, almost casually, and the flame bounced back toward our attacker as if it had hit a rubber wall.

The thing yelped in pain, and once again I thought maybe it would give up and go home. The thing was either determined or extremely stupid, because it growled again; darting toward us with flames shooting from its hands like bullets.

The Accounting Guys continued to deflect the flames back to our attacker, and each time they hit the creature, bits of its body melted off until it looked like a plastic toy left in the sun too long. Despite the damage, the thing kept fighting its way forward until it stood directly in front of Accounting Guys, who didn't move a muscle.

"You will let us pass," the thing hissed. I had a hard time making out the words since so much of its face was gone. "We will win. We will take the girl." It pointed what remained of its finger at Rachel, who recoiled. "You will move."

The Accounting Guys shrugged. "No," they said simply. "We will not."

What happened next was almost indescribable. One moment the Accounting Guys stood in front of us, solid and imposing as always, and then they vanished, replaced by two pillars of light.

No, more than light. They'd become prisms in a shaft of sunlight. A dazzling colorful miasma of brightness that shimmered and expanded turning into rainbow-colored rays of light that shot off in all directions, the reflection so bright I shielded my eyes.

The sparkling, luminous prisms bounced off the walls and the ceiling, and almost seemed to dance around the figure of the server-thing as it writhed and screamed. A noise like a clap of thunder struck so loudly, I clasped my hands over my ears in pain.

A second later it ended. I mean completely over. The Accounting Guys, no longer shimmering like a kaleidoscope designed by someone on acid, were back to their solid and intimidating selves, the lobby empty of demons, appearing as serene and pristine as always. Even the front doors were intact.

A general sense of relaxation permeated the room. "What the hell was that thing?" I asked as soon as I felt calm enough to speak without shrieking.

"An efreet. A kind of demon," Valerie said. I stared at her, amazed. She looked disheveled and unhappy, but was otherwise completely unscathed. "Or a genie, I think. One of those, I can never remember."

"Are you okay?" I asked her stupidly, in the face of evidence. She looked perfectly healthy, with no evidence of the attack marring her features.

"I'm fine." She grinned. "Can't be killed or permanently injured, remember? Although," she grimaced, "I wish 'didn't feel pain' was included on that list. That hurt."

"You, however, are injured," said the Accounting Guys.

I looked down at my blistered hand. Now that the excitement was over and I could afford to pay attention to detail, I felt the throbbing pain.

"Come with us. You need medical aid. Rachel and Valerie, go upstairs, the partners are waiting for you. We will be along shortly."

I followed the Accounting Guys into the elevator where we stood quietly, the tinny, easy listening music humming in the silence. We got off on the HR floor and were halfway down the hallway, when I finally had the nerve to ask, "Exactly what are you?"

They stopped walking, and turned to face me. I looked back at them and sensed, more than ever, the sheer "otherness" of them. Their eyes were dark and deep, the chill of age radiated from them. Their twin gazes penetrated my mind, into the core of my soul. My hand seriously ached at this point, but I didn't care.

"What are you?" I asked again, almost in a whisper.

"You truly want to know?"

I nodded, holding my breath in anticipation, if not outright fear, of the answer. They stared at me for a few more moments, and I tried not to look away.

"We are…accountants."

They turned, and continued to walk toward Angela's office. I stood there dumbfounded for a moment, then heaved a frustrated sigh and followed them.

I couldn't figure out at first why we were going to HR instead of a hospital or something, until I remembered Michael's words about Angela being a nurse with special healing skills.

He wasn't kidding, either. She stared at my hand for a moment then went to work with lightning fast efficiency. She didn't do anything a regular nurse wouldn't do, but even before the ointments and the bandages, I swear the moment she touched my hand the pain subsided, almost like, well, magic. I felt certain the burns on my hands were already beginning to heal.

As she worked on me, Lisa came into the room. Her eyes widened when she saw my blistered hand. "What happened?"

"I got burned." I wasn't sure how much I should

tell her. I figured she knew what went on in the Foundation, after all she'd witnessed to the zombie attack, but something told me most of the details regarding recent events were kind of secret. Besides which, it would be way too hard to explain.

"Oh, bummer."

Angela finished wrapping my hand. "It's not too bad, all things considered," she said. "No permanent damage. Be sure to put some ointment on it at least twice a day. I'll give you some to take with you."

Angela bustled out to get an extra tube of ointment, and Lisa cleared her throat. She looked like she had something on her mind. "Lisa," I said, when it didn't look like she would actually say anything, "Is everything okay?"

"Did you hear about Rachel?"

"What about her?" I asked warily.

"Did you know she will make her choice, soon?"

"She mentioned it to me."

"I was here when Barbara Chose." Once again, I actually heard the capital letter clang into place. It must be a skill a person acquires when working for the Foundation, making ordinary words full of portents. "Part of our job in HR is preparing for the Door."

I knew I probably shouldn't ask, but curiosity got the best of me. "What exactly happens, anyway? I mean, if you are allowed to tell me."

She moved closer to me, lowering her voice to a confidential whisper. "There's a room at the end of the hallway here. No windows, no other doors, at least not until it's someone's time. Then the Door appears in the wall, and the conduit walks through. The Door stays open until the decision is made, and then it closes, and disappears. It can take days, Angela tells me, but Barbara's Door disappeared almost immediately. Sad, but after all, everyone knew she'd already made her choice."

I didn't know what else to say, so I changed the subject. "Is the Door…is it there now?"

"No," Lisa said. "What do you think Rachel will do, when she goes through?"

I hesitated a moment before answering. While I couldn't think of any real harm in telling Lisa what Rachel believed, I didn't think I had the right to discuss something that didn't have anything to do with me. "I don't know," I said simply.

Lisa looked like she wanted to continue the conversation, but Angela returned with the ointment and told me the partners needed me upstairs as soon as possible.

I waved goodbye, and headed back to my own area, wondering vaguely what might happen next, and hoping I wasn't in for another discussion about terminating my employment with the Foundation. I didn't think I could handle another one of those.

Valerie met me as the elevator doors opened. "We're in the conference room," she said. "It's pow-wow time."

Michael was quite concerned when he saw my bandaged hand, but I waved him away, telling him I was fine. I was, too. Any lingering doubts I might have had about Angela's supernatural healing powers disappeared along with the pain, and I had a strong suspicion if I took my bandage off tomorrow, I'd find my hand completely healed.

"They're getting bolder," Michael said as soon as

we were all seated. "To attack in broad daylight, so near to our headquarters."

"I have a question." I grinned sheepishly. "I seem say that a lot recently."

Michael smiled gently. "That's understandable. It's quite a learning curve. What's your question?"

"Why didn't the people in the restaurant notice us being attacked? No one moved until I pulled the fire alarm."

"Magic," he said, and we both laughed. "Seriously though—remember you told me about Stacey putting the circle around your table? Whatever sent that efreet used something similar to keep mortals from noticing anything amiss. If not for Valerie's brave action and your quick thinking, by the time your real server came back to the table he would have only noticed you were gone."

Great. So not only would it have killed us, it would have made us look like we skipped out on the bill. What a jerk.

"Besides, like I've said before, you'd be amazed at how many things people don't notice," Valerie added. "Which, by the way, makes our job a bit easier."

"It is still risky, even without mortals noticing," Ralph said. "And why attack so close to the office? They must know the women are protected." He looked at Rachel. "Perhaps they are stepping up their plans, hoping to gain victory before Rachel makes her choice."

"But wouldn't they be glad?" Valerie asked. "Once Rachel's gone, we'll be sitting ducks."

"I won't be gone," Rachel said, exasperated. "And I bet they know that. I bet they understand I know what my choice will be, and they're trying to stop me before I make it, because then we'll be more protected, not less."

"I suppose that is possible," Samuel said in his soft voice, "but it is far more likely they are striking now, while we struggle with the idea of your…" He hesitated, just for a moment, and I saw a flash of anguish in his eyes. "Decision. Chaos is their byword, after all. They will seize any opportunity to increase disorder and confusion."

"Actually, I think Rachel might be right," I said, surprising myself. Michael and Ralph I felt comfortable enough with, but Samuel made me nervous. He was so imposing I found it difficult to relax around him, despite the fact he'd never been anything but kind on the few occasions we interacted. Still, I'd never even dared initiate a conversation with him before, and downright contradicting him was not something I ever thought I'd do. Nevertheless, I pressed on.

"That thing, the efreet, it stood right in front of me, and turned away to go for Rachel. And later in the lobby, it even said it wanted Rachel. Why would it do that? Maybe…well, I think maybe they know Rachel is strong enough to choose to stay here, on earth, and if she does, the Foundation will be even stronger." They all stared at me. "Won't it?"

"Efreets are not overly bright," Michael said finally, an element of doubt creeping into his voice.

I pressed on. I'd thought about this while Angela bandaged my hand. "I know Rachel is more vulnerable right now, but she probably can't be killed easily, because she still carries part of Samuel's soul right?" The three partners nodded in unison. "Valerie can't be killed at all, so he didn't bother going after her." She raised her eyebrow at me. "Not before you got in his way, I mean. My point is I'm the weak link. I'm still on probation and still mortal and probably even more vulnerable than Rachel, yet it didn't attack me. And I would think the, er…whatever sent it would know I'm the weak link and want to kill me." Despite all my concern, I was rather pleased at how calm I sounded when discussing my own possible assassination. My voice barely quavered at all.

"Anyway," I continued, "I think maybe the…whoever is planning these attacks believes Rachel is more important to stop because she is actually capable of making a decision that will make it even harder for them to, um, do whatever it is they want to do."

Rachel stared at me with a look of new-found respect. "See?" she said triumphantly. "I told you. Even the creatures fighting against us believe I will come back. So, let me do it. Now. Tonight. Then all this will be over."

"It doesn't work like that," Samuel said quietly.

"Why not?"

"You have to wait for the right time. Trust me."

"Why? You don't trust me. Barbara got to choose her time, why can't I?" To my surprise, Rachel looked like she wanted to cry. "Please, Samuel, please. I want to do this. I need to do this. You'll see I'm right. You have to believe me."

"Rachel, it isn't a matter of believing you. It's about the rules."

"You're the leader. You make the rules."

"Not these rules."

"Why not?"

"If it's any comfort," I said. "Lisa told me the Door isn't there yet, so you couldn't do it tonight anyway." They both turned and stared at me. I think, in the midst of arguing they'd forgotten anyone else was in the room.

"She is right," Samuel said. "I have, as you asked, put the wheels in motion, but it takes time. The Door will be ready on Monday. That is the earliest you can do it."

"Really?" Rachel's face lit up, making her look even more beautiful than usual. "Honestly? Oh, Samuel. You won't be sorry, I promise you."

He cupped her face in his hand, bestowing a gentle kiss on her forehead. "Go now," he said after a moment. "Michael, Ralph and I have things to discuss."

The three of us left the conference room, all lost in thought. In my case, my mind whirled with speculation regarding the nature of Rachel and Samuel's relationship. They'd been together for a long time, true, but the intimate look they exchanged when Samuel had his hand on her face struck me as much more than a simple close friendship.

If Rachel and Samuel were together, that meant there was no reason I couldn't have a more intimate relationship with Michael someday. I'd tried to keep myself from dwelling too much on the idea, but I knew Michael being as interested in me as I was him wasn't my own wishful thinking. He kissed me after all. He just never did anything about it afterwards.

I thought at first a partner/conduit relationship might be against company policy, but if Rachel and Samuel were…together, that wouldn't be true, so maybe he didn't feel the same way I did, despite the kissing. Then why did he kiss me? I sighed in frustration and resolved to ask Valerie about Rachel and Samuel at the earliest opportunity. At least then, I'd know for sure.

The opportunity arose about an hour later, when we both went to the restroom at the same time. Not a coincidence, I confess. It seemed like as good a time as any to accost her with yet more questions.

"Samuel and Rachel?" she said, grinning. "Oh, yeah, you guessed it. They've been together for, oh, gosh, at least a hundred and fifty years. They don't live together though. They like having their own space."

"Oh. And, um, there's no rule or anything?" Silently, I cursed at the ridiculously hopeful tone of my voice. Valerie obviously noticed, because she laughed.

"Oh, sweetie, don't feel embarrassed. It happens, it's part of the whole bonding thing. We conduits can't help but fall at least a little bit in love with our partner. Everyone handles it differently. I, for example, dated like a fiend, especially in the beginning." She flashed an impish grin. "It helped distract me from my crush on Ralph, and it was loads of fun."

"Why…um…" I wasn't quite sure how to phrase my next question, but Valerie, as always, knew exactly where I was going.

"Why didn't Ralph and I ever get it on? Various reasons, not the least of which is the fact he is gay."

Valerie laughed at my gobsmacked reaction. "Angels might not be human," she said, "but they share many human traits, including coming in all flavors of sexuality."

I pondered that a moment. It made sense. And

possibly answered the whole "homosexuality is a sin" question at any rate. Can't argue with an angel.

"I admit I was quite disappointed when I realized Ralph would never be interested in me romantically, but now Ralph and I are best friends. Better, even. He's like my brother. I know I can go to him whenever I need something, advice, a place to stay, or a hug when I feel sad. He's the most fantastic person I know."

"That's sweet," I said, meaning it. "It must be nice to be that close to someone."

"Give it time, Gillian. You and Michael will find your way once all this is over and you're permanently bonded with him. He and Barbara were close. It broke his heart when she left."

"Were they…um…"

She laughed again. "No, they weren't 'um.' I think he felt fatherly toward her. To tell you the truth, I'm not sure how often Michael even goes for 'um.' I've certainly never seen any signs of 'um' in him." I must have looked disappointed, because she grinned and added, "Yet, anyway."

I had a lot to think about, and as I worked my way through the day's correspondence, I kept obsessing about my nascent relationship with Michael, and where it might lead. I was attracted to him, certainly, or at the very least attracted to his supernatural and angelic good looks. Maybe that's all it was, an unrequited crush based on nothing more than a one-sided, superficial attraction, and I totally misread those few moments when I believed he might actually like me back.

I gave myself a mental shake. *Like me back.* What a grade school thing to think. Next thing I know, I'd pass him a note in gym.

I stapled some papers together, slamming the stapler a little harder than I probably needed to, and continued to try to talk myself out of dreaming of a romantic…okay, sexual relationship with my boss. I was done with men, remember? And sex wasn't all it's cracked up to be, at least in my limited experience. Besides, sharing the kind of closeness Valerie talked of, a familial relationship, that sounded appealing, too. Perhaps that's what I wanted with Michael. It's something I never had before.

My mother and I were close, in a way, but never what you would call intimate. We talked about clothes, and books, and places we wanted to go, but real, emotional stuff she avoided. Any time I tried to tell her something that made me sad, she'd change the subject or take me out for ice cream to "take my mind off it." Eventually, I learned not to share anything too painful. Good news I could share; anything sad I needed to deal with on my own.

It might be nice, I thought, to have someone who'd listen to even negative thoughts and give me a hug when I needed one. If my mother ever learned to face the bad things, maybe she wouldn't have killed herself. Or maybe she would have anyway. Depression is a tricky thing, I knew, and there were no easy answers, no matter how often I thought of ways I might have helped her.

I squashed those sad regrets that always boiled up whenever I thought of my mother, and turned my thoughts back to Michael. Yes, having him like a brother, like a family would be nice. Being intimate with him, while not without its appeal, might be too complicated.

Valerie told me days after vampire visits were reserved for work that didn't require too much energy, giving everyone a chance to recharge, so I didn't have much to distract me from my thoughts. I continued wrestling with my conflicting feelings without any real success. By the end of the day, I was glad to head home, or at least to the condo, where I could continue my internal argument in peace. As I packed up my things, hoping we'd have a nice, attack-free walk home, Michael came to my desk. "Gillian, I'm taking you home."

"That's okay," I said. "I'm walking with Rachel and Valerie, we should be okay."

"No. Not to the condo," he said. "I'm taking you home. My home."

Chapter 9

I never fully appreciated the expression "mind-boggling" until that moment when Michael made his announcement. My mind was well and truly boggled. I kind of gaped at him a moment, not sure exactly how to process this turn of events. It didn't help that Valerie stood next to me, and I heard her trying not to giggle.

"Oh, okay," I finally said. "But why?"

"We've decided, at this point, it is safer to have you all near us, where we can personally protect you. This goes for you as well, Valerie." Michael raised his hand to cut off her protest. "Yes, I know you aren't the one in danger, but it doesn't mean you won't find yourself in difficulty. The creatures who oppose us will not hesitate to inflict pain on you if they thought it would help their cause."

That seemed to give Valerie something to think about because she looked graver than I'd ever seen her, and ran off to talk to Ralph.

"Are you all right, Gillian? You look a bit confused," Michael said.

"No, I'm, that is, no, I'm fine." I babbled. "I'll wait until you're ready to go then?"

"I won't be a moment. And don't worry; it's only for a couple of days. I know I've been saying this quite frequently, but we'll get past this and everything will go back to normal. I'm sure of it."

I nodded dumbly. The word "normal" ceased to hold any meaning for me at this point. I went back to my desk to wait while Michael finished up his day, and tried to imagine what might be in store for me over the next couple of days.

What kind of a place would an angel call home, anyway? An image rose in my mind of Michael perched atop a fluffy cloud, harp in hand and halo on head, and I giggled.

I supposed if they lived among humans, they'd live like a human, and money was certainly no object, so he could live anywhere. I hoped he didn't live in one of the sprawling ranch homes on the Main Line. I'd had enough of that during my time as William's wife. I pictured Michael in a trendy loft in the city, one of those converted factory places, perhaps.

With a pang of homesickness, my thoughts turned to my own home. I missed my little house, with its tiny rooms and its quiet charm. I'd only been gone for less than a week, but it seemed like years, decades, even. So much had changed so quickly. I hardly felt like the same person who purchased that home and its promise of a simple life not so long ago. I had to admit, though, I liked this new me better.

Michael came out of his office, his coat thrown over his arm. "Are you ready?" he asked.

No, I thought to myself, but I nodded, grabbed my own coat and followed him into the elevator and down to the parking garage located beneath our building.

Based on the drama of the last few days, compiled with knowledge gleaned from the various movies and action television shows, I more than half expected something to attack us in the parking garage, but the short walk remained uneventful. No mysterious car chased us through the levels, and evil creatures from the depths of hell completely failed to appear from behind the pillars.

My ex-husband and his father owned a couple of antique cars in addition to whatever top of the line model they drove. William liked to talk about them at some length, so I had a passing familiarity with fancy cars, but generally speaking motor vehicles didn't impress me much. A car's job was to help me get from to point A to point B. Anything else was irrelevant, and I probably couldn't tell one car model from another on a bet.

All that being said, I fell immediately in love with the car waiting for us in Michael's reserved parking spot. An antique, I got that right anyway, it looked like the kind of car you'd see Grace Kelly or James Bond in, tooling around the English countryside.

"It's a 1948 Jaguar XK 120," Michael said when I asked him about the model. "One owner and I'm that owner." He gave me a boyish grin, and I laughed. Apparently, even angels could be gear-heads.

My ex-husband would drool with envy, I thought as Michael unlocked the car and, ever the gentleman, held my door open so I could fold myself into the seat. Like most sports cars, the car was a two-seater, small and intimate. Michael's hand accidently brushed my thigh when he shifted into gear, and a rush of heat raced through me at his touch. It took a few moments of deep breathing to calm my nerves and libido.

"So, where exactly do you live?" I asked as we pulled out of the garage onto the darkening city street.

"Out in Durham," he replied. "We all live in the

same general area. Rachel calls it 'Middle of Nowheresville,' but it's far enough from the city, and still fairly rural. All the partners need to get away from the city and man-made things for at least a few hours a day." The way he said it made it sound like more than a personal preference, and, after a moment of hesitation, I asked him why.

"Have you ever noticed how draining spending a day in the city can be?" I nodded, and he continued, "The reason is, for the most part, what's underneath the city is more city; subway cars, basements, sometimes even more buildings, depending on which city. A city is not connected to the earth at all.

"You see, everyone, supernatural and mortal alike, draws energy from the earth, and when you are separated from it, even just because there's a subway tunnel between you and the dirt, you lose connection with that energy, and you draw it from other people instead. It's more powerful at first, which is why people find the city so exciting, but also energy is drawn from you, and, over time, will drain you of energy."

"Oh." I thought about it for a moment. "That makes sense." And it did. William and I spent the early days of our marriage going into the city for various reasons. I'd start the evening full of vigor, and end it completely exhausted. I never thought about why that happened.

"In the country," Michael continued, "what's under your feet is land, more or less. Everyone, human as well as non-human, needs that connection to the earth to re-energize, but especially the partners. It's how we regain our strength, our power…" He turned to me and gave me a brief cheeky grin. "Our magic. Even fifty or sixty years ago, we could find dozens of places to recharge, but these days, it gets harder and harder to find a place completely connected to the earth."

"Which is why you live in Middle of Nowheresville, Pennsylvania," I finished for him.

He flashed me another grin. "Exactly."

I thought about what he said as we made our way out of the city. My mind went, again, to my mother, and how she always preferred living in the city, or at least the center of town whenever we moved somewhere. She said she liked being in the middle of things, of life. I guess she liked that energy, that buzz of excitement, like Michael said, drawn from other people. If instead we'd lived in the country, somewhere she could replenish herself through the earth, maybe she'd...I clamped down on that line of thought. I'd been doing that quite a bit lately, wondering what my mother might have done better in her life to change the way she ended it.

In an effort to distract my thoughts, I turned my attention to the road and nearly had a heart attack.

Highway 676, known by locals as "the Schuylkill" was notorious for heavy traffic, especially at rush hour, but Michael's Jaguar sped along at a rapid pace, unhindered by the plethora of cars around us.

The hood of Michael's car touched the Honda in front of us, and I instinctively braced myself for the crunch of metal, squeaking in surprise when we simply kept moving forward. I saw the details of the car's interior as we drifted through it—a forgotten stuffed rabbit on the floor of the backseat, the oblivious driver singing along to show tunes, the cellphone on the dash—and then we were out. I twisted around in my seat, and watched the Honda, stuck bumper to bumper with the other cars on the road.

I turned to stare at Michael. "You said you liked commuting like a normal human," I said in mocking accusation. "What gives?"

"I *am* commuting like a human," he said, laughing. "I simply don't like being stuck in traffic."

It might be a faster way to travel, but flitting like a ghost through other people's commute made me a bit carsick, and I breathed a sigh of relief when we left the city traffic behind, and the drive became more mundane. Strip malls and small towns gave way to tree-lined roads and hilly farmland, and pretty soon it did feel like we were in the middle of nowhere. I wondered again about what sort of home Michael lived in; a farm house, most likely, considering the neighborhood. He might live in one of those "McMansions" that sprang up everywhere farmland used to be, but I honestly couldn't picture Michael in such a suburban setting.

I didn't have much longer to wonder. After maneuvering down a dark road that twisted and wound its way up a small hill, Michael turned into a gravel drive, and I got the first glimpse of his home.

"Here we are," Michel said, stopping the car in front of a two-car detached garage. "What do you think?"

"It's wonderful," I said, instantly in love with the authentic Pennsylvania farmhouse and its stone siding and slate roof. Elegant without being pretentious, just like Michael.

Bright white shutters framed the large windows, and a wide porch spanned the entire length of the house. I used to dream of houses like this when I was growing up, usually when our turn of fortune meant squeezing into a small city apartment.

I followed Michael inside, unsurprised to discover the interior as tasteful and elegant as the exterior, all oak floors and simple furniture. It looked like something in a home and garden magazine. Did he decorate the normal, human way, or simply snap his fingers and copy a picture? It's what I would do if I had magic powers.

When Michael showed me to the room where I'd stay, I gasped in delight. An elegant, four-poster bed dominated the room, covered in a thick, beautifully-made quilt and piled high with pillows. The two tall, thin windows were framed in dark wood, probably oak, and the walls papered in a print of tiny antique-pink roses that didn't look as nearly as frilly as I would have thought.

Immediately, I trotted over to one of the windows, delighted to see it had a window seat, another feature in the dream house of my childhood. I knelt on the bench and opened the window, eager to catch a glimpse of the nature Michael and the partners needed so badly. Darkness prevented me from seeing much, but the sounds of a rushing creek caught my ears, making me smile. It seemed like an idyllic place to live.

"Right then," Michael said, and I jumped, startled. I'd almost forgotten he was in the room. "I'll leave you to get settled and then we can have some supper."

"Get settled?" I turned around, a feeling of mortification surging through me. "I left my bag at the condo. I don't have any clothes!" I couldn't believe I'd forgotten to pack. My nervousness about going to Michael's house obviously outweighed any practical consideration. "Or a toothbrush or anything."

"Relax, Gillian," he said in a soothing voice. "Everything is taken care of. Your clothes are in the dresser, and there is a toothbrush for you in the bathroom."

I stared at him. "How?"

He tilted his head, and gave me another boyish grin. "Magic, remember? Dinner will be ready in half an hour."

After he left, I opened the dresser and sure enough, my clothes were folded neatly in the drawers, far more neatly than I'd ever do it, truth be told. Smiling to myself, and trying not to dwell on the fact Michael might have seen my underwear, I shut the drawer, and checked the closet to see what else he might have teleported over.

The closet was long and narrow and empty, so apparently my entire wardrobe didn't come with me. I assumed it meant he didn't expect me to remain a guest for long in his home, and perhaps he did think this whole drama might end soon, and I could go back to living in my own house, with my own things. Try as I might, I felt more disappointed than relieved. Some part of my imagination still dreamed of a romantic relationship with Michael; as much as the logical part of my brain fought against it, and despite my best efforts, my thoughts over the last couple of hours kept drifting to fantasies of Michael and me playing house together for an indefinite amount of time.

I sighed, pushing those thoughts aside, and tried instead to focus on the present. Spending time outside the office with Michael promised to be interesting. It might not be the torrid romance of my fevered imagination, but the opportunity to get to know him a bit better would suffice.

Emotions rationalized to my satisfaction, I washed my face, dabbed on a bit of makeup, and ran a vengeful comb through my curls. A surreptitious peek under my bandage confirmed my hand was already well on its way to healing, as I expected. After one more glance in the mirror to make sure I looked presentable, I wandered through the unfamiliar hallway and down the large front stairs into the foyer where I stopped, completely unsure which direction to go.

The foyer was somewhat hexagonal in shape with several closed doors along the walls, and I had no clue as to which door led to the dining room. My first choice was completely wrong, instead of the dining room I stood in what looked like Michael's study. A large mahogany desk sat across the room, framed by a large picture window, and large shelves full of books lined the dark green walls. Ordinarily, I'd have stayed to examine the type of books an angel had on his shelves, but didn't want to keep Michael waiting. As I turned to leave, a painting caught my eye, making me stop in my tracks.

The portrait looked centuries old. I didn't claim to know much about art, but my former mother-in-law took great pains to teach me how to tell an original from a fake by pointing out things like brushwork and texture and other artsy terms. Most of it flew right out of my head, but she'd done it enough times I was at least confident the painting was original and not some art-store poster. And why shouldn't it be? Michael had been around for centuries. He probably got the painting from the artist himself all those years ago.

Something about the young woman in the painting intrigued me, and I stepped in for a closer look. She was attractive, or at least what the fashion of that time considered attractive, wearing a simple black velvet gown that looked expensive. She wore her reddish hair parted in the middle and gently pulled back from her face, covered in some kind of a veil. The only jewelry she wore was a round gold pendant, with the letter "A" etched into the center. Her light brown eyes looked pensive, almost sad. In her hands, crossed awkwardly in front of her, she held a rolled up scroll of some kind.

Did Michael know her personally, and if so, who was she and why did he have her portrait? I peered closer, searching for a clue in the faint writing on the scroll the woman held. I took a year of Latin in high school, and recognized the word "amor," but the rest of the words were faded and difficult to read.

"It says 'love transcends time,' roughly."

I jumped about a foot and turned to see Michael leaning in the doorway, a faint frown on his face. Embarrassed to realize I'd been trespassing into his private life, I stepped quickly away from the painting, blushing with shame.

"Michael, I didn't mean…I'm so sorry," I babbled. "I went the wrong way and then the painting caught my eye, and I wanted to get a closer look. I didn't mean to intrude. I'm sorry."

To my relief, Michael's face relaxed into a smile. "No need to apologize, Gillian. You are welcome to go anywhere in this house."

"Thank you." I hesitated then added, "She's beautiful."

Another frown creased his features, quickly

replaced by his usual calm demeanor. "Yes, she was quite beautiful. It is a lovely painting, isn't it? The artist never became famous, unfortunately, but he did wonderful work."

"She looks sad, though."

"It's a style choice. Besides, have you ever sat for a portrait? It's hard to sustain a smile for that long. She was quite happy when she sat for the portrait, believe me."

I turned to look at the painting again. She still didn't look terribly happy to me, but I took his word for it. "Who was she?" Another pained look crossed his face, so I hastily added, "If you don't mind telling me, I mean."

He shook his head. "I don't mind. It's probably something you ought to know anyway, considering the circumstances. She's…she's a part of my past, part of my beginning. I tell you what. Let's go eat dinner, and I'll tell you my entire life's history."

I agreed eagerly, and followed him into the dining room. On the table sat an enormous roast chicken, a basket of dinner rolls, several baked potatoes and three kinds of vegetables. "How many people are you expecting?" I asked, laughing.

Michael shrugged, looking chagrined. "I don't often have company," he said. "I guess I got a bit carried away."

Not enough time had passed since we arrived to prepare all this food and set it out the normal way. Of course, a cook or housekeeper might be tucked away somewhere, but I didn't see any signs of life other than the two of us. I contemplated asking where it all came from, but decided against it. He'd just say "magic," anyway.

We sat down to eat, but instead of getting into the serious stuff, Michael told me stories of his adventures in Europe long ago, and of the various people he met and helped along the way, both the regular, forgotten people of history and the famous. A natural storyteller, I sat enthralled as he spun his tales. The story of him acting in one of William Shakespeare's plays had me laughing so hard I almost choked on my peas. Still, the whole time he spoke, a part of me waited impatiently for him to get to the story of his own life, and the woman in the portrait. I suspected she played an important part in Michael's history.

Dinner finished, we moved into his comfortable sitting room where a fire already roared in the fireplace. Michael poured us both a glass of wine, then sat down in the chair across from mine, his face serious.

I sat up straighter in my chair, and my heart beat faster in nervous anticipation. By telling me his life story, all of it, I knew Michael showed me a level of trust, indicating a more personal relationship than simply one of boss and subordinate. This moment may likely alter the course of our relationship, opening a door I could never close again. I knew my feelings were at risk, in a way far more painful than a simple physical relationship might bring. Nonetheless, I wanted to know. I wanted to know about Michael's existence, the identity of the woman in the portrait, and anything else he wanted to tell me, regardless of what it would do to my heart.

"To understand where we come from, you need to understand there are worlds parallel to this one, other dimensions, some call them; thousands of different worlds with different rules. Although, some worlds are remarkably similar to yours. You follow me so far?"

I nodded, unwilling to interrupt his flow. He smiled and then continued. "My world was one of light and happiness and beauty and joy, everything glowed and sparkled like diamonds in the sun." He stopped, and his eyes had a faraway look. "That's not even close to an accurate description, I'm afraid. There are no words—no human words can ever adequately describe my home world. Suffice it to say, my world is truly beautiful, a paradise. We were not shaped like humans, as we are now, as you know, but made of pure energy, immortal and infinite. We knew nothing but peace and harmony. It was…"

"Heaven," I said.

"Heaven is a good way to describe it."

I tried to imagine a world made up of nothing but light and joy. I pictured a vivid blue sky and rivers of crystal clear sparkling water, verdant trees and colorful flowers dotting a rolling green landscape, and shimmering, sentient pillars of light flitting from place to place in perfect harmony and happiness. "It sounds wonderful."

"It is." A wistful look crossed his face again for a moment, but then he continued, "We were always aware of other worlds. We could see them. Watching those worlds evolve and grow was our version of entertainment, I suppose you could say."

"Like reality television," I said.

Michael laughed along with me. "In a way, yes. One world we were particularly fond of, a world with the potential to become a peaceful, joyous place, not unlike our own world. Although a primitive world and the denizens who lived upon it nothing like our own people, we enjoyed watching these creatures as they developed and evolved, certain one day the world would be its own type of paradise, like ours.

"Unfortunately, we were not the only ones watching. Remember when I rescued you from the shadow man, and I told you my kind banished them and others like them from our world?"

I nodded. "You said something about them finding new worlds to invade, or something."

"Yes. There are always new worlds, new life, and creatures like the shadow men envy the newness, the optimism of that infant world. They long to rob it of joy and hope and replace it with nothing but cruelty and chaos. They attacked our world, once, but we defeated them. They, and others like them, including a few of our own kind who allied themselves with the Creatures of Darkness, were banished from our world forever. Unfortunately, we only succeeded in keeping them out of our world; our power couldn't keep them from other dimensions. Before long, these beings punched a hole in the fabric of the universe and poured into the new world we watched—your world—and began to fill it with their own brand of hatred and fear."

Michael paused and looked at me with a quizzical expression on his face. "I realize this is quite a bit of back story. I hope it isn't overloading you. You've had a lot thrown at you lately."

I shook my head emphatically. "No, I'm...interested. Go on." Interested wasn't the world I should have used. Entranced was more appropriate. I pictured it so vividly in my mind's eye. The beautiful world full of creatures of light, watching over my own little planet as it began, a battle against the evil forces, the triumph, and then the evil creatures entering my world.

"When we saw those creatures invading that new world, some of us decided it would not stand. That world, a world with the potential someday to become a paradise in its own right, could not be destroyed, not if we could prevent it. To do this, some of us had to leave our home, and live among the natives of the world we wanted to protect, become their guardians. Others had done so in the past, to save other worlds, and we knew it could be done, and done successfully.

"Unfortunately, by the time we got there, the evil, for want of a better word, had already settled in, and we soon found it took all our effort to keep it at bay."

"The creatures, the humans, on this planet were so innocent and new, yet so eager to embrace everything the Creatures of Darkness offered; the violence, the power, the rage. Temptation was a hard thing to fight, and we were barely strong enough to survive, let alone prevail." A look of almost indescribable sadness, tinged with anger, crossed Michael's face. He looked for a moment exactly how one expected an avenging angel to look, terrifying and beautiful all at once, and for the first time I truly sensed his inhumanity.

"So why didn't you leave?" I asked hesitantly, almost afraid I would anger him with my question. "I mean, nice sentiment and all, and speaking as one of those humans, I'm glad you did, but didn't you ever want to give up? Why did you stay?"

"Because we knew those same humans, so eager to embrace the dark also had the potential for good. We saw it, sensed it, and we knew, despite the hardship and the sacrifice, they were worth fighting for. We needed to stay. We had no choice."

"So exactly how long have you been here, on earth then?" I asked.

"Oh, many millennia, I think. I've rather lost track. You must understand for the first several thousand years we remained creatures of energy, invisible and intangible to the people and animals of this planet. We did what we could, stopping the Creatures of Darkness and offering what hints we could to the people who populated this planet, teaching them to embrace the power of good instead of the temptations of evil."

"Sounds like a science fiction movie," I said, then immediately wished I hadn't.

Michael laughed. "You can find the truth anywhere," he said. "Even in science fiction. At any rate, around the early Middle Ages, we found it necessary to take a corporeal form."

"Why? I mean, it sounds like floating around like a ghost made it easier to get things done."

He laughed. "It did, at first. Then something happened, something we didn't foresee and didn't expect, and it severely affected our way of doing things."

"What happened?"

Michael took a sip of wine, either to ease his throat—he had been talking awhile—or to intensify the dramatic tension. "The people of your world, they seemed to have the power to shape reality."

I blinked at him. "They shaped reality? How?"

"We weren't visible, but we were noticed, and as the people of this world grew and developed, they made up stories to explain the things they sensed, but couldn't see. They told stories, and those stories tapped into the essence of what we were. That union of human imagination and the life force of my compatriots, as well as our enemies, caused bits of ourselves to break away and become sentient, turning into things like spirits, gods, faeries, kelpies, demons and monsters."

He took another sip of wine as I thought over everything he said. "So basically, gods and good creatures came from you and your kind, and the demons and things came from the other guys?"

"More or less. We think some of the more ambivalent creatures, like your friend Gerald, sprang from a combination of both parties."

"Okay. Let me get my head around this. My ancient ancestors sensed you and the others around them, and they called you gods and angels."

"Among other things, yes."

"And when they…named you, I guess you could say, bits of you broke off and became what they thought you were?" He nodded. "And we have legends of demons and stuff because of the bad guys you fought."

"Broadly speaking, you are correct."

"Oh." I found the idea fascinating, and one at any other time I would love to discuss further, but at the moment I wanted to turn the story back to Michael. Specifically, Michael and the girl in the painting. "So then what happened?"

"We slowly lost ourselves to the belief as each new god took something away from me and my kind, until we thought we might be completely eviscerated. Fortunately, we discovered we could protect ourselves by taking a corporal form. We still had the same sort of power, but with our essence in what you could call a protective shell, the human imagination could no longer access it.

"The solution did not come without its share of problems, however. Being human for the first time brought with it all kinds of human emotions we weren't quite sure how to deal with. You can't imagine how it is to feel, truly feel for the first time, all the emotions humans take for granted, happiness, sadness, fear, joy, love, sex." His grin was so wicked when he said that, I blushed. "That was a new one for all of us."

"Is that why you have girl conduits?" I teased. I thought of Ralph. Why he didn't have a male conduit, if that were the case. "It isn't, is it?"

"No. The conduit link has nothing to do with sexual desire. There's something about the male/female dynamic that keeps the link strong, we don't know exactly why. And we didn't even know about the link for the longest time. Our first mortal bodies didn't last any longer than a regular mortal's. We started over again, but found each time our body died, we'd be weaker and unable to defend against the chaos as effectively as before. Unfortunately, our enemies quickly learned how to use that weakness. We needed to find something to keep us from dying, from becoming vulnerable.

"It took some trial and error, but in time we found the right…formula you could call it, and discovered making a link with a human let us retain our mortal form indefinitely. Unfortunately, our human conduit would eventually reach the end of his or her life span, albeit a much longer one than a normal human's, but we learned as long as we found another conduit before the lifespan of our body ended, we retained our mortal body without interruption."

"And the girl in the painting was your first conduit." I guessed.

"Anne. Her name was Anne." He looked away, but I saw both love and anguish in his eyes. I knew right then who, and what Anne was to Michael, and probably why he didn't indulge in "um" often, if ever. *Damn.*

When he looked back at me, the heartbreak I'd seen a moment ago was gone, replaced with his usual calm demeanor. His voice betrayed no emotion as he continued with the story. "Anne was my first successful long-term conduit. She, quite literally, made me who I am today."

"And you loved her." I swear I didn't mean to say that out loud.

"I was very much in love with her, yes," Michael said. "In a way, I'd never been before or since. Anne helped me navigate all those human emotions I was still trying to get a handle on. She was smart and beautiful and willing to embrace everything our strange way of life offered, the good and the bad." His eyes softened at the memory. "Anne was intelligent and kind, a women truly worthy of being loved." My unreasonable and bourgeoning jealousy of Anne mostly disappeared when Michael added, "You remind me of her a bit." I tried not to preen too much.

"Anne stayed by my side for over two hundred years, and she believed when her time came to make the choice, she would stay with me forever." Michael fell silent, and I bit my lip to keep from blurting out something meant as comfort. I already knew how this story ended, trite platitudes wouldn't help.

Michael let out a deep breath and smiled sadly. "I waited for days, weeks maybe, I lost track, but Anne never returned."

Tears welled in Michael's eyes, and I turned away to give him a few moments of privacy. I stared at the flickering flames in the fireplace, struggling with emotions of my own. I understood, now, why Michael didn't pursue a relationship with any of his conduits. He had his greatest love, and lost it. Maybe you only get one chance at love like that, human or angel. A plaintive voice in my head questioned where that left me, but I brushed that rather pathetic thought aside.

We sat in silence for several minutes, until curiosity got the best of me. "Why didn't you go through the Door after her and convince her to come back?" I asked. "Maybe she would have if she'd seen how much you wanted her."

"I could not. I told you, we stayed in your world to fight because it was the right thing to do, but we also had no other choice. You see, when we chose to become this world's guardians, we gave up our right to go home again. When the Door opens, I can't step across its threshold. None of the partners can."

It took a minute for the implication of his words to sink in. "Wait. Are you telling me the Door Rachel will go through leads to your world?"

"We don't have any incontrovertible proof, mind you. As I said, I and the other partners cannot see into the Door, but based on what others have told us, I believe the world our conduits choose to stay in is the one we chose to leave."

Michael stayed quiet as I thought this through. "But you said the conduits see their loved ones when they go through the Door, that's one of the reasons they stay. That's why Barbara chose to go early, so she could find her daughter. Does that mean your world is heaven for regular humans? How did that happen?"

"Again, we're not certain, but we think in crossing to your world, we built a bridge, of sorts, to our own. We believe it follows the same process as when the humans managed to create beings from our essence. They created their various beliefs from our presence so it's logical the belief in a heaven would lead them to our home. Our world became the utopia your ancestors dreamed of. In that way, at least, we were successful in helping humans because my world truly is paradise."

"And you can never go back?" He shook his head. "But why not?"

"The gateway out of our world is like a one-way street. Once denizens of my world step through it, it closes to us forever." He must have seen a horrified look on my face, because he added, "It's okay. I knew what I was doing when I came here all those years ago, and I don't regret it."

"But it's just so sad."

"It isn't, I promise you. I've had my share of joy and happiness to balance any pain and loss I may have experienced. I wouldn't trade my existence here, or the work I do, for anything." An expression of fondness, mixed with a tinge of sadness crossed his features. "The way I look at it, all the conduits who were my links in this world are now in my own world, and so, in a way, I'm there too. It's a great gift."

We lapsed into silence while the fire crackled and burned in the fireplace and rain, simple, autumn rain, not murderous elemental rain, drummed down on the roof, both of us lost in our own thoughts.

I stared at the fire, trying to process everything Michael revealed to me. Foremost in my thoughts was the disappointment of knowing Michael might never love me the way I hoped. I knew I was being petty and selfish focusing on the loss of any possible romantic relationship when Michael, by all accounts, had exiled himself from paradise to save the world I lived in, but my heart ached just the same.

After a while our conversation continued and turned to more mundane things, like our favorite books and what movies we thought the stupidest ever. We discussed the finer points of a meeting we set up in the morning with a group of witches who wanted to start a coven in New Jersey. All covens had to register and incorporate through the Foundation. Apparently, too many witches together caused all sorts of problems if they didn't think they're being monitored. "Power corrupts," was how Michael put it.

As much as I enjoyed my alone time with Michael, I knew I'd fall asleep in my chair if I didn't go to bed soon, so we said our goodnights, and I went to my room where I fell asleep practically the moment my head hit the pillow.

I had, perhaps not surprising, a strange dream. I stood in the middle of what looked like a medieval village during a market day. People milled around me, a cacophony of voices filling the air as various peddlers shouted their wares. The dream was amazingly vivid. The pungent smell of animals up for auction assailed my nose, the afternoon sun warmed the top of my head, and I felt the wetness of the mud as it squished beneath my bare feet.

"Would the mistress like to sample my wares?" a voice said so close to my ear I jumped.

I turned to see a tall man, dressed all in black, standing by an empty cart. His vivid blue eyes seemed to sparkle with a mixture of amusement and malevolence, and his long blond hair looked out of place in the medieval setting. I recognized him at once.

"Hey. You were in my dream before."

He executed an elaborate bow, grinning wickedly. "Indeed."

"You tried to make me marry a zombie."

He laughed. "I did. For your own good, of course. I wanted you to change your mind about working with the Foundation. It's not good for you."

"How would you know?"

He raised an eyebrow. "Because I'm the reason it's not good for you." He held out a beautiful ring made of silver, carved with intricate symbols, the same ring he almost forced on my finger in my wedding dream.

The air around me thickened, got colder, and I found myself shivering. I wanted to turn, to walk away, but my feet were rooted in place. The…man, for want of a better word, stepped closer, menacingly.

"I'm here to give you one last chance. Run away. Go back to your normal life. It's the last chance you will have to save yourself." He grabbed my left hand so tightly I gasped in pain. "This is your last chance for redemption."

I knew, as I did before, if the ring touched my hand I'd be lost. I struggled to escape his grip, but in vain.

Someone grabbed my shoulder yanking me from the man's grasp, nearly dumping me onto the muddy ground. An unfamiliar female voice whispered in my ear, "Turn. Run. Now!"

I turned and dashed blindly through the village, narrowly dodging cows and people, and almost made it to the forest before my legs tangled in my skirt and I fell in an ungraceful heap. I knew before long my tormentor would be upon me. "Okay, Gillian, wake up now." I told myself. "Come on. WAKE UP."

And I did.

I opened my eyes, grateful to see Michael's guest bedroom and not a medieval village. I waited until my heart wound down to its normal pace, then closed my eyes, falling back into a, thankfully, dreamless sleep. I woke up again a couple hours later, refreshed and calm, the scariness of the dream already fading into the back of my mind.

Then I saw the ghost standing by my bed.

Chapter 10

I didn't panic or scream or dive under my covers or anything, not because I was particularly brave, but because she looked so solid, so alive. At first, I assumed she was a person, a housekeeper or something, coming to wake me up to start the day.

Not until my sleepy brain caught up with what my eyes saw did I realize something wasn't quite right. The woman standing by my bed wore a dress a housekeeper would probably not wear in this day and age, for one thing, and Michael never said anything about actually having a housekeeper. I struggled into a sitting position.

"Who's there?" Not the most original thing to say, I know, but it was all I could come up in the heat of the moment.

The more I stared, the more I realized there was something…well, otherworldly about the woman standing in front of me. I had the strangest sensation she was at once close and far away, and she looked lit from within by some kind of supernatural glow in an eerie, but not completely unpleasant way.

It, or she, smiled. "You can see me? That's interesting. I'm so pleased. I thought I'd have to drop hints in a dream. You have good sight."

"So they keep telling me," I muttered. "Who are you?"

"I'm Anne," she said. She spoke in oddly accented

voice, kind of a mixture of what I assumed cockney sounded like and something from the deep south of America.

"Michael's first conduit?" She nodded. I stared at her another moment. "Um…aren't you dead?"

Okay, it might not be the most tactful thing to say, but in my defense it was the middle of the night after a long, confusing day and a vivid nightmare, and she *was* dead.

"Yes, I left this world long ago," she said, moving gracefully to sit on the foot of my bed. I tried not to recoil from her, wondering at the same time how a ghost could actually sit. "But I can follow the link from…where I am to where you are, when necessary."

"There's a link? What link?"

"We conduits are all connected through our host, in our case, through Michael. Sort of a spiritual bond, if you will. When you become a full conduit, you'll be able to sense all the women who came before you."

"Oh, wonderful. That's not creepy at all," I said, rolling my eyes.

She laughed. A pleasant laugh, but there was something eerie built into a ghost laughing. I shivered a little, pulling the covers a bit higher to cover my shoulders. "The other girls tell me it's not unpleasant at all. They say it's like never feeling lonely. Generally, we former conduits try to help out the current one with tips and encouragement, usually through dreams and premonitions. It's a pleasant change to speak to you directly, I must say."

I thought back to what Michael told me, about the Door leading to his own, lost world. Somehow it made sense that all the conduits who stepped through would find each other. I envisioned a bunch of women gathered around, drinking coffee and gossiping, watching over me as I stumbled through my job. I have to admit it sounded kind of nice. Well, uncomfortable, honestly, but with overtones of nice.

"Are you in Michael's world? Is it heaven? Harps and angels and clouds and things?" So many questions vied for first place, but I was extremely curious about the whole heaven thing, for various reasons. It seemed like a good opportunity to get some answers plaguing mankind for ages. Maybe I could write a self-help book.

"No harps and clouds," she said with a smile. "But if you define heaven as a place of joy and contentment, where you are surrounded only with people who love and care for you, then yes, it really is like heaven."

"It sounds wonderful."

"Indeed it is a wonderful place." She smiled wistfully. "It is such a shame the partners are never able to return. I would like to see Michael again."

"Why don't you, then? I mean, you're here now. Why don't I go get him?"

She shook her head, the same pensive look she had in the painting crossing her face. "He can't see me, and I can't see him."

"Why not?"

"For the same reason he can't go back. The sacrifice the partners made when they chose to become the guardians of our world means they can no longer even glimpse the world they left behind, and since I am now a part of that world, we are separated forever. Although, you..." She looked thoughtful a moment, but then shook her head. "But no, if he came in here now, he couldn't see me."

"You could talk to him, through me, though, couldn't you?"

She smiled wistfully again. "That would not be wise."

"Why not?" Any residual fear I might have had talking to a ghost faded as I warmed to the topic. "Obviously, the fact I can see you is kind of a big deal, so why not take advantage of it? I don't mind being the go-between." Truth be told, I did mind, just a little bit. My feelings for Michael made it difficult for me to be one hundred percent happy at being forced to listen to Michael declaring his love to someone who wasn't me, but the romantic in me easily overrode that petty and jealous thought. I liked the idea of bringing some measure of happiness to Michael, and Anne, too for that matter.

But Anne shook her head. "I do not think it wise. I fear it would cause him pain, and I don't wish to do that to him again."

"How did you cause him pain?" She smiled sadly, and light dawned. "Oh. Because you didn't come back."

She nodded. "I am afraid any conversation Michael and I engaged in would become recriminations. That would not be kind to either of us."

I saw where she was coming from. After all, she'd promised she would come back through the Door. "Why didn't you return?" A blunt question, perhaps, but I had to know. "He loved you, and you loved him. Why didn't you come back and stay with Michael forever? Then you'd both be happy."

"I've asked myself many, many times, but rarely

do I regret my decision, although the love Michael and I shared was a wonderful thing." She sighed, quite literally a ghostly sound. "I had a beautiful life, Gillian, but by the end I was truly weary of living. I no longer wanted to deal with struggles we faced on a daily basis. There were so many attacks in those days, and the world I stepped into offered, oh, so much Gillian, the beauty, the peace, the purest sense of love." Once again, she looked lit from within, the expression on her ghostly face full of such fierce joy, giving me an inkling of what the world must be like, to evoke such emotion. "I had to stay, Gillian, I simply had to. I loved Michael, more than anyone or anything I'd ever loved before, but ultimately, I suppose, I didn't love him enough to give up paradise, to give up the peace it offered to me."

"Is it…who else goes there? I mean…" I took a deep breath, working my way up to the question that had been in the back of my mind almost since the start of this bizarre conversation. "Did my m…I mean, did Barbara find her daughter when she went through the Door?" I silently cursed myself for chickening out, but I did want to know about Barbara.

"She did. She's with her daughter and her parents now. She's happy. She's sorry for the mess she left behind, but she isn't sorry she made the decision. Is that what you wanted to know?" With one more, steadying breath, I tried again.

"My…my mother. Is she there, do you know? Would I find her if I went through the Door?"

"Are you sure you want to know the answer to that question?"

"Yes. She's my mother. I want to know if she

found the peace she sought for so long." I stopped; the implication of what she said sank in. "Do you think there's a chance she didn't get there?"

Anne gave me a look full of understanding and pity, and I turned my head away before I burst into tears. "There's always a chance, I'm afraid," she said gently. "There are so many other worlds, and as far as I understand it, many choices a soul can make at the end of her life."

"So she could be somewhere else?" I began to regret following this line of questioning, but since I did, there wasn't much sense in taking it back. And I guess I did want to know, once and for all, if the decision my mother made was the right one.

She'd been raised with the belief people who killed themselves went to hell, and yet she did it anyway so she must have truly believed it was the only way to end her pain. For my part, I hadn't been raised to believe in either heaven or hell, and mostly convinced myself it didn't exist. I'd also convinced myself my mother's suicide brought her the peace she needed, because to believe otherwise was too painful.

Now, with all the dizzying and belief-defying events of the last few weeks, I was no longer certain as to what I believed, and the thought of my mother suffering even more than she had in life filled me with dread.

I didn't want to know the answer, but at the same time I needed to know. "Could she be somewhere bad? Some kind of hell?"

"I honestly cannot answer that question, but I can tell you the choice was hers. She would not be forced into a world she didn't want."

I thought of my mom, all the times she sank into a depression, certain she didn't deserve any goodness or happiness in her life. I could, all too easily, imagine her choosing hell because that's what she thought she deserved. Anne must have sensed my thoughts because she said, "Gillian. This is important. Trust your mother. Believe in her. Trust your heart."

"But I…"

"Gillian, I am running out of time. Listen to me. You will face grave danger soon, and you must be prepared."

I blinked at the abrupt subject change. "I've been facing danger for weeks now."

"This is…bigger."

"Bigger? How big are we talking? Dragons?"

She laughed, but her expression turned serious as she said, "We do not know. The enemies are worried and nervous, which means they will resort to more desperate measures. Rachel, and her determination to stay on earth, has made them nervous for centuries, and with her choice coming up in a matter of days, they are running out of time."

"So they do think she's going to come back." I felt rather proud of myself for being right about Rachel. "Wait. What do you mean centuries?"

"There is an old legend describing a day when a human conduit will become a guardian, and that decision shall usher in the beginning of a new age, a time when the forces of good will become stronger than ever. The Creatures of Darkness don't like that idea, and Rachel, it seems, may well be the one to make that change. Up until now, the most the partners could do is hold them back. Should Rachel actually return, it would turn the tide and loosen the foothold they have in this world. This worries them, those creatures of the Dark. They've been trying to stop her, trying to scare her into changing her mind, but they have not succeeded."

"Good for Rachel." I punched the air. "She'll be thrilled."

"Gillian, listen to me." Anne's sharp tone brought me up short. "You've managed to thwart them so far, more than they expected, but desperation will drive them and you are still the most vulnerable. If they can't stop Rachel, they will come for you. You must be on your guard."

"Oh." I swallowed the lump of fear forming in my throat. "That's…bad."

"The problem is…" She hesitated, as if having a hard time finding the words. "Do you remember the story of Troy?"

"Um, yeah? The Greeks and the big horse?"

"Troy fell because they believed the Greeks left. They let down their guard, and they didn't believe the warnings they were given. Soon you and the others will think the enemies have given up."

"Why?"

"It's…let's call it a spell. That's not strictly true, but I don't have time to explain further. This spell will keep everyone, even the partners, from seeing the truth."

"If the partners fall for it, what makes you think I won't?" I asked reasonably.

"As the newest person in the Foundation, you are the least susceptible to this spell. You must be aware of anything that might seem strange or unusual, stay strong and try to convince the others the truth they all believe is actually a lie."

"So I'm Cassandra in this scenario, then?"

"In a way," she said, smiling. "It helps that your sight is so good. Because I warned you of this, you will have a weapon to fight against the lies when they start to happen. That is my warning and my advice. Heed it well."

"I will. And thank you for explaining it clearly, all direct and to the point and not phrased in a badly rhymed couplet that doesn't make any sense."

She laughed again. "It would be more fitting with the theme, wouldn't it? I must go, but remember I and all the other conduits are watching over you, and care for you. Trust in that, trust in your own mind, and, above all, remember to trust your own heart."

"I will. Can I…should I tell Michael we spoke?"

She smiled again, but sadly this time. "That is up to you. If you do, please, tell him…tell him I've never forgotten."

Before I could say anything else, she disappeared, leaving me alone. Well, as alone as possible, since apparently all the past conduits were looking over my metaphorical shoulder. The jury was still out whether or not that was a good thing, as far as I was concerned.

I scrunched down in my bed, and pulled the covers up past my ears, in the classic "making sure monsters don't get me" pose favored by children throughout the world, and closed my eyes.

Chapter 11

I was so sure I would lie awake for the rest of the night, but before I knew it, I opened my eyes again to the sun shining in dappled patterns through the window.

I felt oddly refreshed, despite my nocturnal visitor, and leapt cheerfully out of bed, ready to face whatever this day planned to bring.

What it brought, initially, was an incredible breakfast cooked by Michael himself. He looked so cheerful sliding bacon and eggs onto my plate I couldn't quite find a moment to tell him I'd had a conversation with his dead girlfriend in the middle of the night. In fact, he seemed more cheerful than I'd ever seen him, perhaps on some level he'd sensed Anne's presence, and that made him happy.

Assuming I actually saw her. In the light of day, the whole ghostly conversation felt more like a dream than something that actually happened.

I tested the waters by telling Michael about my medieval dream with the recurring blond guy. By the time we finished talking about it, breakfast was over and we needed to get to the office, and it seemed even more awkward to mention Anne's possible visit.

I tried, on more than one occasion, to bring Anne up in a casual way as we drove back to the city, to see if I could work the visitation naturally into the conversation, but I kept getting distracted by Michael's mode of transportation.

Morning traffic on the Schuylkill wasn't any better than on the trip out of the city, and in the daylight, I saw the other drivers quite clearly as we ghosted past them. We made a game of it, counting the number of people drinking coffee, eating breakfast, and talking on their cell phones. We saw one person actually shaving his face as he drove, making me glad we could slide through him, although I feared for the more mundane drivers. The only thing worse than rush hour traffic on the Schuylkill was rush hour traffic and an accident.

We were having such fun, it didn't seem right to bring up ghostly warnings and old lovers. Finally, I decided my best course of action was to run it past Valerie and Rachel first and get their advice before saying anything to Michael.

At the time, it seemed like the right choice. Perhaps if I'd told him right away things might have ended differently, but I suppose I'll never know.

I cornered Valerie and Rachel in the break room around mid-morning to tell them about Anne's nocturnal visit. When I finished, they looked at me skeptically, and my heart sank a bit. If they didn't believe me, who would?

"I can't believe Michael's first conduit could visit you," Rachel said, not unkindly. "I mean, if they could, I'm sure other conduits would have mentioned it before now."

"She does have good sight, though," said Valerie. "I suppose it's possible she could see a spirit hovering nearby."

"Or she dreamt it. That's more plausible."

"It seemed real," I said, but without much

conviction. The more I thought about it, the more I thought I must have dreamed the whole thing. "But do you think it's true? That the old conduits watch over me? Over us?"

Valerie looked thoughtful. "I suppose. I mean, now that you mention it, I have sometimes felt someone watching over me, especially when I'm in the middle of a stressful situation. I have had the occasional dream that I realized later foretold things." She shrugged. "I suppose it could be all of Ralph's conduits watching over me. It's a nice thought, I guess."

"I guess," I echoed, still not quite sure. It made going to the bathroom feel a bit awkward, that's for sure. I thought of Anne's warning. If it wasn't a dream, then I needed to warn people. I said as much to Valerie.

"What was the warning?"

I frowned, trying to remember exactly what she said. The details of what she said kept slipping away from me, much like trying to remember a dream. "She said…she said the enemies were more desperate because…" I stopped and glanced at Rachel, remembering what Anne said about her. "Because they believe Rachel will choose to come back through the Door, so they need to strike before she makes her choice."

Rachel looked beyond pleased. "But that's not exactly proof what you saw was real, Gillian," she said. "It's common sense, at this point. We know I'm coming back, and it's only logical to think the enemies will want to up their game before it's too late." The smug look crossed her face again as she added, "When I come back, we'll be stronger than ever before and the enemies will have to slink back where they came from."

"Maybe it's your subconscious way of dealing with everything going on lately," Valerie said. "It makes sense you'd warned yourself to be careful."

"So you don't think I saw a ghost?"

Valerie shrugged. "I'm sure they exist, but honestly, out of all the supernatural things we've ever dealt with in the time I've been here, I've never, ever seen a ghost." I must have looked unhappy because she gave me a one-armed hug and added, "But, as the man said, there are more things on heaven and earth. I'm still constantly surprised by the things I have to learn."

"If they are up to something, and you did see Anne's spirit, then you've done what you were supposed to do," Rachel said. "You've warned us, and we're on our guard. Try not to worry so much."

I smiled. "Okay. Thanks." I felt better having talked about it, and knowing they had my back made me feel like a burden lifted from my shoulders.

Valerie and Rachel agreed I still needed to tell Michael. My visit with Anne might be nothing but a dream brought on because of Michael's story. Still, if learned nothing else over the last few weeks, I knew how important it was not to discount anything, no matter how minor. Michael needed to know I had a warning, even if it only came from my subconscious and not from his former lover.

I sighed, thinking of Anne and Michael and their tragically beautiful love story. That, more than anything else, was why I hoped the visit was real. I wanted to tell Michael that Anne still loved him, to tell him she missed him as much as he obviously missed her, and, even though she regretted her broken promise, she was happy now. I wasn't being noble. I liked the idea of being able to offer him a little bit of happiness, knowing I could do something to give him joy.

We were so busy with the witches and everything, though, I didn't have an opportunity to speak with Michael until the end of the day. He cheerfully responded to my knock and I entered, surprised to see him with his feet up on the desk, whistling as he read over some paperwork. He looked more relaxed and happy than I'd ever seen him, and a shiver slid down my spine.

I don't know why someone I cared for being happy would cause warning bells to go off in my head, but I couldn't shake the feeling something was seriously amiss.

Michael smiled, motioning me to sit down. "Gillian, come in, is everything okay?"

"Fine," I said. "I wanted to tell you…"

"I have some good news," he said, obviously not hearing me. "We got a message today, the other partners and I. The threat is over. The enemies have retreated. I think we scared them off after that last attack."

I stared at him, unsure what to say. "Isn't it…I mean are you certain?"

"Of course. We have ways of determining such things. I'm not saying they won't try again, mind you, but for now we can relax. Take a breather, as it were. You can get settled in and Rachel…she can make her decision in peace."

"But…"

"So, you don't have to come back to my house this weekend, if you don't want. It's not that I didn't enjoy having you there, but I'm sure you'd like to get back to your own house, finally. I know you've missed your own things."

I carried on staring at him. He seemed cheerful, almost manic. Those warning bells in my head were now a cacophony, and I still had no idea what to do about it. How could I, a mere mortal, convince him, a millennia-old angel of light, he might be wrong? I struggled to remember Anne's warning. Something about Greeks, wasn't it? No, horses. Something about a horse. "Trojans!" I shouted.

"I'm sorry?"

That was it. Anne said they planned to trick people into thinking they left. "I mean, what if it's a trick?"

"A trick?"

"Yeah, a trick, a ruse, like the Greeks did to the Trojans. They pretended to go away and then hid in the horse, and the Trojans brought it into the city and the Greeks attacked when their guard was down. Maybe the…the enemy thingies are doing that." I still didn't have a handle on what exactly we were up against. Michael called them Creatures of Darkness, bringing to my mind an image of your stereotypical devil with pitchforks and horns. Why not? If Michael and the others were called angels, it kind of stood to reason they'd have a counterpart.

"I don't think that's the case," Michael said, interrupting my semantic musings. "As I said, we have ways, and we've been dealing with them long enough to know."

"But…"

"I appreciate your concern, Gillian, and you are smart to think of all the possibilities, but we're safe for now. They've pretty much run out of time, anyway.

You'll be complete in a couple of weeks, and Rachel…" He stopped looking quite so confident, but rallied, and continued. "It will all be fine. Honestly. Trust me."

"I do trust you, but…" I stopped, not quite sure how to get through to him. Maybe if he understood Anne told me, he'd believe me. "You know how everyone always says I have good sight?"

"Yes, of course. And you do. And if you are going to say I should trust your vision with this, I do. And, if it will make you feel better, you can continue to stay with me." I didn't quite appreciate his amused grin. Did he honestly think I was working an angle?

"It's not that," I said sharply, feeling every bit the Cassandra. "I have to tell you something, and it's something I think you ought to know." I took a deep breath. "Last night…"

His phone beeped, and I signed in frustration. He pressed the intercom button and Lisa the HR Assistant's voice came over the phone. "Michael, sorry to disturb you, but is Gillian there? She wasn't at her desk."

"Yes, I'm here," I answered. "What's up?"

"I'm at the reception desk, filling in, you know, and you have a visitor."

"I do?"

"It's someone named William. Your ex-husband, he says. He would like to speak with you."

"William? Are you sure it isn't Gerald again?"

"Yes. I asked Stacy to do her witch thing and check. He's human."

On the whole, I'd have preferred Gerald. I might have expected this. After calling me the day of the elemental attack, William left me a drunken message three days in a row, asking me to please call him it was important. With everything going on, self-pitying my ex-husband wasn't high on my priorities, so I didn't call him back.

"Anyway, can you come see him?" Lisa asked. "He refuses to leave until he sees you."

I sighed, and considered asking the Accounting Guys to deal with him, but then changed my mind. Knowing William, he'd keep showing up if I didn't nip it in the bud right now.

I looked at Michael. "Go see him, get it over with," he said, apparently reading my mind. "We'll finish our conversation when you get back."

"Fine," I said, rather ungraciously, and to Lisa I added, "I'll be right there."

I found Lisa waiting for me at the front desk, but no sign of William. "I put him in the conference room in the HR department," she said. "I figure it's nice and private. I'll take you there."

"Thanks," I said. We walked in silence to the HR area as I mentally reviewed all the possible scenarios of what William could possibly want, and what I would to say to him. Stalking my house on occasion was one thing, but coming to my place of work to try it again went beyond annoying, although typical of him. He always lived life like he was the only one who mattered; other people's rules and desires meant nothing to him. He probably wanted to see how pathetic my job was, so he could point out how much better off I was when married to him. That sounded like something he'd do.

Assuming it was actually William waiting for me. I still half hoped to find Gerald instead, come to talk about my wish again. A mystical faerie would be easier to deal with for me than William in self-pity mode. Gerald I could yell at, at least.

"Here you go," Lisa said, breaking into my thoughts. "He's in there."

I followed her into a windowless and completely empty room. I turned to Lisa who'd shut the door and stood in front of it, looking rather pleased with herself. "What's going on?"

"You'll see in a moment."

"I'll see what in a moment? Where's William?"

"Oh, he's not here. I needed an excuse to see you, and I knew he was the right button to push. Just like Barbara's button was her daughter."

"Lisa, what are you talking about?" I stared at her, exasperated. I was distracted, still worrying about William, and wanting to get back to Michael and tell him about Anne and her warnings. I wasn't fully processing her words. I can't believe how thick I was.

"Did you know I found Barbara's daughter for her? Simple, really, the access we have at this place is unbelievable. As soon as Barbara and I became friends"—she made little sarcastic air-quotes—"I knew what I had to do. I had to find her daughter."

My stupid brain finally caught up. Something wasn't quite right. "That was nice of you," I said carefully, a prickle of fear creeping up and down my spine. "It's sad her daughter died so soon after they found each other."

"She had to die, you see. We knew it would be easy to manipulate her emotions once her daughter died."

She still stood in front of the door, Lisa in her

sensible shoes and inexpensive skirt, but for the first time since I met her she was smiling, an evil smile. It might have taken me a few minutes to catch up, but the vague uneasiness I'd had since we stepped into the room blossomed into full blown fear. "Are you telling me you killed Barbara's daughter?" I kept my voice as calm as possible, hoping, I suppose, she would laugh, tell me she's kidding, and everything would go back to normal.

"Yes. Well, I didn't do it all, of course. He told me how to tamper with her car so the brakes wouldn't work, but he arranged the rest of the accident by causing the other car to run that red light." She giggled like a school girl, an innocent sound chilling me to the bone. "Tragic accidents are so easy for him. But getting Barbara to leave the Foundation, that was all me." She giggled again. "That was the important bit. Barbara had to want to leave this world, and he knew the key to get her to go through the Door. All part of his plan."

Something in the way she said "he" indicated the word was more than a mere pronoun. "Who are you talking about? What plan?"

"His plan to destroy the Foundation," Lisa said slowly, like speaking to a child. "Barbara's daughter needed to die, so Barbara had a reason to leave this world, at the right time, opening the two biggest partners to attack. It took some convincing, her loyalty to Michael and the Foundation was strong, but we were friends." Out came the air-quotes again. "She listened to me when I told her she would be happier with her daughter, in paradise. I also kept Michael vulnerable by picking unsuitable replacements. Angela trusted me to pick the right people, you see."

"Seems like too many people trusted you," I said, trying surreptitiously to edge my way around Lisa, hoping to make a break for it and escape.

"I'm trustworthy." She giggled again, and I couldn't repress my shudder. "I seem trustworthy, anyway. It's why he likes me. No one questions quiet little Lisa. One more failed conduit and Michael would be completely vulnerable and open to attack." She frowned. "Unfortunately, you slipped under my radar and Angela got to you first. Once we saw you weren't going to run screaming like the others, we had to accelerate the plan. Especially since Rachel, bless her egotistical little heart, is so certain she will return. It made the others nervous. Not him, though. He knows exactly what he's doing."

"Who's 'he'?" Lisa only smiled, so I tried a different tack. "Who are you then?" I needed to come up with some sort of exit strategy. I could try pushing Lisa out of the way and making a run for it, but if she wasn't human, if she was something like the efreet thing, it might not end well for me. I took a deep breath and did my best to stay calm and stall for time, hoping my sluggish brain would come up with a good plan soon. "Are you one of the…" What did Rachel call them? "The enemies?"

She laughed again. "No. I'm one of you. I'm a conduit. You think your partners are the only ones who can offer eternal life?" She shook her head. "That they are the only ones to connect to humans? They are so arrogant."

Good. She's human. Maybe I can push her out of the way and run for it. "So you're a conduit for…whom, exactly?"

"Someone far, far greater than your precious partners. I've been with him for over fifty years, and when he takes over this world, he promised I'll be by his side, forever, as his queen. I have, after all, done something no other creature could do."

"And what's that?"

Lisa actually rolled her eyes at me. "What do you think? I infiltrated the Foundation. I'm the Trojan horse."

I blinked, startled at her use of that phrase. "Were you spying on me?'

"Spying on you? No. I mean, I heard your little talk with Rachel and Valerie in the break room. You three think you are so special, you never even notice when other people are around." She laughed derisively, jealousy plain on her face. I wanted to dispute her, but she wasn't wrong. I hadn't noticed her in the break room. Maybe I was being elitist. I shook my head. My personal flaws weren't important right now. Besides, Lisa was clearly a psycho.

"I heard you tell them about your ghostly visitation," Lisa continued. "They didn't believe you, did they? Michael didn't either, I'll bet. It's working. The partners have let down their guard and opened the gate, and now we're going to sack the city. Just as soon as I get rid of you."

"Michael knows I'm down here. He'll…"

"What? All he knows is you're meeting with your ex-husband, safe inside the Foundation's walls with me, sweet little Lisa, the HR assistant."

I didn't have anything to say. She was right. Michael had no reason to think anything was wrong.

"Besides," she continued, "he and the other

partners don't have a care in the world right now. Any sense they might have that something is wrong is blocked, and even if he notices, or cares, he'll be too late." Her eyes flickered to something behind me. "Ah, there it is, right on time."

I couldn't help it. I turned to see a huge iron door, rusted with age but still imposing, surrounded by an archway lined with ancient-looking stone. A feeling of dread crept through me as it slowly creaked open, revealing nothing but blackness beyond. "That's not…" My voice nearly squeaked in terror and I stopped, and took a deep breath, and tried again. "Is that Rachel's Door?"

"No," Lisa said behind me, her breath tickling my ear. "It's yours." And before I could even scream, she pushed me through.

Chapter 12

Not floating, not falling, I hung suspended in the dark. No, not dark—dark is the absence of light, and this was the absence of everything. I couldn't see a thing, not even my hand when I held it inches in front of my face. When I shouted, nothing came out, at least not anything I heard. A complete void, a word I never truly appreciated until that moment.

Eventually, I felt something underneath me and realized I sat on some sort of surface. It didn't feel like I'd landed, more like the ground appeared beneath me. After a moment, a faint light surrounded me, brightening in slow increments until I could finally see around me.

The dirt was gray and gritty, more like ashes than sand. Surrounding me were tree-like things, dark and dead, nothing but shadowy scribbles against the pale light. I looked up, half expecting, or hoping, to see the door above my head, but saw nothing, darkness stretching out forever.

I heard whispering all around me, voices far enough away I couldn't understand what was being said, but close enough I kept turning around to see if someone or something was nearby. The whole place radiated a sort of sadness I still can't quite describe.

I think, on the whole, I preferred the void.

I didn't cry. I didn't even feel particularly scared—

bemused, possibly. I absolutely refused to let the idea I was trapped in some sort of dark world with no escape occur to me.

If it did, I might start screaming, and I didn't think I'd ever stop.

Besides, I was sure Michael would find me. He always found me. Every scary moment that happened to me since this whole saga began ended with someone coming to my rescue. I couldn't—I wouldn't—believe this time was any different. Michael would find me. I held on to the thought for as long as I could.

I lost all track of time as I sat on the ashy ground listening to the whispers until I came to the conclusion sitting around waiting for rescue was a pathetic way to behave. Besides, the ground was cold and uncomfortable and I, believe it or not, was bored. "She could have at least chucked a book down with me," I muttered as I struggled to my feet, my attempts at humor to lighten the situation failing miserably.

I picked a random direction and walked for a while, not sure what I should look for or what I thought I'd find. I trudged along, wondering where I was and trying to ignore the unpleasant sound the ashy dirt made under my feet. Every once in a while, I thought I heard something, but when I looked around I saw nothing except the dirt and the blackness and the trees.

The trees were particularly horrible. The trees, with their dark, knotted bark and twisted branches looked far more frightening than anything fanged and drooling could. The way they stood there, bare and unmoving, and every time I looked at one I was overcome with such a feeling of dread and sadness, I turned away. Like one of those nightmares when some ordinary object feels terrifying, but you can't say exactly why.

I did my best to push the unpleasant thoughts aside as I continued to move forward. Many times, I wanted to sit down on that gray barren ground and cry, but I didn't. I couldn't. I couldn't give up, not even after walking for what seemed like hours, with no sign of rescue. No signals from the blank sky above me, or joyous shouts from my friends calling my name. No telepathic link to Michael telling me not to worry, and he'd be here soon. I kept moving, keeping my gaze firmly fixed on the ground in an attempt to avoid looking at the trees, hoping to stumble across something, anything to lead me out of this terrible place.

The whispering continued all around me as I walked, and I began to think I heard words among the whispers. I told myself my imagination made the whispers sound like words. Human brains do that; "pareidolia," I think it's called. I told myself the whispers were nothing but the effect of the wind through the trees. Ignoring the fact there was no wind and the trees weren't moving.

It didn't help. The whispers seemed to get sharper the more I tried to ignore them, and soon all I heard was words, sad words full of pain and sorrow. "I'm sorry," came floating to me, over and over again. "I'm so sorry."

Covering my ears didn't help block out the sound so, eventually, I did my best to ignore them as I trudged on. Then a new word came through, a word that stopped me in my tracks.

"No one is calling your name," I spoke aloud, immediately regretting it. My voice echoed oddly in this place. I continued to move forward, telling myself over and over it was my brain trying to interpret the sounds. It's easy to misinterpret whispers. I'd almost convinced myself no one whispered my name.

Until they shouted it.

Startled, I turned toward the sound, facing the trees for the first time. During my endless walk, the light around me continued to brighten, and I saw the trees clearly for the first time. I froze, whimpering in terror, fighting the urge to throw up everything I'd ever eaten.

I remember reading Dante's *Inferno* in high school, and one part always disturbed me, particularly after my mother's death. In one level of hell, all the people who committed suicide were turned into trees. Something about them not respecting their bodies in life, so they lost them in death.

What I saw in front of me might not be exactly like Dante's forest, but came close. The trees weren't made out of people, more like cages made out of trees. The trees themselves looked like human flesh, the bark blackened in places and dripping with blood, branches gnarled into various shapes; some like a gun, some a noose, one suspiciously looked like a train. Within each nightmarish tree, I saw pale faces peering out, trapped within the bark, bloodless lips whispering incomprehensibly. The forest contained hundreds of souls trapped in hundreds of trees, old men, young women, teenagers, all kinds of people, all with identical looks of pain and regret on their faces. I stared in horror, unable to look away, two things racing through my brain like a mantra. My mother killed herself, and someone shouted my name.

I ran straight into the woods, shouting for my mom.

Every few minutes, I heard her shout my name and I changed direction, branches whipping across my face and tangling in my hair as I ran. It seemed as if the trees reached out for me or perhaps trying to stop me, a secondary, if disturbing thought as I ran on through the macabre forest. Hopes of my own rescue and escape vanished, replaced with only one goal, one hope. I needed to find my mom.

"Gillian!" I stopped so quickly I almost fell. The voice was right by my ear and unmistakably my mother's.

I turned, my heart in my throat, and for the first time in ten years, looked into my mother's eyes.

"Hi, baby," she said. It was her, really her, my mother, twisted in the bark of that demonic tree, smiling at me; a sad, pained smile, as familiar to me as my own.

"Mom." I swallowed the lump in my throat. "Mom, what are you doing here?"

"What do you think I'm doing here?" she said, a touch of her old wryness tingeing her voice.

"Why, Mom? Why did you do it?" I hadn't meant to ask. I wanted to get her out of that prison somehow, but the words tumbled out. "Why did you leave me?"

"Baby, I'm so, so sorry. I just…I couldn't take the pain anymore."

I swallowed hard, fighting against the conflicting emotions surging through my mind. "So, why didn't you talk to me if you were hurting? Why didn't you get some help? I could have helped you, or tried to, at least, if you had let me."

"I'm sorry, I'm so sorry." Around us other voices echoed her words. "I didn't want to burden you. I did what I thought was for the best."

"And this didn't burden me?" I shouted. I didn't want to, but the anger and the pain I'd pushed aside for so long came bubbling to the surface. "I was sixteen, Mom. Sixteen and alone. You left me. I could have helped you." My voice broke. "I could have helped."

"Oh, darling, I don't think you could."

"If not me, then why not see a doctor? Someone might have been able to…" I didn't finish my thought. Stop her? Help her? Maybe she didn't want any help. "You could have talked me, at least."

"Why are you here, Gilly? You're not dead, are you?"

I laughed through my tears. My mother always changed the subject when she didn't want to talk about her feelings. Funny how some things never changed, even in another dimension. "It's a long story. I'm kind of trapped here, I think." I gave an abbreviated account of my recent adventures, and, despite everything else, a warm, almost contented feeling filled my heart.

I was actually talking to my mom again.

Looking back on it, I think if a way back to the Foundation opened right in front of me, I'm not certain I would have walked through. I wanted to tell my mother so many things, to share the years of my life she missed, to tell her how much I loved her, how I'd missed her every day of my life since she died. Despite the fear and the dark and the impassioned whispering of all the imprisoned souls, I think could have stayed there forever, with her, and been happy.

No wonder none of the conduits ever came back.

"There's some kind of entrance farther into the forest, just beyond here," my mother said when I'd finished. "I can sense it. I don't know where it leads, but I'm sure it's better than here. Perhaps you can find your way out. Go now, before…just go."

"I can't leave you here."

"Yes, you can. You have to."

"No. No, I don't." I grabbed a piece of the bark imprisoning her, and tried to tear it apart, but when I did so my mother screamed in agony, and I pulled back, horrified.

"There's only one way you can free me," my mother said sadly. "And it isn't worth it. Go. Find your way back, live your life. Be happy."

"No. I can't," I said, beginning to cry again. "I can't lose you again."

"Ah, Gillian, there you are. I'd wondered where you'd gone."

The voice came from behind me, smooth and gentle, with just a hint of menace. I swallowed hard, then, steeling myself, turned to see what new horror this world brought.

In a flash of insight, I knew exactly who, or at least what, he was. He was the man from my dreams, the man I'd seen in the graveyard and probably even the person standing on the deck below me in the condo the day before the elemental attack.

The one behind all this.

Looking at him, I had a hard time believing he was evil, though. With his handsome face, long blond hair and blue eyes, he looked a bit like a Tolkien elf, or perhaps a romantic poet; and his smile reminded me of Michael's. I found it disconcerting to think he was the creature behind all the horrible things happening lately. I guess what they say about books and their covers is true.

"You must be the person Lisa told me about," I said finally, pleased to notice my voice barely faltered. "Her 'partner.' "

He bowed formally. "I am indeed. I am, to forestall any further questions, the counterpoint, of your Michael. The devil to his angel, if you will."

I looked over at my mother, who appeared terrified, a rush of anger swept through me. This…*thing* in front of me imprisoned my mother in a tree. All my fears melted in the heat of my anger. My hands balled into fists as I fought to remain calm. "What do you want?" I practically snarled. "Why am I here?

"You've proved much too hard to outright kill, and, frankly you're not that important to our cause. Separating you from Michael was the easier choice. With his conduit in a different plane of existence, Michael will be so much weaker, and therefore the protection around Rachel rendered practically nonexistent. We will stop her before she steps through the Door." He stepped closer to me, and I stiffened. "I'll take you back, when your partners have fallen, if you'd like. You can watch the world burn."

"You think Rachel's going to come back, don't you?" I said. "That's what you and your, your minions are fighting against. If she comes back, the Foundation will be even stronger."

His eyes narrowed, and I knew I'd hit a nerve. A bit of a hollow victory, but there you go. "Moot point, my dear," he said. "We are already winning. After all these millennia, the world will finally be ours."

"Why my world? Why not stay here and, I don't know, conquer this world? It seems more your speed."

"Oh, we've been here for too long. We've used it all up. We want your world with all its pain and evil and malevolence. There's so much more to do there."

I heard a sob behind me, and turned to look at my mom, who was crying, and I no longer cared any more about the battle for earth. They'll win, or we'll win. At that moment, I simply didn't care. "Whatever. Let my mom go."

He looked nonplussed. I guess he expected me to plead for the earth, or beg him to send me home, or something. "I can't do that."

"Yes, you can. I mean, if you used her to get me here, then mission accomplished. You don't need her any more. Let her out. Please, let her go."

He gave an elegant shrug. "It's not that simple. We have rules in this world. If you want something from me, you must challenge me."

"Challenge you to what?"

He smiled. "A drinking game."

Now it was my turn to be nonplussed. "A what?"

"A drinking game." He waved his hand and a table appeared in front of me, upon which stood a large golden goblet, rimmed with red jewels like rubies. As I watched, the goblet filled with a dark amber liquid. "Drain the cup, and if the drink leaves you standing, you win the challenge."

"And if it doesn't?"

"If you fall to the ground before the game is over, you stay here with me, forever." He smiled again, looking predatory. "An intriguing prospect for me, I must say."

"Whatever would Lisa think?" I said as sarcastically as possible, given the circumstances. "So that's it? Drink and try not to pass out?"

"In a nutshell."

I looked at my mother. She shook her head urgently, her eyes wide and frightened, and I gave her the most reassuring smile I could muster. I might never have reached the level of professional drinker like my ex, but I admit to a few drinking binges in an attempt to keep up with him, back when I still thought I could save my marriage. I managed to hold my own. I even won at beer pong a few times, so how hard could it be? "Okay. I'm in."

Taking a deep breath, I grabbed the goblet and lifted it to my lips. I expected the drink to taste bitter, or spicy, but instead it tasted like honey and lavender. I gulped it down, wondering as I did so what the catch would be.

I found out about a second after I put the cup back on the table. Everything around me blurred, and when my vision cleared I stood on the playground of the school where I'd spent sixth grade; one of the worse school years of my life.

The popular girls of the school surrounded me, as they often did, jeering at my old clothes and unfashionable haircut. "Silly Gilly," they called me, over and over again. Tears stung my eyes, making them laugh even harder. I wanted to stand up to them, but I was too shy, too afraid of what they might do if I tried. Instead I ran away, toward the field beyond the playground, and stumbled over a rock, nearly falling to my knees. I looked down at the rock, and back up at Sarah, the girl who teased me the most.

She laughed at my tears, and the thought came to me, quick as lightning, to pick up the rock that had nearly tripped me and throw it at her head. That would stop her laughing. She deserved it. She had no compassion, no kindness in her heart. I picked up the rock. Sarah laughed. "You are nothing, Gillian," she said. "You're weak, and you're stupid, and you will never be anything important to anyone."

"Shut. Up," I said, gripping the rock even harder. I pictured it in my head, so clearly. I saw myself leaping at Sarah, knocking her to the ground, smashing the rock into her mocking, cruel face.

"Do it. Give in. It will make you feel so much better." I don't know if the voice was Sarah's or my own. "Take revenge. Win for once, Gillian."

I looked at Sarah again, and for an instant I stopped seeing her as a bully who tormented me, and saw her as she was, a scared little girl who needed to put others down to make herself feel stronger.

"No," I said. The rock thudded to the ground. "I can't. Just…go away and leave me alone."

The world spun again. I stood in the graveyard, at the open pit that took mother's body. I wasn't crying. I was angry, and I was hurt. The woman from child services stood next to me, looking stern. "Listen to me, Gillian, you are being unreasonable. You're sixteen years old, and not nearly bright enough to survive on your own. You're too much like your mother. You must come with me."

I pulled away from her. My foot slipped in the mud surrounding the grave, but I righted myself again before I fell. "No. I want emancipation. I don't want to go into foster care."

"Gillian, you can't survive on your own. You're a silly, stupid little girl, and you know it. You don't know what's best for yourself."

She stood perilously close to the edge of my mother's grave, and I wanted to push her as hard as I could, make her fall, to make her shut her condescending mouth.

Once again, I saw myself giving in to my anger; I saw her fall, saw her hit her head on the edge of the wooden coffin.

"Gillian, you will never be able to take care of yourself." I took a step forward, but stopped myself, and stared hard at the woman in front of me. She was condescending, yes, and she seemed unable to feel any sort of compassion, but I saw the pain in her face, the sadness in her eyes. She wanted to help, to save the world, but the tragedy and dysfunction she saw every day wore her down, making her lose faith in herself, in the world.

"No." I turned away from her, from my mother's grave and once more the world around me changed. My vision cleared to reveal the bedroom I shared with my ex-husband. William was there, his eyes red and his face flushed from a night of drinking. "Of course, I stayed out all night!" he shouted. "Why would I come home to you? You're nothing. You're boring and stale, and I never should have married you." He stumbled toward me, his hands grasping at me, pulling me toward him, making me almost fall. I grabbed the edge of the bedside table to steady myself and braced for what I knew would come. Generally after insulting me, he'd try to kiss me, then tell me the kiss was terrible and I was frigid and dull.

The heavy lamp I kept on the bedside table sat near my hand in invitation. It would be so easy to pick it up, and smash it over his head. My fingers itched to do so, but I pushed the thought aside. William was a sad little boy who never managed to grow up. "I'm sorry," I said, pulling myself out of his grip. He stumbled, but I helped him sit on the bed. "I don't need this anymore." I smiled sadly at my ex-husband, and headed toward the door. "Goodbye, William."

The world shifted again. I was back in the woods with Michael standing in front of me. I nearly cried in relief. "Michael! You came. I knew you would!"

"Did you? I can't imagine why. You've pushed people away from you your whole life. 'Leave me alone.' That's your mantra, isn't it? Why do you think you were sent here?"

"Lisa…"

"Oh, yes. She works for me. You weren't working out, so I asked her to get rid of you. I can't have a conduit constantly shutting me out. It doesn't work that way."

"I didn't shut you out."

"Didn't you?" His smile, something I'd come to love in the past few weeks, looked bitter and cold. "What about the cruelty lurking in your heart? Do you know how much hatred lives in you? Didn't you see it? I did. I know you wanted to throw that rock, push that woman, and smash your drunken husband on the head. It's all in you, waiting there under the surface. I can't have that kind of evil in a conduit."

I felt the blood rushing to my face. The shame and hurt his words brought surged through me. He was right. I did think those terrible things, I did. I remembered those moments; they weren't visions sent to torture me. They were memories, real memories. I wanted to hurt those people as much as they'd hurt me.

I took a step toward Michael, my arms outstretched, silently pleading for him to forgive me, but he turned away. I wanted to drop to my knees and beg, and almost did.

And then, once more, my vision cleared.

The thing in front of me wasn't Michael. It wasn't a memory, and it wasn't real. The devil, or whatever he was, tried to trick me. I stood straighter, more securely and faced the thing in front of me. "Sure, they were in my mind, those dark thoughts. Those kinds of thoughts race through everyone's mind sometimes. But I didn't do it. I didn't do those things. That's what makes a person good. It isn't a lack of darkness. It's facing the darkness, and turning it away."

I smiled, feeling more confident than ever. I was winning this contest, and I knew it. "I'm not alone, either. I have Rachel and Valerie and Stacey, and Angela, and Ralph and Samuel and the Accounting Guys and…all the other conduits who have gone before me." I looked at the Michael standing in front of me and nearly laughed. "And I have Michael. And you're not him."

The world spun again, and the original forest returned with my mother behind me and the blond man in front of me once again, looking less confident. My head ached, but my heart sung, I was elated. I'd won. The drink didn't make me fall.

"Congratulations," he said dryly. "You've had an epiphany."

I turned to my mother, still trapped within the bark. "Mom. Get out of there. You're free now." She shook her head, tears streaming down her face. "Mom?"

"I'm sorry, Gillian. I'm so sorry, but I can't. I don't deserve freedom."

"What are you talking about?" I stepped as close as I could and reached into the cage to try to stroke her face. She felt as insubstantial as air. "That's stupid. Stop punishing yourself, Mom, I know you're sorry. You were always sorry. You spent your whole life apologizing to me, and punishing yourself. Just let it go."

"I tried, sweetheart, I really tried, but the pain always came back, and I couldn't cope. I was never as strong as you. I knew you'd be okay. I knew you'd find the life I could never have. I wanted you to find happiness, and I didn't think you could find it with me."

I looked at my mother's face, remembering all the times I'd come home to find her crying in her bedroom. I'd do everything I could think of to cheer her up, but it never worked. Other times, though, we were happy. I knew we were. The games we played when driving from one home to another; the stories we made up about the wonderful life we would have once we got there. I remembered the times, as few as they may have been, when my mother pushed aside her own pain and sat with me when I was sad or hurting. All the love and the sadness and the joy and the pain wrapped around me like a blanket, and I broke down in sobs.

"I know you can never forgive me for all the pain I caused in your life, but believe me, you brought me the only happiness I ever knew. I was a bad mother, I know, but you were a wonderful daughter."

"No. You're wrong. You tried your best, Mom. I know you did. I didn't understand. All I knew was you left me." All the sadness, all the pain I'd kept in check ever since the day I walked in and found her lying in a pool of blood in front of her closet, her eyes staring up into nothingness, came pouring out of me. I couldn't have stopped the tears even if I tried. "But I know, I know, Mommy, you loved me. I always knew."

I sank to the ground, wrapping my arms around the rough bark that held my mother, sobbing like a baby. I understood, finally, I could either spend the rest of my life resenting the things my mother didn't give me, or embrace the things she did. "You did the best you could, Mom, and I'm sorry, too. Don't say…don't say I can't forgive you because I can. I do. I forgive you, Mommy. I love you, I'll always love you, and I forgive you."

As I chanted those words, willing her to understand, the bark surrounding her disappeared and I felt the solid form of my mother in my arms. I looked up, into my mother's face as she smiled, her hands stroking my hair like she used to when I was a child. "Thank you, my darling. Thank you. I will always love you." She leaned forward to whisper in my ear, "Trust your heart." Then she disappeared.

I sat alone on the ashy ground, wiping the tears from my face. I still didn't know where I was, or what might happen to me, but at the moment I hardly cared. I saved my mom. Finally, after years of guilt, I saved my mom. Anything else almost didn't matter.

"You think you've won, do you?"

I jumped, startled. I'd completely forgotten about the stranger. "I did win. My mother is freed. You let her go."

"Oh, Gillian, silly girl. I did nothing of the sort."

"But you said if I challenged you and won, you'd

set her free."

"No, I only said if you wanted something from me, you must to play the game. I wasn't the one holding her here."

"What are you talking about?"

"Look around you." He waved his arm at the forest surrounding us. "All these tortured souls chose this place out of guilt and pain; they have absolutely nothing to do with me. Your mother was here because it's where she thought she belonged.

"Your mother, all these people are here because they think they deserve this place. When they can forgive themselves, or when they are sure the ones they left behind forgave them, they can move on."

"You're saying my mother's guilt and fear led her to this place?"

"Yes. And your anger, your resentment kept her here."

"So it's my fault she was trapped?"

"In a way, yes," he said, his voice almost kind. "Your forgiveness freed her."

"So the game meant nothing?"

"I didn't say that. And I never said the game was over." He took a step toward me and held out his hand.

"You're on the ground, Gillian Burke. I win."

Chapter 13

"I…you…" I fumbled, numb with shock. "That's not even remotely fair."

"And who ever said anything was fair?" he replied, still smiling. "Didn't Michael warn you about making deals with supernatural beings? Always make sure you know the rules before you enter into anything."

"You…" I couldn't think of anything harsh enough so I settled for, "asshat." I ignored his still out-stretched hand, and pushed myself up off the ground. I wanted to argue with him, but, unfortunately, he was right. I walked right into it, and now I was stuck.

I stared up into the empty sky, the hope that somehow Michael or someone would rescue me fading fast. I was trapped in some unknown world, alone except for some sort of psychopathic creature whose motives I didn't know or understand, and I couldn't see any way out. Despair, stronger than I ever experienced before, washed over me until I looked at the tree that so recently held my mother, and the despair was joined by a modicum of peace. If I hadn't been sent here, I wouldn't have seen my mother again. I wouldn't have freed her. My situation might still be dire, but I couldn't completely regret it. Not if it meant seeing my mother one more time, and knowing she may have finally found the peace and happiness she sought for so long.

"Why don't you let me take you back to my home?

There's no need for you to stay out here in this forsaken place. I'll even feed you."

I wasn't listening to him. I remembered what my mother said to me, something about an entrance just beyond her prison. I doubted it would lead to my world, that would be too much to hope for, but it might definitely lead me away from this one, and from my captor. That was good enough for me.

I turned in the direction I hoped she'd meant and broke into a run. I didn't bother to check to see if the man followed me; it would only slow me down. I ran faster than ever before, ignoring the gnarled branches slashing against my face and grabbing at my clothes until the trees finally parted, and I stumbled into a small clearing where I skidded to a halt, gasping in surprise.

There in front of me was a Swiss chalet, looking unbelievably out of place surrounded by all the creepy trees. Bright red and white roses spilled merrily from the window boxes, their rich sent filling my nose, the bright green roof dotted with pure white snow.

My music box had grown life-sized and completely real, its door open invitingly.

Hope gave me strength and I dashed toward it, practically leaping through the opening only to bounce off what felt like solid concrete and landed solidly and painfully on my back.

Groaning, I got up and this time approached the entrance cautiously. Gingerly, I reached out my hand and met solid resistance. I pushed, carefully at first, then harder, until I pounded on the invisible barrier, but to no avail. I couldn't get through.

I stepped as close as I could and peered through the doorway, hoping for, well, I didn't know what, exactly.

Maybe someone on the other side with a key or something, someone who could get me through, or at the least get a message to Michael. I was grasping at straws, I knew, but the alternative meant the loss of my last hope, a fact I wasn't quite ready to face.

I knew right away what world lay on the other side, and my breath caught in my throat at the sight of it.

If the shadow man I'd experienced in the graveyard contained of all the fears and worries I'd ever experienced, the feelings I got looking through that door was of every happy thought and joyful moment I'd ever had, transcended and made solid. I didn't see the sparkling, crystal river or glimmering trees of my imagination; the world beyond that door exuded a beauty that defied description, full of shimmering colors more vivid than I ever could have dreamed, a whirling kaleidoscope of peace and joy and pure, unadulterated love. I thought I saw glimpses of actual people, but I couldn't be sure. If I looked too long at something, it would merge and flow into something else entirely. My mother *was* there. I knew that as well as I knew my own name, the pain of not being able to break through and join her almost unbearable. I lost all track of time as I stood there, tears running unchecked down my face. I didn't even turn when I heard the footfalls of my captor behind me.

"Do you honestly believe Rachel will turn this down?" I asked softly. I was nearly as convinced as she was that she would stay with Samuel, but looking through that impenetrable barrier, seeing what awaited her there, I was no longer certain.

"It is foretold, so yes."

"Why can't I get in?" I didn't mean to sound so

plaintive.

"Because Michael cannot."

"And I'm linked with him." Knowing that made me feel the tiniest bit better about my predicament. Knowing we were connected, even slightly, gave me hope.

"That and it isn't your time yet." His voice lacked the tinge of malice I'd already come to expect, sounding almost like pity. That was enough to make me wipe my tears and turn away from the door. I wasn't going to have a creature like him pity me.

"Worth a try, anyway," I said, hoping he couldn't hear the despair in my voice. "At least I got to see it."

"It is beautiful, isn't it? Even I miss it, sometimes."

"You're from that world, too? But...you're so evil."

He laughed. "You could call me evil, if you must. The elders certainly thought I was, the reason I'm here now." He stepped past me to bang on the invisible barrier. "See, I can't get in either. Unlike Michael and the others, however, I didn't leave by choice."

"Oh, come on," I said derisively. "Don't tell me you were kicked out of paradise. That's just so...so...Milton. Next you're going to tell me your name is Lucifer."

He laughed again. "No, but feel free to use that name. I rather like the idea."

"I'm not calling you Lucifer," I said, exasperated. "That's too ridiculous to contemplate." I no longer felt particularly terrified at the idea of being trapped with this creature. There was no room for it any more. I'd lost my last hope of escape, trapped in this world of sadness and loss, but worrying or crying wouldn't make me any more unstuck. I needed to be brave and deal with the situation at hand, and hope another means of escape presented itself in time. "I'll call you Luke."

"Luke, then. That's as good a name as any, and we'll be together awhile, so you'll need to call me something."

He grabbed my hand and, before I knew what he was doing, he'd slid a ring on my finger, the same silver ring from my dreams. "Of course," he said with a lewd grin, "you could always call me Master."

As I was about to offer a hopefully witty retort, the world around me shifted and the next thing I knew I stood in what can only be described as a room in a medieval castle, complete with tapestries on the wall and a roaring fire in the cavernous fireplace. My sarcastic comment died on my lips. "What the hell?"

"Welcome to my humble abode," Luke said, dropping gracefully into an armchair in front of the fire. "Make yourself comfortable."

"How did you do…oh, never mind, I don't care." I tried to take the ring off, but to my complete lack of surprise, it wouldn't budge. I flopped in the chair opposite him, feeling completely exhausted. Too many things had happened in a short amount of time for me to worry about what the ring might mean, or what would happen next.

Besides, if truth be told, despite what I knew about him, and everything he'd done, Luke was difficult to completely hate. He was…intriguing, I had to admit, charming even. A bit disturbing, but it made it hard to maintain a state of constant fear.

"So, tell me about your master plan. It's generally what supervillains do in this situation, right?"

"What do you want to know?" He waved his hand and a tray appeared on the table before us, laden with fruits and candies and nuts. "Care for some refreshment?"

I shook my head. I was famished, but I'd learned my lesson. I wasn't going to eat anything in this place, just in case. For all I knew, eating food would trap me here forever, like Persephone in Hades, or turn me into a statue or something. I didn't want to take any chances. "So who are you? Not Lucifer, I'm sure. Are you really the same kind of being as Michael and the other partners?"

"It is true. I am from the same world as your partners, but, unlike them, I didn't want to save your precious earth."

"Why not?"

"We didn't need another world like ours, so peaceful and tranquil and boring." He nearly spat the words. "I agreed with the, what did Michael call them, the shadow men. The ones from this world, and others, who want to feed on the anger and chaos and hatred your kind excels at creating. I fought against my people, in the beginning, and I was expelled for it. Not that I cared. My world was too tame for the likes of me."

The pained look on his face betrayed the lie. He did care he was barred from his home world. It almost made me feel sorry for him.

"What about me?" I asked. "I still don't quite understand why you need me here."

"With you in a different dimension than Michael, the link you share is weakened. It will...help."

"So why not kill me?" A question I wasn't sure I

wanted answered, but I had to ask. "Why keep me alive like you're some kind of Bond villain?"

"Several reasons, not the least of which you are currently more valuable alive than dead. I can use you as leverage, if necessary."

I took a steadying breath, biting back a sarcastic retort. He may act the genial host now, but I didn't want to piss him off. "Do you think if you can keep Rachel from coming back, or going through, or whatever you're trying to do, you'll defeat the partners? All of them? I mean, there's more than three partners in the world, right?"

"We're punching a hole in the wall. It might be a small hole, but it will be enough. Eventually, the walls will crumble, and we will prevail."

"You've been trying for thousands of years, though. It must have gotten frustrating, losing all the time."

Okay, so I wanted to piss him off a little bit.

"We didn't lose all the time," he said sharply. "We had victories; Salem, Nazis, the Spanish Inquisition."

"I guess nobody expected that one," I said before I could stop myself. Luke simply poured himself more wine. Huh. Not only was he evil incarnate, he had a lousy sense of humor.

"Getting Lisa into the Foundation, working for our side right under the noses of your precious partners, was our latest little victory for the cause."

"Lisa said she was your conduit. Is that true?"

"Not exactly. She's more like a 'thrall' if I may use an old-fashioned word. You know what that means, right?"

"Enslaved, correct?" I hoped I was right. I didn't

need a supervillain laughing at my weak vocabulary skills on top of everything else.

"Yes, more or less. In this situation, the difference between a thrall and a conduit is, while you draw from Michael as much as he draws from you, for Lisa it's a one-way deal."

"You draw from her, and she gets nothing in return?" That seemed crueler than anything else he'd said so far.

"Not nothing. She hasn't aged in fifty years after all, and if I choose I can give her power, strength, skills. Things I need her to have so she can carry out my orders." He leaned forward in his chair, and his voice took a seductive tone. "If she's good, I might give her a little something in return, and if she's naughty…if she's lucky she gets nothing."

It didn't seem like a fair relationship, and I almost felt sorry for Lisa. Almost. "She said she helped you kill Barbara's daughter."

"Oh, indeed she did, quite willingly, too."

"But why did you have to kill Barbara's daughter?"

"Lisa told you already. We wanted to give Barbara a reason to leave her position as Michael's conduit, and the only tie she had left to mortality was her daughter. Lisa, working on my orders, made sure to introduce Barbara to her long-lost daughter, and then, when we were sure the bond was strong enough, we killed the daughter in a car crash Lisa created." He took a sip of his drink and popped a couple of grapes in his mouth, a nonchalant gesture that made his words seem much more chilling.

"That's a lie, though. Lisa said you did stuff too, to make the accident happen. You didn't need Lisa's help at all."

"Ah, but getting blood on one's hands, even by proxy, brings that person that much closer to our side. Tapping into the evil lurking inside makes it so much easier to control that person. Helping me was her blood sacrifice, if you will." He grinned, but there was no humor in it. "She wanted to help me, little, human Lisa, with such greed and jealousy and vengeance lurking in her heart, making her so easy to corrupt."

"You say human like it's a bad thing."

"It's a weak thing, humanity. So willing to embrace the dark as long as they think there's something in it for them. People like Lisa are the ones that drew us to this world in the first place with their rage, their capacity for violence, and their greed. It's wonderful."

I chose not to rise to that argument. I wasn't quite up to the challenge of defending humanity at this point in my life.

"When I met Lisa fifty years ago," he continued in the same, mocking tone, "she was a sad, bitter young woman, cast off from her family for engaging in immoral behavior. She believed the world owed her for her own misery, and I offered her the chance to take what she thought she deserved, in exchange for her help. She's no different than most of the humans on your world. You all think the same way. You think the world should be fair, and you get so angry when you find that it is not." He made a scoffing sound. "And this is the race of creatures your partners want to save."

"We're not all like that, and you know it," I said, angry on behalf of my world and my fellow humans, even as I thought he might be a little bit right. "There are plenty of people in the world who do good things, for good reasons, or at the very least do their best not to do wrong."

"Perhaps. But the potential for evil is in there, in all of you, waiting to come out."

I thought back to my trial with the drink. I may have lost the game, but I learned the lesson. "So is good, even in the most evil of people, if you choose to look for it. Your lot only looks for the bad things."

Luke sighed. "Now is not the time to get into a psychological debate, my dear. We'll have plenty of time later." He leered at me, and I resisted the urge to stick out my tongue at him. It would be a childish move and probably wouldn't end well. "At any rate, the accident I arranged scored yet another victory against the Foundation, serving as the impetus for getting Barbara out of the way and leaving Michael vulnerable. And it was kindness, don't you agree? Letting Barbara go be with her daughter for eternity?"

I shrugged. I'd seen that world; in all honestly I couldn't say Barbara made the wrong choice. "So basically Lisa is your slave, and in return she gets to live forever? Is that all you promised her in exchange for her committing murder?"

"No, of course not. I promised her everything, offered to give her whatever her heart desired, eventually, if she would do this one more thing." His voice turned cold, mocking. "And I always had one more thing. She did as I asked every time, partly because she wanted her rewards but mostly…" He leaned closer to me with a lascivious grin. "She did what I asked of her because she loves me with every fiber of her being. She yearns for me, Gillian, rather like you yearn for Michael. That's what made using her so easy."

"Hey," I protested weakly. "I don't yearn for Michael. Not in the way you mean. Not to that degree at least." No point in lying to the bastard. Obviously, he saw right through me.

He laughed and took a sip of wine, silently miming at me to see if I wanted one of my own. I shook my head emphatically. I had enough of his drinks for a lifetime.

"Surely you understand her position, though. I promised, if she got you here, she was guaranteed a special place in the coming years, ruling beside me as my queen. That's her greatest desire."

"Why isn't she here now, then? She got me here. Why isn't she sitting next to you being all adoring and stuff?"

"I still need her back in your world, keeping an eye on your partners and your Foundation, sabotaging any attempt they may make in defeating my forces who are, even now, gathering for attack. That's my next one more thing. After, perhaps I will bring her here. I'm a bit bored with her though. She's so pliable, so willing to do whatever I ask. There's no challenge left." He winked at me again. "I think perhaps I'd rather keep you instead, make you my conduit." He pointed to the ring on my finger. "You're already halfway there."

I looked down at the ring with a feeling of dread. "Is that what this is? You've marked me?"

He smiled slowly, staring at me in such a sexual way I crossed my arms over my breasts in defense. "Yes, I think I rather like that idea. You'd fight me. It could be…interesting."

"Okay, that is beyond disgusting," I said, trying not to let the implications scare me. I hoped my voice sounded severe and not horrified as I continued, "You sound like a villain in a bad romance novel."

He leaned forward and took my hand, raising it to his lips. "If that's what you want me to be, I'm willing to play along."

"Ugh. No," I said, yanking my hand back. Luke might be handsome and more than a little charming, and I definitely understood why Lisa thought she loved him, but the evil-is-sexy thing only went so far, and I'd reached my limit.

"If I understand you," I said, getting back to the subject at hand. "You make all these promises to get what you want, but you have no real intention of granting Lisa's wish." And just like that, an idea popped into my head. I tried not to dwell on it, afraid he might read it in my eyes.

He laughed and took another sip of wine. "Are you certain I can't tempt you with some food? I assure you there are no lasting consequences."

I shook my head. "Actually, I'm kind of tired. Is there anywhere I can go take a nap or something in this place?" My voice quavered a little bit, but I didn't think it mattered. He wanted me at least a little bit afraid. I needed some time alone to think through my tenuous plan and, hopefully, put it in action somewhere he wouldn't notice. *If I fail, at least he won't know I tried.* I rather suspected his congeniality would fade in the face of outright defiance.

To my relief, he offered to show me to my room.

I barely took note of my surroundings after he left. Instead, I took a deep breath, steadying myself for the task ahead. I needed to get myself out of there, and get Lisa away from the Foundation. If my plan worked, Luke would not be pleased to see her. I felt another twinge of sympathy for the woman, but I squashed it. She sent me here; she had to face the consequences of her actions.

One more deep breath. This was it. My last ditch effort to escape this world and get back to Michael.

I closed my eyes, crossed my fingers, and whispered, "Gerald, if you can hear me, I'm claiming my wish. I wish to be back in my own world and Lisa McGovern, our HR person, to take my place in this world. And Gerald, this is important so please don't pull any of your elf tricks. Just get me home."

For a split second, I didn't think it worked until, for what seemed like the one-hundredth time, the world around me changed. The walls blurred and twisted into a spiral taking me with it, my body stretching in several different directions at once, then snapping back like a rubber band. It should have been painful, but I barely had time to register any sensation before it stopped and I found myself sprawled on the ground, solid and whole.

At first, I couldn't tell where I landed because I was busy throwing up, and after, when I was in better condition to take in my surroundings, all I saw was a pea-soup fog surrounding me, making it impossible to identify any kind of landmark. Tears of frustration pricked my eyes. After all that, I still didn't make it home.

"Good use of a wish, there. I'm quite impressed."

"Gerald? Is that you?" Please be Gerald, I prayed as I desperately peered through the thick fog in an effort to find the owner of the voice.

A shadowy figure stepped closer to me until he was near enough I could make out his features. Relief flooded through me at the sight of Gerald's familiar face. Even if I wasn't home, at least I wasn't alone. "Where the hell am I?"

"You are home, my lady. Your wish is fulfilled."

I wanted to collapse with the happiness of the news, but instead threw my arms around the faerie, hugging him tightly. As far as I was concerned, he could imitate my ex-husband any time he wanted. "Thank you. Thank you so much for saving me."

"You are quite welcome." Gerald's voice was tinged with laughter, and I backed away, embarrassed.

Details of my surroundings became clearer as my eyes adjusted to the fog, and I realized with delight we stood in the middle of Rittenhouse Square. "Why is it so foggy?"

"Because of all the magic in the air, lady. Evil things are afoot, dark forces are amassing, mounting an attack on the Foundation. Many of us are lending assistance, but the partners are weakened."

"Weakened? Why? What happened?"

"Among other things, Rachel stepped through the Door, and you've been missing for two days."

"Two days?" It seemed like only a few hours since Lisa pushed me into that other world. I didn't think there would be anything I could even do to help, but I knew I had to be there, with the others. No, not had to, wanted to. I needed to see Michael and my friends, to stand by their side during the battle, regardless of the outcome. "I have to find them. I have to find Michael."

"Allow me to help you, lady," said Gerald. I must

have looked slightly skeptical, because he added, "No strings attached, I promise. I want to fight against the Creatures of Darkness as much as you. I can see in this fog. I will lead you."

I nodded in agreement, and we slowly made our way through the fog-covered streets. "So what's with the fog, exactly?"

"It's a shroud, blocking the regular human world from the goings on of the supernatural one. The Foundation's building may be on fire, but those outside the fog will not notice."

"The building's on fire?" I cried. "We have to get there!"

"I don't know if it's on fire,' said Gerald patiently. "I'm using that as an example."

"Sorry, I'm a bit on edge. I spent two days stuck in some alternate universe and no one noticed, remember?"

"They noticed, I promise you. Not long after you'd gone, Michael felt his link with you weaken, and when you failed to return to work on Monday, Michael grew suspicious of the story he'd been told."

"What story?"

"From what I understand, Lisa told Michael you went home with William to talk, and planned to spend the weekend with him, to try to work things out."

"How could anyone think I'd run off with my ex-husband?" I cried, ridiculously insulted by the thought. "Didn't anyone think that was strange?"

"Humans always do strange things," replied Gerald sardonically, "and at the time no one had any real reason to doubt Lisa's story."

"At the time?" I stopped walking, surprised and

pleased. "So they figured Lisa out? They knew she worked for Lu...for the enemy?" Luke's ring still circled my finger. As hard as I tried, I couldn't slip it from my hand. I worried saying his name out loud might help him find me again, a thought that made me start to shiver uncontrollably. I couldn't go back to that place. I couldn't.

"Right before Rachel's ceremony on Monday, Michael confronted Lisa and got the truth from her. Eventually." The harmonics in his voice as he said "eventually" made me wonder exactly what Michael did to make Lisa confess. "Samuel was rather miffed when he realized they'd been duped."

Miffed. Something told me miffed was an understatement. "So then what happened? What did they do to her?"

"Complete chaos," Gerald said, navigating around a group of businessmen I didn't see until they were almost upon us. "Not long after Lisa confessed, a battalion of demons burst into the office, right as Rachel's Door opened."

"Were you there?"

"I was indeed. It is traditional for some of the long-term clients of the Foundation to attend the ceremony, to say goodbye, should the conduit choose not to come back. I, fortunately, managed to escape the initial onslaught, and then I heard you calling me. Clever of you, by the way. I couldn't interfere directly. I had no way of finding you in that other world, even if I'd known you were there, but the wish superseded everything."

"More desperate than clever," I said dismissively, not wanting to talk about my adventure any more. "But tell me what happened to Rachel. They didn't…" I faltered, more than a little worried about the answer. "Did she make it through the Door?"

"She did. She is quite a remarkable woman. She fought off her attackers with strength I'd never seen before, so determined was she to get through the Door." Gerald chuckled. "I watched her take out the Kappa blocking her path by kicking it right between the eyes, spilling the water stored in its head, rendering it powerless. She made it through right before I made my own escape."

I was impressed. *Go, Rachel.* "So you don't know if she came back?"

"I very likely would not have seen the outcome even if I had not left. As it did for you, time moves differently in that world. A few minutes there could be a day or two here. Meanwhile, the dark forces continue their onslaught on the Foundation, hoping to press their advantage."

"And punch a hole in the universe," I muttered, remembering what Luke said.

"That seems the general plan, yes."

"Is Michael…is he okay? Do you know?"

"I believe it's been a hard battle for Michael, being physically weakened due to you being in a different world. Although…" His voice took on a twinge of amusement. "I think he took a bit of comfort knowing you were simply lost and not off with your ex-husband after all."

In spite of my worry, I smiled at that, hoping Gerald wasn't currently reading my thoughts. They weren't particularly pure or noble at the moment.

"Now you are back," Gerald continued. "I believe

he will find the strength to fight even harder," Gerald said. "Look, there he is now."

I don't know if Gerald did some faerie trick, or because we were closer to the source of all the magic, or even if I was getting used to all the fog, but I saw the tableau in front of me quite clearly.

I saw various snapping, snarling creatures surrounding Michael, being kept at bay only by the sword in his hand. The hilt of his sword looked made of stone and wrapped with a band of leather, but the blade wasn't like any earthly material. It looked vaguely metallic, but whenever Michael lunged at a creature the blade would bend and flicker as if made of white-hot flame.

I couldn't take my eyes off Michael as he expertly parried and thrust his flame-like sword at his opponents. Frightening, awe-inspiring and dead sexy. With one sweeping arm movement, Michael managed to disarm and decapitate three unidentifiable creatures, making me want to simultaneously cheer and throw up. I might have stood there indefinitely watching Michael, but one of the creatures evaded Michael's guard, swiping his legs out from under him. Michael fell to the ground, his head smacking against the pavement, and his sword flew from his hand landing several feet away.

I cried out in terror as the creatures descended upon him, and then, quite obviously thinking with something other than my brain, cried out once more, and leapt into the fray.

Chapter 14

I'd like to say I jumped in, and with strength I didn't know I possessed, smote those demons and saved Michael's life.

I'd like to say that, but I'd be lying.

Instead, I smacked into one of the demons so hard I bounced backwards onto the pavement, knocking the wind out of me.

On the plus side, my ill-thought-out attack distracted the demons long enough for Michael to roll on his side and dodge the claws of the beast about to disembowel him, grab his lost sword and jump to his feet in one fluid movement.

Michael stood before the demons, sword aloft, his handsome face set like stone and a strange, almost feral smile on his face, looking every inch the avenging angel, powerful, terrifying and beautiful. The demons, obviously bright enough to know they were on the losing side, backed away, but to no avail. One by one, Michael's strangely flickering sword sliced through the creatures surrounding him like they were mist. Each time the sword struck a demon, the creature shuddered and exploded in a shower of…I'm just going to call it dust. When the air finally cleared, I saw no trace of the demons other than a scattering of ashes on the ground.

I barely had time to catch my breath before Michael pulled me to my feet, hustling me into the relative safety of the building.

"Gillian!" The delight in his voice filled me with joy, as did the bone-crushing embrace. "You're back! Where were you? What happened? Are you okay?"

Before I could answer any of his questions, he pulled me into another hug, and I melted into his embrace, hugging him tightly in return, and trying hard not to cry.

"I am so sorry," he said at last, releasing me. I let go a bit more reluctantly. "You tried to tell me on Friday, but I didn't listen, and when you left…I had no reason to disbelieve Lisa." His face darkened with anger. Perhaps I did Lisa a favor getting her out of here. "Then on Monday all hell broke loose, and I couldn't take the time to try to find you. I am so sorry. I should have listened to you."

"It's not your fault," I assured him, equal parts pained and pleased by the anguish on his face. I didn't want him to blame himself, naturally, but I rather liked the idea he cared enough about me to want to take the blame in the first place. "It wasn't anyone's fault. Something made all of us ignore the warning signs, which is why Lisa could, um, send me away."

"Where did you go?"

"Darned if I know," I said with a shrug, briefly describing what I'd seen in that world, in case that gave him a clue. When I finished Michael shuddered and pulled me close once more. "I'm so, so sorry," he said again.

"It's okay," I replied, my voice muffled by his chest. I pulled away from him and gave what I hoped was a brave smile. "Honestly, I'm fine. None the worse for wear." I thought I meant it when I said it, but looking into Michael's concerned face seemed to do something to my emotions and before I could stop myself I burst into tears.

Once again, I found myself engulfed in Michael's arms. He held me tightly, whispering comforting words, but that made it worse. So I pushed him away, turning my head until I could look him in the eyes and not burst into tears again.

"Sorry," I said, when I felt composed enough to talk. I gave a watery smile. "I guess the whole thing was more traumatic than I thought. But there were some good bits, too." I gave him an abbreviated account of meeting with my mother. "So, in some ways, I'm not completely sorry. If I hadn't gone there, I would never have saved my mom. I wouldn't have known…" I felt tears threatening again, so I stopped that line of thought.

"Anyway, Lisa kind of did me a favor, sending me into that world, and I even got to see…" I hesitated, unsure if I should tell him about the glimpse I had of his lost world, and decided against it. "I mean, I met the person behind all the attacks, the person Lisa worked for." I repeated everything I remembered about Luke's master plan, and at Michael's prodding, gave a detailed description of Luke's appearance.

"Him?" Michael almost spat the word, his mouth tightening in anger. "I should have known. It's been at least three hundred years since his last defeat. I thought he'd given up at last. I should have known better."

"He told me he was Lucifer,"

Michael snorted. "He would."

"I called him Luke." That made Michael smile in spite of his apparent worry. "He said he came from your world. Is that true? Who is he?"

"He's…He's a long story I don't have time for now. He's one of the reasons we've been fighting against the Darkness for so long." He shook his head, still looking surprised. "And Lisa worked for him? How did we not know?"

"She was Luke's conduit, sort of," I said. "I mean, I still don't understand it all, but I think she stayed human enough to slip under your radar, but attached to him enough she willingly did his dirty work." I told him about Barbara's daughter and Lisa's part in her death. The look on his face chilled me. I had no doubt of Michael's inherent goodness, but I knew if Lisa showed up right now he would kill her.

"I still can't believe Lisa sent you into that other dimension, and we didn't sense anything." Michael sighed and ran his hand through his hair, his normal gesture of frustration or confusion, and my heart warmed at the sight. For a while, I thought I might never see that again. "I looked for you when you didn't come back to my office, and Lisa was at her desk, working on paperwork, as calm as you please. She lied to me, and I didn't even notice."

"Gerald said she told you I went off with William." I couldn't keep the hurt out of my voice, even though I tried. It still rather annoyed me he would think I ran back to my ex so easily, that he thought I was so malleable.

He nodded his head, looking rueful. "She did. And I believed it without question. I still can't believe we didn't spot the lie, or the fact she was a marked conduit. Or she opened a Door without us noticing. That's big power."

A sudden tremor shook the building, reminding me we were in the middle of a battle. A shout echoed throughout the lobby as the Accounting Guys ran past us and out the door, waving double-headed axes. "Giants," they said by way of explanation.

"Did Lisa tell you how she managed to open a dimensional portal without any of us noticing?" Michael asked. I'd rather expected him to rush out after the Accounting Guys and join the fight, but I guess getting to the bottom of the mystery was more important than giants to Michael. Fair enough.

"A spell," I said. "I called it the Trojan Horse spell. It made everyone think things were okay, even though they weren't. I tried to tell you, but then Lisa came and…well, you know the rest."

"It's all my fault." Michael said grimly. "I should have been on my guard. You could have…Gillian, again, I am so sorry. Can you ever forgive me?"

"Of course, I can. There's nothing to forgive. I mean, if anyone acted stupidly, I did. I knew about the spell. I should have been more on *my* guard. I'm the one that let Lisa get the drop on me. I was the one with the warning something was wrong, and I didn't try hard enough to convince you. Anne warned me people wouldn't believe me, and I would have to try hard to get anyone to listen. I…oops." I hadn't meant to mention Anne.

"Anne?" he whispered. If I thought Michael looked surprised at any of my other revelations, it was nothing compared to the look of utter shock on his face now. "My Anne?"

The building shook again, so violently I had to grab Michel's arm to keep from falling, and something large but indistinct flew into building with a resounding thump, nearly shattering the glass before it melted away. There were giants out there, and demons and who knew what else in other parts of the building and the city. I didn't know what happened to Valerie and Ralph, or Stacey or Roger, or anyone. We didn't have much time, but this…this was important.

"Yes, your Anne. She visited me last night. I mean Thursday night to warn me about the Trojan horse spell."

"Did she say anything else?" The hopeful look on Michael's face made him look vulnerable and more human than I'd ever seen him. "Did she…did she mention me at all?"

My heart ached with the pain of knowing Michael couldn't, or wouldn't ever love anyone the way he loved Anne. I felt ashamed of my jealousy, but love is never the most reasonable of emotions, and I loved Michael enough to feel the pain of knowing he may never feel the same way about me. I loved him enough to want him to be happy, to know Anne loved him as he did her.

"Anne told me she loved you more than anything, but she couldn't give up the beauty and peace of that world—your world. She said she was sorry she hurt you, Michael, but she wanted to rest. She's happy there."

The look of love and longing on Michael's face as I spoke was almost too painful to bear, and I had to swallow hard to keep from crying.

"She isn't completely gone, you know," I said. "I mean, you said it yourself, if all your conduits are in your old world, then a part of you is there, too, with her.

Besides…"

I bit my lip, hating the anguish in Michael's eyes, and not sure if I could say or do anything to take some of his pain away. Taking a deep, steadying breath, I pressed on. "I'm connected to Anne, to all the conduits, apparently, so maybe, if you wanted to tell her something, you tell me, and the message will get through to her."

Michael looked at me a moment, then rested his hands gently on my cheeks. "Thank you, Gillian." His eyes darkened and, after a heart pounding moment, bent his head toward mine. I stopped breathing, and closed my eyes as his lips touched mine. I don't know why he kissed me, and I didn't care. It might be the last time he ever did so, and I didn't plan on wasting time wondering.

"Gillian!" Valerie's delighted voice screeched through the lobby, and Michael pulled away. I was happy to see her, but more than a little miffed she'd interrupted my kiss.

"Thank all the gods you're okay! Where have you been? Did someone disguised as your ex-husband kidnap you? That was my guess. Where did you go? Are you okay? How did you get out?"

Before I could offer any answers, she pulled me into a bone-crushing hug. It might have been amusing if I hadn't noticed she was shaking badly, with unshed tears in her eyes. "Are you okay, Valerie?" I asked as soon as I could breathe again. "What's going on? Is Ralph okay?"

"He's fine. He's outside somewhere, chasing down a dragon. Roger and I are guarding the Door, watching to see if…when Rachel will come back."

"Any sign of her final decision yet?" Michael asked hopefully.

"No. Nothing. We eliminated the most recent attack of the shadow men." A dark look crossed Valerie's face. What did she do to eliminate them, and how much did it cost her to do so? "It seems to take them about a half hour to regroup, so I came down to see if Ralph returned yet. We're holding our own, but it's hard. Poor Roger. He's getting tired. I'm not certain we can keep those things away much longer. It's just…it's hard."

I gave her a hug. She looked beyond exhausted. "I'm here now. That should help, right? What can I do?"

"Are you sure you're up to it, Gillian?" Michael asked. "You've been through a pretty traumatic time yourself."

"I'm fine. I want to help. I…" Sudden pain shot through my entire body, almost like I'd been mildly shocked. I looked around to see if it happened to anyone else, but Michael and Valerie looked unaffected. "Did you feel that?"

"Feel what?" Valerie asked.

"I'm not sure." Another, stronger shock bolted through me, and I cried out in pain.

"Gillian, what is it?" Michael said, instantly concerned.

"I don't know, I…" The next shock was so strong it brought me to my knees. Before I could say anything else another shock hit me, even worse than before. "What the hell?" I managed to say when the pain subsided.

I tried to stand up, but another excruciating jolt

ripped through my body, knocking me flat. I tried to focus on Michael's face, but the world spun, he looked like he was at the end of a long tunnel, falling away from me. Another bolt of pain flashed through me, and I screamed in terror.

I knew what was happening. Luke was trying to drag me back.

Chapter 15

"Gillian!" Michael shouted, his voice tense with anxiety. "Take my hand! You can do it. Come on."

I barely made out his features through the searing pain blinding me, but made a wild grab, nearly sobbing in relief when Michael's warm hand clasped my own. The shocks jolted through my body at an almost continuous pace, but I was beyond pain now. The only coherent thought in my head was I didn't want to go back there. I couldn't. Luke wouldn't be quite so polite this time around.

I clung tightly to Michael's hand, the only solid thing in the whirling world around me, and prayed to whoever might listen I withstood the torture. I pictured Luke holding onto my feet, trying to pull me down, while Michael held onto my arms, pulling me up, until I thought I would break in half from the force of it.

Gradually, after a million years or so, the pain subsided, and I could breathe again. The world came back into focus, and I saw the welcome sight of Michael, leaning over me, stroking my back and whispering soothing words.

I waited a few more seconds until I no longer felt like vomiting, then stood up, letting go of Michael's hand rather reluctantly. "I'm okay now, thank you," I said.

"No. Thank you, Gillian." I saw Michael's face

tighten as he looked beyond me at the person who'd spoken. "Allow me to congratulate you on your clever little escape. I salute your ingenuity. I may not even punish you."

I turned to see Luke standing before me with a sardonic smile on his lips and a malevolent glint in his eyes. Lisa stood beside him, her head bowed. She looked like she'd been crying. I wanted to hate her, but something in her expression made me feel more pity than anger. I didn't imagine Luke reacted with pleasure when she showed up in my place.

"She is my conduit," Michael said, stepping in front of me. "You have no claim."

"Oh, do you think so? She played a game, in my world, and lost. That gives me a claim to her soul." He smiled and once more a jolt of electricity shot through me, dropping me to my knees again.

I was an idiot to even think I could challenge him to a game, much less win. He was too powerful, too talented to lose to someone like me. I shouldn't have left his castle. I didn't deserve Michael. I was worthless, useless. I…

Michael pulled me to my feet, and as he did so a warm pulse of gentle energy ran through me. "He's manipulating your emotions, Gillian. Whatever thoughts you are having now are not yours. Fight them. He has no hold on you, I promise."

I closed my eyes and let Michael's energy sweep through me, pushing out all the negative emotions, all the self-doubt. I felt myself relax, growing stronger and more confident.

"Thank you," I whispered to Michael, giving his hand a squeeze. I don't know what he did, what he gave me, but I felt stronger and more confident than ever before, like I could take on the world and win. I turned to glare at Luke. "And you, bastard. You are going down."

"You will not win, brother," Michael said in a far more formal voice than mine. "You know that. You tried to stop Rachel and failed. You tried to take my conduit and failed. You are running on borrowed time, brother. Leave now while you still have your dignity."

Brother? Did he mean that literally or as some sort of formal address? I hoped I had the chance to ask Michael someday.

"I am not leaving," Luke said. "Not when I am so close to winning this world once and for all."

"Then it comes down to you and me." Michael's sword reappeared in his hand.

Luke raised an identical sword. "I wouldn't have it any other way, my brother."

I hadn't even noticed the sounds of the battles raging outside until they stopped, as if the two men squaring for battle championed both sides now, no other fights necessary.

With a strangled cry, Valerie ran toward the elevators. I briefly contemplated following her, but something told me Michael needed me to stay with him. I guess it was a conduit thing. Besides, I was too exhausted to move.

Michael and Luke stood unmoving for a long, expectant moment until the crash of their swords shattered the eerie silence surrounding us, and the battle began in earnest.

Both men equally matched in swordsmanship, their swords spun and parried and thrust so quickly they practically blurred. I might have found it thrilling if it were a movie or play rather than reality, and if the outcome didn't have quite so much riding on it.

A few minutes in, Michael scored a hit when his sword sliced Luke's hand. Luke only laughed, but Lisa cried out in pain, clutching her own hand. After a few moments of waffling, curiosity won out and I went over to her. "What happened?"

"I'm his conduit," she said bitterly. "I take his injuries." Sure enough, her hand bled profusely. I looked at the fighting men, wondering if that happened to me as well. "Oh, don't worry," Lisa said, apparently anticipating my train of thought. "Michael would never dream of hurting you."

As if to prove her point, Luke managed to get past Michael's defensive parry and his sword stabbed Michael's shoulder. I cried out as Michael staggered for a heart-stopping moment before regaining his balance and blocking Luke's sword. My own shoulder remained unharmed, and Michael's didn't look like it bled, either.

"You see? He uses your energy to protect himself, but he also uses his energy to protect you. He's too noble"—she spat the word—"to do it any other way. Unfortunately, that's why he will lose. My master uses all the energy, his and mine, to fight, but all Michael can do is balance the energy. To tip it either way would cause harm to you or him."

Sympathy stirred in my heart. I couldn't absolve Lisa for her part in Luke's nefarious plans, but I understood a bit more why she did what she did. Luke manipulated her negative emotions as well as her love for him only to drain her dry and leave nothing in return. A bit like my relationship with my ex-husband actually, only rather more dramatic.

Michael's sword sliced across Luke's chest, and Lisa slumped to the ground with a muffled cry, a ribbon of blood staining the front of her shirt. I stared dumbly at her, horrified at the sight, until my brain finally kicked into gear. She might be evil, or at least easily manipulated, but I couldn't stand there and watch her bleed to death.

I lifted her shirt to inspect the damage. Fortunately, the cut was long, but not deep, and after another moment of dithering, I ripped a strip of cloth from my own shirt as a make-shift bandage in an effort stop the flow of blood which sounds a lot easier in theory than in practice. I fussed over her until I knew she wasn't in mortal danger, then turned my attention back to the sword fight.

In movies, sword fighting looks rather like a dance, but the battle in front of me lacked any kind of real elegance. The two combatants wasted no time with showy blocks, but hacked at each other with vicious intensity. Michael stumbled and nearly fell, then regained his balance and slashed at Luke's thigh, and blood came pouring through Lisa's jeans.

This time the cut ran deep, and I worked frantically to stop the flow of blood, afraid she would bleed to death before much longer. "Isn't there anything I can do to help you?"

Lisa shook her head, wincing in pain as another cut slashed her arm. I tried my best to stanch that wound, tears of frustration welling in my eyes. I wanted to tell Michael to stop, to scream that the wrong person was being wounded, but if he stopped Luke would win, a scenario he undoubtedly counted on.

Blood blossomed over Lisa's eye, and I ripped off more of my shirt to tend to her, blessing the fact I'd worn cotton. "There must be something we can do, some way to break the link or something. He can't keep doing this to you."

"Stop being so nice to me, there's no point."

"Lisa, you're going to die if we don't do something."

"No, I won't."

"Come on, Lisa. I know what it's like to love someone who doesn't deserve it. You can't let him do this to you."

"I have to. He needs me. He won't let me die." She turned away, speaking so softly I almost didn't catch the words. "Not until he wins, anyway."

Her voice held such anguish, despite my better judgment all the hatred and anger I had toward her melted away. "Lisa…"

"No. Go away. I'm your enemy, remember? I'm on his side. I don't regret anything I did."

Everyone kept saying what good sight I had, and now more than ever, I knew they were right. As I gazed down at Lisa, I saw through the bitter woman who believed the world owed her favors and beyond the girl who thought love was something bought and sold, discovering within her that spark of divine nobility Michael and all the other partners spent so many eons fighting for.

We humans seemed to reach for the bad things so easily, but, perhaps in different circumstances, Lisa might have cultivated the better parts of her nature, and would not have ended up the way she did. In spite of everything she'd done, all the hurt she caused, I felt certain she still had the capacity for good.

"I don't believe you, Lisa," I said quietly. "I think you regret what happened, and what you did to make it happen, and for whatever it's worth, I understand, and…and I forgive you."

She let out a little sob and turned away, curling up in a ball. Feeling more helpless than ever before in my life, I turned my attention back to the fighting, offering a quick prayer for it to end soon, without any more damage to Lisa. I was running out of shirt.

Unfortunately, it didn't look like we'd ever get past a stalemate. As long as Luke kept using Lisa's energy, Michael couldn't beat him, and with Michael using both our energies to avoid injury, the fight could go on indefinitely, and Lisa would continue to suffer.

Michael fell to Luke's sword once more, but managed to dodge the attack and jump to his feet, his return blow cut a deep gash in Lisa's cheek. "This has to stop," I said fiercely. I stood up, ready to tell Michael to stop fighting, but Lisa grabbed me. "Wait. There is something I can do."

I knelt back at her side. "What is it?"

She smiled faintly. "The link. It works both ways. I can't break it, but I can send something the opposite way."

"Send what?"

She reached into her pocket and pulled out a vicious-looking knife. "This." She took my hand, her eyes wet with tears. "Thanks, Gillian," she said softly, and plunged the knife into her neck.

I shut my eyes a moment too late, and I knew the sight of all the blood spurting from her throat would haunt me forever.

Behind me, I heard Luke shout a curse. He'd fallen to his knees, clutching at his own throat. I looked back at Lisa. Her eyes wide and unseeing, her body covered in blood, but she was smiling.

I closed her eyes, something that looked far easier in the movies, by the way, and using the remains of my shirt I attempted to clean her up as much as possible. I didn't hear Luke approach, but I wasn't surprised to see him by my side.

He didn't look any weaker, but his expression was frightened, and I knew Lisa's theory was right; she'd somehow weakened him with her sacrifice. He knelt down by Lisa's body, bowing his head, an expression of sadness on his face, and I thought for a moment perhaps he did care for Lisa, at least a little, and a tendril of sympathy curled around my heart.

Luke touched her face, almost tenderly, but then his face hardened and he snarled, "You bitch! How could you do this to me!" Immediately, I stopped feeling sorry for him.

"Give it up. Leave this place. Nurse your wounds, maybe try to find forgiveness." Michael stood behind Luke, his sword raised. "It's over."

"Perhaps you are right, brother," he said, his voice weak. "With my conduit gone there's not much else I can do." He sighed and pulled the knife from Lisa's throat. "Except this."

With snakelike speed, he plunged the knife into Michael's chest. "Go on, Michael, take your conduit's energy to heal yourself." Before I could even scream, Luke grabbed my throat. "But can you do that and still save her?"

Even in the midst of my pain and terror, I had to

admire Luke's reasoning. To keep me from strangling to death, Michael had to use his energy, which would weaken him, and if he took my energy to keep from bleeding out I would strangle to death. Luke used the balance against us, forcing Michael to choose. Sacrifice his life mortal body for my life, or let me die.

It was the last ditch effort of a desperate man, and would probably work. Michael's sacrifice of his mortal body to save me would result in our world being overrun and destroyed by Luke and his minions.

Yeah, well, two can play the sacrifice game, I thought. I was not part of the Foundation yet, still mostly mortal despite Michael's exchange of energy. If I died, Michael could use all his energy to heal himself and save the world.

I'd like to say I felt noble, brave and selfless, but I didn't. I was frightened and sad, and didn't want to die. I didn't want to leave my friends at the Foundation, and I especially didn't want to leave Michael, but I knew I had to. I closed my eyes, visualizing the world I'd glimpsed in the forest, mentally reaching out toward the images I'd seen, all the beauty and peace.

I forced myself to stop fighting Luke and thought of Anne, and my mother, and anyone else who might be in paradise, waiting for me to join them. I was going to a good place. That was some comfort.

Then I saw through the black beginning to blur my vision a dark haired-slightly plump woman appear next to me. I knew she wasn't real, because Luke stood right next to her and he didn't react, but when she took my hand in hers, and I felt the warmth of her skin and the gentle pressure of her fingers as they grasped mine.

Next to her stood another woman, and next to her

another woman, and then another, all indistinct and kind of overlapping each other, rather like images in a funhouse mirror. They circled the foyer, hand in hand, until at last I saw Anne, standing next to Michael. She smiled at me, and took Michael's hand in her own.

As it did when I stared into the paradise, Michael's world, wave after wave of love and peace and joy crashed over me, emotions so strong it took several seconds before I realized I could breathe again and the pain had vanished.

Luke lay curled on the floor by my feet, writhing in agony. The energy, the emotions of almost overwhelming sense of peace and love and joy continued to fill the room like a physical presence. As it grew in intensity, Luke, shrieking and cursing, grew smaller and more indistinct until finally he faded away completely. With a tiny metallic tinkle, the silver ring slipped from my finger, spun for a moment, then disappeared.

I struggled to my feet, smiling at the figure I somehow knew was Barbara. "Say hi to your daughter for me," I said to her, and she laughed silently then faded away. One by one, the other women disappeared, until the only one left was Anne, still holding Michael's hand.

He could see her. I don't know how, but he could see her.

As I watched, Anne lifted her hand and stroked Michael's cheek. He closed his eyes, and, timidly, like he was sure she would disappear if he moved too quickly, he placed his hand on her face. Tears sprang into Michael's eyes, and his face shone with a fierce love almost painful to see. I felt like an intruder, peeking into a love so pure, so true, there was no hope of ever matching it. It didn't make me as sad as I might have thought it would, instead, I felt privileged to witness it.

Finally, with one last, sad smile, Anne faded away. Michael dropped his hand to his side and stood unmoving, lost in his thoughts. Tears still shone on his cheeks, but he smiled.

The sounds of the battle raged outside, reminding me demons continued to try to break through, and work needed done, but I couldn't bring myself to say anything. All I managed was to stare at Michael, my own mixed emotions raging a war of their own in my heart.

A few moments later, Michael blinked, looking as if waking from a dream. He turned to me with a smile, taking my hands in his. We stared at each other a moment, then he kissed me lightly and briefly, and I went shivery with the shock. "Thank you again, Gillian."

"For what?" I managed to say. "I didn't do anything."

"You, your vision opened the Door, so the conduits could get through. I saw…I finally…"

"Yeah, yeah, I have good sight. I've heard," I said lightly, hoping to keep him from crying again, and it worked because his face cleared, and he laughed.

"So what do we do now?" I asked.

"The others will be weak now their leader is gone. It's simply a matter of sweeping up the pieces." He sighed wearily. "I hope we have the strength left."

"Oh, I think we will."

We both turned, startled, to see Valerie and Roger

stepping off the elevator. Grinning ear to ear, they moved aside to reveal the person standing behind them.

Rachel.

Chapter 16

The private karaoke room at the Fuji Mountain restaurant was rather elegant. Although some might argue the big banner reading "Welcome Gillian and Goodbye Rachel and Samuel" hanging crookedly across one wall might have lowered the tone a bit.

I sat curled up on one of the long sofas lining the wall, an untouched drink in my hand, listening in amusement to Roger singing a truly painful rendition of "Werewolves of London." What he lacked in talent, he made up for in enthusiasm as everyone else clapped and sang along with the chorus, even Samuel, a frankly astounding sight.

"Hey, Gillian, when are you going to sing?" Valerie flopped down next to me, making me jump and nearly spilling my drink.

"Right after never," I replied, smiling. "I can't sing."

"Neither can Roger," she said. "That's not stopping him." She looked fondly at her boyfriend, now attempting to belt out "Bohemian Rhapsody." "Although maybe it should." We both laughed.

Roger finished the song and relinquished the microphone to Kim, one of his IT employees. I had no idea if she was a human or not, but she sure could sing.

I finally took a sip of my drink, and closed my eyes, thinking back, as I'd been doing every few minutes for the last week, of the moment when Rachel strode out into the lobby, proud and determined.

She looked the same, still Rachel, but now she had an indescribable aura of power, of magic, as Michael and the other partners did. The legend, then, was true. A conduit who chose to stay in this world became a partner.

I felt a bit intimidated watching her, until she flashed me a friendly smile with the tiniest bit of condescension, and I knew that while she may have changed into something new, at heart she was still our Rachel.

Meanwhile, she continued to march purposefully across the floor, heading to the battle still raging outside. A sword, the twin to Michael's, appeared in her hand.

As she passed us, Michael wordlessly fell into step with her and a moment later, Ralph and Samuel, reacting, I suppose, to some sort of psychic link, appeared next to him. Together the four of them went outside to face the attackers.

If the loss of Luke took the fight out of most of the demons and monsters, Rachel's fated appearance on the battlefield completely unnerved them. I saw demons pause mid-attack and disappear into the fog, leaving our allies fighting nothing but air. Some sort of leafy creature fighting with Gerald simply disappeared, causing him to nearly punch a wall.

The giant the Accounting Guys were in the process of subduing took one look at Rachel and the partners and literally shrank into nothing. Almost comical, despite the trauma of the day, to see these formidable creatures turn tail and escape like so many schoolyard bullies fleeing at the sight of the teacher. The creatures slower on the uptake were quickly dispatched with minimal fuss by Rachel and the partners.

Unfortunately, the shadow men seemed made of stronger, or at least stupider, stuff, and weren't quite ready to give up the fight.

We didn't even have a moment to celebrate our victory before a battalion of those creatures amassed, forming a ring around the building, hundreds upon hundreds of them filling the streets and the sky, overlapping like a geometrical and demonic optical illusion.

Valerie and I stood in the ruined lobby, wrapping our arms around each other for support as the terrifying effect of the shadow men washed over us. I wanted to run and hide, but held my ground, my desire to see what happened next stronger than any feeling of terror the creatures might throw at me. I wanted to watch this epic battle unfold.

Seemingly unaffected by the shadow men, Rachel and the partners formed a circle, facing outward, fingertip to fingertip. Faintly, I heard their voices chanting in that strange angel language, a language Rachel now appeared to know.

As they chanted, a tiny ball of light appeared in the midst of the circle, growing larger and larger until it burst like a sonic boom.

The entire world shook, and I fell to the ground, trying to find some part of the floor not threatening to change places with the ceiling. The light surrounding me continued to brighten until I had to either shut my eyes or go blind, and even then the light invaded my vision to an almost painful degree.

I tried vainly to shut out the anguished cries as the light eviscerated the shadow men and any remaining demons and creatures in its path. I knew the horrible, dare I say demonic, noise would echo in my dreams for the rest of my life.

The last of the screams died away, and I cautiously opened my eyes. The mystical light disappeared taking the fog with it, leaving behind only the late afternoon sunlight and an eerie silence. Slowly and painfully, I struggled to my feet to make my way outside.

With the fog completely lifted, I saw for the first time the amount of damage the rampaging hordes had unleased on the neighborhood.

Cars were smashed, big chunks of masonry gouged out of the surrounding buildings lay scattered in pieces on the ground, and the street and much of the sidewalk were torn up so badly I couldn't see any level surface left. It looked, understandably, like a war zone.

I listened for sirens, screams, anything to indicate the rest of Philadelphia knew a large swath of the city now lay in ruins, but heard nothing, no sound at all. The silence struck me as almost more disturbing than anything else so far. What happened to the rest of the city?

I looked at Valerie, who followed me outside. "Where are all the people?" I asked, but she shrugged and shook her head.

I wanted to cry. We saved the world, but at what cost? How many human lives were sacrificed as collateral damage to our fight? "Shouldn't we look for survivors or something?"

"Go back inside." It took me a moment to realize Rachel spoke. Her voice sounded different, stronger, more commanding, echoing with power, brooking no arguments. As one, Valerie and I hurried back into the building then turned to peer out the window, anxious to see what happened next.

The partners and Rachel stood as still as statues, their eyes closed, their fingers still touching. I was unsure if they were even breathing. For several minutes, they stood unmoving, a hazy sort of glow branching over them like a dome. For a few moments, everything seemed to freeze in place then, like a movie rewound to the beginning, the damage around our building reversed and disappeared. Chunks of street and sidewalk rose in the air like gravity decided to take a vacation day, then gently dropped, becoming whole once more. Smashed out windows and walls of the surrounding buildings repaired themselves, all the dents and dings in the damaged cars popped and disappeared until the entire street was whole once more.

"Look at the sun!" I cried, nudging Valerie sharply in the ribs. It had been late afternoon a moment ago, but now the sun was high in the sky, indicating it wasn't much after twelve. "Did we move backwards in time?"

"Sort of." My heart leapt in joy at the sound of Michael's voice as he and the others came staggering into the lobby, looking weary but triumphant. Throwing caution to the wind, I dashed over and threw my arms around his neck.

"We didn't go back in time, but the rest of the world did," Ralph explained while gathering Valerie into a strong, brotherly hug of his own.

"Does that mean everything that happened today didn't happen?" Even as I asked, I glanced over to see Lisa's body, still lying in a bloody heap on the ground, and I knew the answer.

"We can't undo what happened to us and our allies," said Michael wearily, "but at least we repaired the damage to the city. Regular civilians are unharmed, and we sealed the rift created by our enemies."

"We couldn't have done it if Rachel wasn't with us," Samuel said proudly. "The three of us didn't have enough power to effect a change this large, especially after such a battle."

Rachel smiled, blushing, then shot a smug look at Valerie and me. "Told you I'd come back," she said impishly.

"I didn't doubt it for a second," I said then, after a moment's hesitation, gave her a hug. She hugged me back, and then Valerie joined in, and the next thing I knew the three of us were laughing and crying and generally acting like sappy idiots.

However, the day, already long and now magically even longer, wasn't over yet. We needed to find the rest of our staff and all the clients who fought with us and tend to their wounds. The Accounting Guys sported matching bruises and identical broken arms, looking pleased with themselves for holding their own against a giant. Stacey's hands were burned from her fight against a dark witch, but she was otherwise unharmed and as cheerful as ever. "I finally got to turn someone into a newt," she said happily.

Roger had broken his leg in several places, but his super werewolf genes were already at work, and he assured me he'd be up and around in no time. Angela and all the other fully human employees were sent home as soon as the attack began. How would Angela react when she found out about Lisa's part in everything? She'd been fond of her, treating Lisa almost like a protégée. That kind of betrayal had to hurt.

We spent the next few hours finding people, healing those who needed it and tending to the bodies of those who never would again. While we worked, I noticed everyone kept glancing over at Rachel with wondering expressions. Clearly no one had the courage to ask her exactly what happened when she went through the Door, but everyone wanted to know.

For my part, although I wanted to know as much as anyone what she endured, and how she found the strength to leave paradise, I tried to content myself with the idea Rachel would tell us in her own time, when she was ready. I hoped it would be soon, because the curiosity ate at me.

Eventually, we, the partners and the conduits, gathered in the conference room for debriefing. I was beyond exhausted, but things needed discussion and questions answered. Sleep could wait a bit longer.

Thankfully, boxes of take-away Chinese food awaited us, and we all ate ravenously, myself especially, since technically I hadn't eaten in days.

I had one important question, and asked it as soon as the opportunity arose. "About Luke. He's not actually Lucifer, is he?"

Samuel answered my question. "He was one of us, once upon a time, but when he looked upon other worlds, he saw himself as a conqueror, not a savior. We banished him into the shadow realms as a result, and he has since spent his existence attacking other worlds and trying to exact revenge upon those of us who vanquished him the first time."

That didn't quite explain my question or the whole brother thing, but I decided it wasn't the time to ask. "So is he banished again now, or dead or what?" Somehow, he didn't strike me as the type to stay dead, but I could always hope.

"Banished is as good a word as any," Samuel said. "We've weakened him, and it will take some time before he regains his strength for another attack."

I imagined Luke in his castle turned prison, plotting his next move and planning his revenge, and I shivered.

Michael must have sensed my thoughts, because he laid a reassuring hand over my own. "It won't be for a long while, Gillian, and when he comes back, we'll be ready."

I returned his smile, doing my best to push aside my worry. After all, we'd won the day. Rachel, against all precedent, had come back, a serious game-changer. Possibly, Luke and his cronies wouldn't try to hurt this world for another millennium, at the very least. For now, we were safe.

The remainder of the week we spent dealing with residual supernatural debris from the battle as well as our regular duties, leading to some late nights at the office. I welcomed the work. It kept me from focusing on things I'd rather not think about until I had more time to process them, and made me tired enough when I slept I didn't dream. I knew, at some point, nightmares would come, but for now I was grateful for the respite.

A few days later, I sat in the break room, scarfing down a sandwich and flipping through a gossip magazine when Angela came in. She grabbed an apple from the community fruit basket on the table and sat across from me, a worried frown playing across her face. After a few minutes of watching her nervously play with the apple, I took pity on her and asked what was wrong.

"I want you to know I am so sorry for hiring Lisa in the first place," she said, her usual rushed manner of speaking curiously subdued. "I didn't notice she was a conduit. I've been working here for years. I should have known."

"Angela, it isn't anywhere near your fault," I said firmly. "She fooled everyone, including the partners. If they didn't notice, you certainly didn't have a chance."

"She was…" Her voice broke, and burst into tears. "She was my friend. I thought she was the only other ordinary person here and it made me feel a little less alone."

I patted her awkwardly on the shoulder, making soothing noises until her sobs quieted. "Angela, you are not ordinary. Not in the way you imply. Most ordinary people couldn't handle working here."

She pulled back and gave me a watery grin. "You know, you're right," Angela said. "I hadn't thought about it before, but you're right."

"Not to mention your healing powers." She stared at me, looking confused, and I had to laugh. "Haven't you noticed?" I showed her my hand, completely unscarred from the burns I'd received only days ago. "An ordinary person couldn't heal me the way you did. As far as I'm concerned, you are as extraordinary as anyone else on staff. And as for Lisa…"

I hesitated, trying to find the words to explain what I sensed when I sat with Lisa, before she died.

"Michael said they came here because they saw

great potential in us, a potential for good, to turn to the light. Lisa had that potential, too, but she made bad choices, and Luke manipulated those regrets to coerce her to work for him. Still, in the end, when it mattered most, she did a wholly unselfish thing. By sacrificing herself, she saved Michael and me and, well the whole world."

I sighed. Angela still looked doubtful. I don't think my incoherent explanation made her feel any better. "What it comes down to is this, Lisa wasn't completely evil. No one is, and I think…no, I'm certain any friendship she showed you was probably real."

"Thank you," Angela said after a few more minutes' contemplation. "I'm not sure I quite believe that yet, but it helps." She stood up, tossing her half-eaten apple into the bin then, much to my surprise, gave me a hug. I didn't think Angela was a hugs type of person. "You've made me feel a little better."

"Glad I could help." And that was that.

Friday afternoon, as I tidied up my desk and looked forward to a quiet, drama-free weekend in my own home, my intercom beeped and Michael asked me to come into his office, his voice grave and serious.

My heart immediately leapt into my throat. Did something happen? Did Luke come back? *Am I being fired now that the threat is over?* My mind reeled with all sorts of paranoid possibilities as I entered his office in great trepidation.

Much to my surprise, the entire senior staff stood around Michael's small conference table, grinning at me. Valerie held a cake.

I turned to look at Michael, standing at his desk. He still looked extremely serious. "What's going on?" I asked stupidly.

"Today is the day you make your choice, Gillian Burke," Michael said, his voice low and serious and deeply sexy. "Your thirty days are over. Should you decide to stay with us on a permanent basis, you and I will be bonded together, and you will no longer, strictly speaking, be a mortal woman. However, should you choose to leave us, you will receive a year's pay and anything else you need to start a new life elsewhere. The choice is yours."

Once more, I felt my life opening up before me. I saw one path clearly before me, one that led to a simple job where I worked a quiet nine-to-five shift then went home to my little house. I met a nice, normal man, one who wasn't a million-year-old angel of light, and we fell in love, got married, had babies and took a family vacation to Ocean City once a year.

Did I honestly want to give up the possibility of that type of future in exchange for two hundred or so ageless years tending to faeries and vampires?

I looked around the room at everyone I'd come to know and care for over the last month. Not, technically, a long time, but so much had happened, I felt like I'd known everyone forever. They were like family, a family I never had, but always wanted. A weird family, mind you, but a family. And there was Michael.

There was always Michael.

"It's a bit dull," I said, grinning, "but I can't imagine working anywhere else but here."

Michael held out his hand, like he did on my first day, and when I took it, instead of the shock I expected, the sensation of being dipped into a warm bath washed over me from the top of head to the tip of my toes. My whole body vibrated with such a strong feeling of power, I actually I checked my hands to see if I glowed.

"Welcome aboard, Gillian Burke," Michael said. "We're glad to have you with us."

The moment of solemn silence was broken by Roger shouting, "Woo-hoo! Party time!"

"Indeed," Samuel said, smiling an enigmatic smile. "We have much to celebrate."

And so here we were, celebrating my permanent employment and our defeat of the dark forces with sushi and songs. It seemed fitting somehow.

Stacey had taken over the microphone, singing "Witchy Woman," with the Accounting Guys doing back up, and I grinned happily to myself. I wouldn't have missed seeing that for the world.

"You should be over there, being the center of attention," Valerie said, not quite giving up on getting me to sing something. "This party is for you, you know."

"It's for me and Rachel," I pointed out. "And I think she deserves the attention more than I do." We looked over at Rachel, deep in conversation with Samuel. "She knew what she wanted, and she got it."

"And now she's one of them, a partner. I still can't believe it happened," Valerie said, and she wasn't the only one. Partners from all over the world popped into our office all week long, everyone eager to meet the "Conduit Who Came Back." An unprecedented event.

"Luke believed it possible." I pointed out. "The reason he was so determined to get to her before she went through the Door. He knew what it meant. He knew it would create a whole new type of angel, stronger than ever before."

Rachel's return meant she and Samuel didn't need human conduits to maintain their mortal bodies, because they were bonded together forever, sustaining each other for eternity.

I found the idea wildly romantic, Valerie not so much. "Sounds claustrophobic," she'd said when she heard the news. "I think I'd prefer to keep my options open."

"And now they're off to protect Hollywood against the forces of evil," I said. Rachel and Samuel were leaving in the morning to open a new Foundation branch in Los Angeles. They would meet three new partners, beings who crossed over recently from their world to ours to help strengthen our numbers against dark forces.

"Judging by the quality of entertainment nowadays they may be too late," Valerie responded, laughing.

After Los Angeles, Rachel and Samuel planned to go to other places, traveling the world, opening offices in areas that needed it, and assisting parts of the Foundation that required some extra support, making sure nothing bad broke in anywhere else.

Michael got bumped up to Samuel's old position, and we expected a female partner from England to take over his vacated position. Valerie eagerly looked forward to having a male conduit around the place.

I hadn't known there were partners out there who were, well, freelance, I guess you could say, but apparently over the world angels bided their time, waiting for the opportunity to form the appropriate triad. This involved quite a bit of shuffling and organizing, and I was heartily glad I didn't have to do it.

A burst of laughter caught my ear, and I turned to see Michael, Samuel and Ralph taking their places in front of the microphones. "Michael seems happier than I've ever seen him," Valerie said.

I nodded in agreement. "He is happy. I can feel it." Now we were bonded, I was much more aware of his emotions, and I knew he felt a measure of peace he hadn't experienced in centuries. "He got to see his true love again."

I didn't turn my head away from the show in front of me, but I felt Valerie's gaze on me. "So it is true about all the conduits? Did he see Anne?" she asked at last.

I nodded again. "He did. Only for a moment, but he saw her." I fished around for the right way to describe what I saw, but failed. I witnessed love in its absolute purest form. I knew that much, but I didn't know how to say it out loud without sounding incredibly cheesy.

"And you're okay with that?"

"Why shouldn't I be? No, stop it," I added, laughing at the incredulous expression on Valerie's face. "Look, I could say I'm jealous, and maybe I am, a bit, but what he shared with Anne, that was important, and I wouldn't want to ever replace it, or her. I couldn't. His relationship with Anne, their love, it made him what he is today, it made him the person..." *Oh hell, I may as well say it.* "That I love. If it means I have to settle for less, in my own relationship with Michael, that's okay by me."

Valerie looked like she wanted to say something else, but, fortunately for me, Roger bounded up and dragged her away to do a duet with him, and I was spared her probing for the time being. What I'd said was true, every word, but I didn't want her to realize the effort it cost me to get to the truth.

The partners finished their song to great applause and laughter and as Valerie and Roger took their place, Michael came over and sat by my side.

"Are you having a good time?" he asked me.

"Of course I am."

He took a long sip of his drink then ran his hand through his hair. Obviously, he had something on his mind, so I waited patiently, knowing he'd get to it when he was ready.

"Let's find somewhere a little more private for a minute," he said, and the next thing I knew we stood on what I could only describe as a cloud, except for the fact it felt as solid as a rock.

"What did you do?" I asked, astonished.

He grinned. "I thought we'd go to a traditional angel hangout. I know you've been picturing it since you met me."

I laughed. "I don't see a harp though."

"I'm more of a guitar sort of person." Michael laughed, but then his face grew serious. "Gillian. This past month has been extraordinary in many ways, and I worry the feelings we have for each other might be a byproduct of the heightened drama we experienced."

I closed my eyes, feeling defeated. I should have anticipated this. The "let's be friends" speech. I needed to stop him before he got to "it's not you, it's me" portion of the talk, but before I could speak, he pressed on.

"But then Rachel's return made me realize something, something about me and my relationship with Anne.

"My love for Anne was the most wonderful thing I'd ever experienced in my entire existence. She proved to me beyond a doubt humanity was worth fighting for."

"I know," I said, "I saw when you…you don't have to justify your feelings to me."

"Hear me out. I loved Anne, and she loved me, but seeing her again, and seeing what Rachel did, made me realize Anne may have loved me, but she didn't love me as much as I loved her."

"That's not true," I said, despite myself. "She loved you. She still loves you. She told me so."

"Yes, I know she did, and does. But in the end, Anne couldn't give up the last of her humanity for me, as Rachel did for Samuel."

I didn't know what to say, so I stayed quiet. He was right. Anne even said it herself.

"Anyway," Michael continued. "What I'm trying to say is for years, for centuries, I was sure I would never recover from her leaving, from losing the love we shared. I'm not certain I even wanted to get over it, over Anne. But now…now I think it's time I let it go. It's time I let myself feel love again."

He ran his hand through his hair again, and swallowed hard. Michael was flustered. I'd never seen him flustered. I got an inkling of what he might be trying to say, and deep in my heart I felt a flutter of anticipation. I bit my lip to keep myself from blurting out something embarrassing and waited as patiently as possible for him to finish his thought.

"What I'm trying to say, Gillian…" Michael grabbed my shoulders and pulled me to him, his lips capturing mine in a soft, long kiss that sent ripples of joy to every part of my body. A kiss full of promise, hope, and the possibility of love.

When Michael finally broke the kiss, I realized, in a dazed sort of way, we were back in the karaoke bar, with the entire office staring at us. Someone started clapping, and then everyone joined in. I think I heard Roger shout, "About time!"

Michael raised his glass to me, giving me that dazzling smile I liked so much. I raised my glass in return, and we clinked rims, then turned to watch Valerie and Roger deconstruct the song "Endless Love." I relaxed back into my seat, enjoying the feeling of Michael by my side.

Anne might have been Michael's greatest love, but that didn't mean she was his only love. Michael might not love me now, not completely, but I loved him with all my heart, and that was enough for me.

Michael took my hand in his, and I leaned my head on his shoulder, perfectly content. I knew his getting over Anne would take more than a moment's revelation, but our love would wait for us when we were ready to grasp it.

It might take some work to get there, but that was okay.

I'd willingly put in the overtime.

A word about the author...

Carol wrote her first "book" in the 3rd grade for a school assignment; it featured an evil scarecrow and contained some truly abysmal poetry. Her teacher liked it, however, and thus her love of writing was born.

When not putting pen to paper (or fingers to keyboard, in these modern times) Carol enjoys acting in community theatre, visiting local wineries with her husband, and spending time with her good friends.

She lives in Pennsylvania with her wonderful and supportive husband, almost-grown son, and two very lively cats.

Thank you for purchasing
this publication of The Wild Rose Press, Inc.

If you enjoyed the story, we would appreciate your
letting others know by leaving a review.

For other wonderful stories,
please visit our on-line bookstore at
www.thewildrosepress.com.

For questions or more information
contact us at
info@thewildrosepress.com.

The Wild Rose Press, Inc.
www.thewildrosepress.com

Stay current with The Wild Rose Press, Inc.

Like us on Facebook

https://www.facebook.com/TheWildRosePress

And Follow us on Twitter
https://twitter.com/WildRosePress